THE
MARK

Also by Kiki Swinson

Playing Dirty
Notorious
Wifey
I'm Still Wifey
Life After Wifey
Still Wifey Material
A Sticky Situation
The Candy Shop
Wife Extraordinaire
Wife Extraordinaire Returns
The Score

Anthologies

Sleeping with the Enemy (with Wahida Clark)
Heist and *Heist 2* (with De'nesha Diamond)
Lifestyles of the Rich and Shameless (with Noire)
A Gangster and a Gentleman (with De'nesha Diamond)
Most Wanted (with Nikki Turner)
Still Candy Shopping (with Amaleka McCall)
Fistful of Benjamins (with De'nesha Diamond)
Schemes and *Schemes 2* (with Saundra)

Published by Kensington Publishing Corp.

THE MARK

Kiki Swinson

Kensington Publishing Corp.
www.kensingtonbooks.com

DAFINA BOOKS are published by

Kensington Publishing Corp.
119 West 40th Street
New York, NY 10018

All Kensington Titles, Imprints, and Distributed Lines are available at special quantity discounts for bulk purchases for sales promotions, premiums, fund-raising, and educational or institutional use. Special book excerpts or customized printings can also be created to fit specific needs. For details, write or phone the office of the Kensington special sales manager: Kensington Publishing Corp., 119 West 40th Street, New York, NY 10018, attn: Special Sales Department, Phone: 1-800-221-2647.

Library of Congress Card Catalogue Number: 2016955137

Dafina and the Dafina logo Reg. U.S. Pat. & TM Off.

ISBN-13: 978-1-61773-970-5
ISBN-10: 1-61773-970-7
First Kensington Mass Market Edition: February 2017

eISBN-13: 978-1-61773-971-2
eISBN-10: 1-61773-971-5
First Kensington Electronic Edition: February 2017

10 9 8 7 6 5 4 3 2 1

Printed in the United States of America

THE
MARK

1

I MESSED WITH THE WRONG GUY

I can't believe I finally got the life I've always wanted. It seemed like it was yesterday when I left Virginia from a life of crime. Even though I was on the run, I met and married the man I love and finally have a baby. No one would've ever told me that I was going to leave Matt, the hustler I'd been with since forever, after all he and I had been through. But him screwing around on me with Yancy changed everything. Taking all the money that he, Yancy, and I stole was the best revenge plot I could've ever mustered up. It felt good to be the last woman standing. It also helped me that after I ran off with the money, Matt and Yancy both got arrested. But Matt wasn't away for long.

Now here I was in my hospital room, looking at a man I'd hoped to never see again. I'd just delivered my baby boy and everything was supposed to be right in my world. But here he is, turning my dreams for the future into a nightmare. After Matt told me he had a couple of people on the outside pay off a couple COs on the inside to help break him out of jail in exchange for some of the $3 million payout, I watched as he walked out of the hospital room with my baby in tow. My entire body cringed at the sight of him holding my infant baby. There was nothing I could do that would calm me down and quell the alarming fear that flitted through my stomach right then. "Matt," I sobbed, barely able to speak. "Please . . . don't do this."

"Do what? Take your son like you took my mother-fucking money?" he chuckled wickedly. I crinkled my eyebrows in response. He stopped laughing abruptly and started talking in a very serious tone. "Bitch, I want back every fucking dime you took from me. And just know that if you don't come off it, you will be making funeral arrangements for this little motherfucker right here," he barked. His words sunk in on me and I felt hopeless. I didn't know what the fuck I was going to do, but I knew I had to come up with his money or else.

The thought of him mishandling or mistreating my baby made me sick to my stomach. Thankfully, he grabbed a few Pampers and bottles of formula to carry along with him. I cried silently, avoiding any unwanted attention. But I knew that if I stayed around here much longer, either the doctors or nurses would know something was wrong after they found out my baby was nowhere around.

Still somewhat medicated, I got up on shaky legs, but I couldn't let that deter me from getting out of there. I got dressed pretty fast and managed to walk out of the hospital without being detected by the staff who were assigned to treat me.

When I arrived downstairs on the main floor, my body felt hot all over. I felt like I could just faint. But I pressed on and got into the first taxi I saw. I gave him my home address, sat back in the seat, and tried to pull myself together. I couldn't help but wonder whether Matt really had Derek like he insinuated, so I called his cell phone and prayed that he'd answer it. My call was picked up on the second ring. "Hello," I rushed to say.

All I got was laughter on the other end. The laughter

came from Matt's voice. "Matt, where is Derek?" I asked. I was completely irritated by his insensitive behavior.

"I already told you where he was. Didn't you believe me?" he replied.

"I wanna speak to him now. I need to know if he's all right," I demanded.

"Hold on. Let me see if he's available." Matt continued his laughter.

The cell phone went silent for five long seconds. Then I heard my husband's voice. "Hello, Lauren, is this you?" Derek asked.

"Yes, baby, it's me. Are you all right?" I whined desperately. I needed answers and I needed them now.

"Yes, I'm fine."

"What about the baby? Is he all right? Has he been crying?"

"He's fine. He's drinking his bottle now," Derek replied, his voice sounding weary.

"Baby, don't worry. I'm gonna get you and our baby out of this okay," I tried to assure him.

"Now that's the spirit I like! Save your man and your baby!" Matt interjected. When I heard his voice, I knew that he had taken the phone from Derek.

"If you put your fucking hands on any one of them, I promise you'll fucking regret it!" I roared. I knew I couldn't actually speak of the money in front of the taxi driver nor the gun I was going to bring along with me when I finally met up with Matt to make the switch, so I said the next best thing. Matt knew what I meant.

"You only have twenty-four hours! So call me as soon as you pick up the money," he demanded, and then the call went dead.

Hearing Matt's usual warning play in my ears now made a huge lump in the back of my throat. Tears sprang up to my eyes, but I fought to keep them from falling. I couldn't let anyone know what was going on with me concerning Matt and my family. Letting someone know would be too risky. And I couldn't let anything happen to my family.

I swallowed hard and closed my eyes because I knew he wasn't going to let this go. I had to think quickly. This thing had gone from complicated to nightmarish. I was now responsible for two lives. Lives of two people I loved dearly.

I swear I blanked out after Matt disconnected our call. I had no idea I had arrived at my apartment building until the taxi driver announced it to me for the second time. "Ma'am, we are here at your destination," the taxi driver said.

I looked at the cabdriver and then I looked out the back-door window and realized that he was absolutely right. I was home, so I needed to pay him and continue on with my mission. I reached into my purse, grabbed thirty dollars, and paid him. Before he could give me my five dollars in change, I had already gotten out of the car and closed the door.

My family's life meant more to me than fucking five dollars. I walked into my apartment building as fast as I could, considering the amount of drugs I had in my system. The building doorman spoke to me upon opening the door. I spoke back without giving him eye contact. He knew I had been in the hospital to have the baby, so he made mention of it. "Ms. Kelly, where's the bundle of joy?" he asked cheerfully.

"He's still in the hospital with his dad," I yelled back without turning around. But the questions didn't stop there. He must've noticed the pain I was in when I walked by him because he asked me if I needed any help. "No, I'm good," I continued. I couldn't get on the elevator and away from that meddlesome doorman soon enough. As badly as I needed help to deal with getting my family back, I knew the doorman wouldn't be cut out for the job.

Thankfully, the elevator was empty when I got on it. When the elevator doors dinged open, the reality that Matt had resurfaced in my life had become a permanent fixture in my mind. I rushed through the elevator doors and sped down the long, carpeted hallway that led to my apartment. The hallway was pin-drop quiet as usual. In a ritzy building like that it was the norm. Although it was quiet and empty, I was looking around like a burglar about to rob someone's house; that is how nervous I felt. I don't know if I was nervous about going in my apartment or nervous about someone being there after I opened up the door.

My heart jerked in my chest as I reached down to unlock my door. Before I pushed the door open, I looked around again, paranoid that someone was watching me. But why? That damn hallway was empty as hell. So I pushed the door open and walked inside. Immediately after I closed the door and locked it, my mind was racing at an unbelievable speed. Trying to hatch a plan to get the money and get my baby and my man back was becoming a little more than I could bear. Deep down in my heart I knew I couldn't fuck this up. The depth of hatred that Matt had for me was indescribable. Not only had I robbed him of the heist he and I crafted together, I'd also left him and started another family. At this very moment, I needed to focus solely on giving Matt what he wanted. And if I didn't deliver the goods to him within twenty-four hours, I knew my family would die.

"Come on, Lauren, you can do this, baby girl," I started telling myself. I needed as much pep talk as I could get. "Get yourself together and go down to this bank and get that money so you can get your man and your baby back. They're all you have in this world. Fuck that money! Let that sorry-ass nigga have it. He needs it more than you."

I looked over at the clock on the DVR and noticed that I didn't have a lot of time before the bank closed. With my bank being ten blocks away from my apartment, I knew I had to hurry up, change clothes, and hop in the first taxi I saw. My family's lives depended on me.

On my way to my bedroom I had to walk past my baby's nursery. Derek and I designed this room ourselves. It was Derek's idea to paint the room blue, white, and yellow. But I picked out the thin-blue-striped wallpaper. His room was simply gorgeous. So when I entered it, my heart dropped at the sight of his empty, white, laced bassinette. Seconds later, tears formed and started falling from my eyes. Next thing I knew, I had broken down and started crying. All of the emotions I was feeling from the kidnapping consumed me. My baby wasn't supposed to be with Matt. He was supposed to be here with Derek and me. "God, please help me get my baby back!" I cried out after I fell down to my knees. "Lord, please don't let anything happen to my baby. He needs me, God! So please let me get him back safely. And I promise I will surrender my life totally to you, Lord!" I ended my prayer.

I think I wallowed in my sorrows for another ten minutes before I snapped out of it. Remembering I now had less than fifty minutes to dress and get the money got me back on my feet and focused. I wanted to take a shower but I couldn't. I didn't have enough time. Nor did I have the energy, so I took off everything I had on and slipped on a pair of dark brown cargo pants with pockets along the leg. Then I slipped on an old brown flannel shirt, two pairs of socks, a pair of tan Timberland boots, and a camouflage-designed cargo jacket. I looked like I was ready for war, but my body felt otherwise.

I looked back at the clock on the DVR and saw that another ten minutes had gone by. Panic-stricken, I grabbed an old backpack Derek owned that was on the floor of the hall closet. And then I grabbed his gun from the lockbox that was hidden in the back of the closet but on the top shelf. I wasn't going anywhere without it.

After I placed the pistol inside the backpack, I grabbed my house keys and two forms of ID from my purse and shoved all three items down inside the right front pocket of my pants. I was ready to get back what belonged to me and I was willing to risk my life to do it.

2

GOTTA GET THIS PAPER

I don't know how, but my adrenaline was pumping at a fast pace as I moved from my apartment to the first floor of my building. Like clockwork, my doorman was waiting at the front entrance to open the door for me. And once again, he made it his business to ask me if I was all right. "Yes, I'm fine. But you can help me get a cab," I told him without giving him eye contact.

"Oh yes, of course," he said, and rushed outside to the curb after he held the door open for me. Within seconds, he flagged down a cab and held the door open for me to get inside. I thanked him and then I instructed the driver to take me to Citibank. The Haitian driver started the meter and then he sped off. I laid my head back against the head-rest and thought about the possibilities that Matt could be hurting Derek and my son at that very moment. My poor babies. All of this shit happened because of me. It was my fault that I put them in this situation and now I had to make some moves to get them out of it.

As soon as the taxi pulled up in front of the bank I paid the driver and asked him to wait for me. After he demanded more money, I handed him a fifty-dollar bill and he agreed to do it. Immediately after the driver took the money, I slid out of the cab as quickly as I could without hurting myself. As I approached the bank, a nice gentleman held the door open for me. I thanked him and kept moving forward. I told a teller that I needed to get in my safe-deposit box, so she walked away from the counter to fetch the bank manager. Three minutes later a white woman approached me and introduced herself. After we shook hands, she escorted me to the vault located on the far side of the bank and led me into the area where the safe-deposit boxes were stored. Once she helped me pull out my box, she left me alone in the room so I could have my privacy. When I lifted the metal flap on the box, I saw exactly what I had come to the bank to get. There before my eyes was all the money I had left from the score. I knew it was $250,000 but I counted it again just to make sure. After I counted it, I stuffed every labeled $10,000 stack of bills into my bag and closed it. The customary thing to do would be to put the metal box back into the slot on the wall but I didn't have time for that. I had to get out of there. Time was winding down and I had to get my family back before Matt killed them.

The moment I walked outside of the bank, I pulled my cell phone out and made the call to Derek's phone. I knew Matt would answer it. "Hello," I heard Matt's voice say after he answered the call on the second ring.

"I have the money," I told him.

"Good. Where are you?" he wanted to know.

"I'm standing outside of the bank," I informed him.

"Come to Forty-Second Street in Manhattan and meet me in front of Grand Central Station," he instructed me, and then the line went dead.

Without hesitation I walked back to the cab that was waiting on me and slid into the backseat. "Take me to Grand Central Station," I instructed the driver.

"As you wish," the driver replied.

While the cabdriver dipped in and out of ongoing traffic, I wondered how this trade-off would go down. Matt only told me to meet him at Grand Central Station. Grand Central Station was a huge place, so he could hide anywhere without me knowing. I was worried that Matt would try to do something underhanded that would jeopardize my getting my family back. I swore on my family that if this were the case, then there would be some problems.

It didn't take the cabdriver long to get me to my destination. As soon as he made a right turn onto Forty-Second Street from Lexington Avenue, my heart started racing at an uncontrollable speed. I was so freaking afraid that I didn't immediately get out of the car when he announced that we had made it to the location. "Are you going to get out or what?" he asked me after I sat there for at least fifty seconds.

I looked at him and then I looked back out the rear passenger window. My feet felt like steel so I couldn't move them for anything. "Ma'am, you're gonna either pay me more money for me to stay parked here or you're gonna have to get out," the cabdriver expressed. I could tell that he was starting to get frustrated with me.

Part of me wanted to ask this man for his help, but then I realized that would be a bad idea. First of all, New Yorkers were known for not getting in strangers' public altercations. That was a no-no. They'd literally let you get killed in broad daylight and walk away from you like nothing happened. And in my case, I figured this cabdriver would do the exact same thing, so I kept my mouth closed and convinced myself that I had to do this alone.

After I paid the driver, I grabbed my bag of money and got out of the car. I didn't see which direction the cabdriver drove off in because I was so fixated on who I was going to walk into in this place. I stood a few feet away from the glass doors and called Derek's number back. Matt answered it on the second ring. "You here?" Matt didn't hesitate to ask.

"Yes, I'm here," I told him.

"Which side? What street?"

"I'm on the Forty-Second Street side."

"Got the money with you?"

"Yes, I got it in my backpack."

"Come inside and go into the women's restroom. Go into the last bathroom stall and wait there until I give you further instructions," he said, and then the call ended.

With my heart rate traveling at an uncontrollable speed, I braced myself because I wasn't sure what was coming next. But I pressed forward in the most courageous manner I could muster and walked inside Grand Central Station. Like always, this place was packed to the max. I surveyed the crowded station high and low for some sign of my husband and child on my way to the ladies' restroom, but they were nowhere in sight. Feeling somewhat hopeless I continued toward the restroom, praying that they would be there.

Upon entry, I saw a white woman at the bathroom sink washing her hands. She didn't acknowledge my presence. She continued to wash her hands and dried them with two paper towels that she pulled from the paper towel dispenser located on the wall near the exit door.

While I looked around the bathroom, I got a whiff of the stench coming from the noisy first stall. I damn near regurgitated all the chicken broth I had for breakfast at the hospital earlier. I almost turned around to leave but when I thought about my family, I quickly came back to my senses. I couldn't let anything deter me from getting my family back. They meant the world to me.

Immediately after I regained my faculties, I covered my nose with my shirt collar and proceeded to the last bathroom stall. The door was slightly ajar so I pushed it back enough to get inside. Right after I closed the door, I heard footsteps walking in my direction. I couldn't see anything but my eyes were on high alert.

The footsteps stopped when they got in front of my stall. I stood there quietly and waited for the person to announce themselves. My heart rattled in my chest. My mind started racing in a million directions and my body felt tense and rigid as I stood behind the stall door.

"Where is the money?" I heard the man's voice ask.

It wasn't Matt's voice, so I was kind of thrown off guard. I must admit, it felt eerie and kind of crazy being there not knowing what was about to happen next. "I got it right here with me," I told him.

"Well, slide it underneath the door," he instructed me.

"Where is my family?" I asked while I held on to the backpack for dear life.

"They're on the other side of the station," he told me.

"When am I going to get them?" I grilled him.

"Stop it with all the fucking questions and give me the money!" his voice boomed.

Very hesitantly, I bent down and slid the backpack underneath the door. The last thing I wanted to do was put my family in any further danger. Right after the guy picked the bag up from the floor, I heard his footsteps as they walked away. I panicked and opened the door. "Hey, where are you going?" I shouted after seeing the back of a guy who looked to be about five-ten with a one-hundred-eighty-pound build. He wore a black hoodie, a pair of dark blue jeans, and a tan pair of Timberland boots.

He didn't look back, nor did he respond to me, so I bolted behind him. By the time he got to the door and opened it, a middle-aged white woman blocked his exit. That stalled him just enough for me to grab ahold of the black jacket he wore over his black hoodie. I yanked on it for as long as I could but my strength was no match for his. He came right out of the jacket and pushed the woman out of the way. She fell backward into the wall behind her and then she slid to the floor. I stepped over her and tried to run behind him. I was no match for his speed, either. As soon as he ran onto the open floor of the station, he sprinted through the crowd. I watched him as he fled on foot toward the Eastside door of the station.

"Somebody grab him!" I yelled as I started running behind him, but after a few steps across the floor I knew I wouldn't be able to catch him, especially not in the condition I was in, so I stopped in my tracks. The people in the station were eerily silent. It felt like I was among a group of fucking robots or androids from some futuristic movie. They didn't even acknowledge that I was speaking to them. A huge lump formed in the back of my throat as tears sprang up to my eyes. I was on the verge of cursing their asses out but when my cell phone started ringing, I was instantly thrown off track. I reached into my pants pocket and grabbed it. I was panting intensely while I fumbled with the phone for a couple of seconds. The people surrounding me began looking at me kind of strange, but I totally ignored them. I was dealing with a life-or-death situation so their stares went right over my head. I almost dropped my phone on the floor when I noticed the call was from my husband's number. "Hello," I said into the phone, sounding desperate.

"You are playing a very dangerous game." Matt's words pierced my eardrums.

I ignored his words. "Look, your guy just ran off with the money so where is my family?" I yelled.

"Are you trying to bring attention to yourself?" Matt asked in a menacing tone.

"Where the fuck is my family?" I screamed through the phone, ignoring his question once more.

"After I get the money in my hands, I will call you back with the location where you can pick them up," Matt told me, and then the line went dead.

Before I could utter another word, Matt was gone just like that. I tried calling the number back but it went straight to voice mail all three times. Panic-stricken, I shoved my cell phone down inside my pocket and headed out the front exit of Grand Central Station.

While I was standing outside on the sidewalk, a dark feeling of helplessness came over me, and my knees felt like they were about to buckle. Matt's words started burning through me and I felt a wave of nausea that I didn't expect. I was also exhausted and in a lot of pain, so I knew I needed to sit before I fell down in the middle of the sidewalk and ended back up in the hospital.

I willed myself to go back into the station because I had no other place to go at this point. Upon reentering the station, I took the first available seat I saw. I sat there for nearly a minute before I was approached by a transit cop patrolling the station. He was a tall, chubby Latino cat with short black hair and big, round eyes. His English was very good. "Ma'am, are you okay?" he asked me.

I was out of it but his words echoed inside of my head. I looked at him with uncertainty. For a moment there, it seemed like I was seeing two images of him. But I quickly snapped out of it when I heard him radio another transit cop. "I think we might need a paramedic," I heard him say.

"Oh no! I'm fine. I don't need a paramedic," I belted out in sheer panic.

"Are you sure, ma'am?" the cop asked.

"Yes, I am sure. I just need to sit here for a moment, if you don't mind," I told him.

"Well, can you tell me why you were running after that man a few minutes ago?" the cop continued to question me.

"Look, it was just a big misunderstanding. I'm all right now."

"No problem, ma'am. But if you need me, I'll be over at the patrol station," he told me.

While he walked away, I heard him tell the patrol cop on the other end of the radio to disregard the medic call.

I stared as he made his way across the station's floor. He watched me and occasionally glanced at the patrons who roamed in and out of the station. I also found myself looking down at my cell phone every two to three minutes just to make sure I hadn't missed a call from Matt. I needed to hear from him. I needed to know that my husband and my baby were okay. The pain in my heart began to beat with a rapid speed. Knots started forming in my stomach. The feeling of not knowing what was going to happen next was starting to consume me. Then I started thinking back to how I got to this point.

I wasn't being greedy. Nor had I done anything sheisty. Matt and Yancy crossed me first. They're the ones who started this whole thing. So why try to kill my family because I fucked you before you fucked me? My husband and my brand-new baby had nothing to do with my actions. They didn't ask for this. So I had to make this thing right and bring them home.

I sat on that bench for seventeen minutes before my cell phone rang again. The ring startled me. I looked down at the caller ID and noticed that the call was coming from Derek's cell phone. "Hello," I said without hesitation.

"The money isn't all here. You still owe some bread," Matt said.

"But I thought you already knew that. What did you think I was living on? I had to eat and pay for a roof over my head," I began to explain.

"Fuck that! Do you think I give a fuck about you eating and having a place to lay your head?" Matt's voice boomed. "You spent over half of the fucking money. If Yancy was here she wouldn't be able to get her cut. And that wouldn't be fair. So you know what that means, right?"

"Matt, why do you care if Yancy's part isn't there? She's

not even around to get it," I tried to explain, but Matt interjected.

"Bitch, you fucked up! Now your family is going to pay for what you did. Say good-bye to your weak-ass husband and your fucking kid!" Matt roared.

My heart skipped a beat because I knew what Matt meant when he told me to say good-bye to my family. So at that very moment, I screamed at the top of my voice, begging and pleading for him to let my family go.

"Matt, please don't hurt my family!" I began to say, until I heard my husband's voice.

"Lauren, I love you, baby," he yelled, and then I heard two gunshots fire one after the other. POP! POP! The power that rang out from discharging the bullets struck my eardrums. I dropped the phone and it fell onto the floor. I felt dizzy for a second but immediately after I regained my faculties, I picked the phone back up from the floor and put it to my ears and screamed "hello" over a dozen times but no one replied. The phone line was completely quiet. And when I looked at the phone screen, that's when I knew Matt had disconnected our call. "No! No! No!" I screamed, while I redialed Derek's cell phone number. It kept going straight to his voice mail. *This is D. Sorry, I'm unavailable. Leave me a message at the tone.* BEEP . . .

"Answer the fucking phone!" I barked, and ended the call. I redialed his number again. But there was no luck. The voice mail picked up again. Instead of leaving a message, I pressed the end button and dialed the number again. I figured if I kept calling he'd answer at least one time. "Come on, come on, and answer the damn phone," I whispered to myself. My palms started sweating profusely. It felt like I was going to drop the phone a few times but I keep my composure.

After Derek's voice mail picked up for the eighth time, I pressed the end button and cursed the day that Matt was born. "Damn that motherfucker to hell! I swear, I'm gonna kill him if he murdered my fucking family! I fucking swear I am. How dare he do this to me after all I've ever done for him? All I've ever done was give that nigga the world! And this is how he repays me? Come after my family!" I roared as the blood boiled in my veins. I couldn't fathom losing my family like this. Not by Matt's hands. He was a fucking low-life son of a bitch! He already fucked up my life long before I left him and ran off with the money. So I couldn't let him come back and wreak havoc on my loved ones. That's savage behavior! I wouldn't ever do it to him. Whatever beef he had with me could've been settled between us. Not my family! Fucking miserable bastard!

3

YOU WIN SOME, YOU LOSE SOME

I hadn't noticed that the transit cop had come back over to where I was sitting until he got my attention. This time he wasn't alone. He had another transit cop with him. This cop was a white, curvy, short woman. "Ma'am, we're gonna have to ask you to come with us," he stated.

"Just leave me alone," I cried out as the tears rolled down my face.

The female cop reached out to grab me but I pushed her hand back in an abrupt manner. "Don't fucking touch me! Just leave me alone!" I spat.

"Ma'am, I'm sorry but you're gonna have to come with us," the female replied as she reached her hands out toward me.

This time I slapped them. "I said don't fucking touch me," I snapped.

At that very moment both transit cops grabbed me and wrestled me to the floor. "We tried to be nice to you," the male cop said as he handcuffed my wrists together.

"Ouch! You're fucking hurting me!" I screamed in agony.

"You put this on yourself," the female cop commented as she and the other officer lifted me from the floor.

I continued to yell and scream obscenities while they dragged me to their back office. All eyes were on me and I couldn't care less. I was dealing with bigger issues. My family was in harm's way by a nigga who hated my guts. So I could only imagine what he did to them.

Once inside the office, I was placed in an iron chair and handcuffed to an iron pole drilled into the wall. Both cops tried to calm me down but it wasn't working. All I could think about was my family. I pictured their lifeless bodies left alone in a run-down hotel room. My heart ached while I thought about not being able to talk to them or hold them and tell them how much I loved them anymore. The way I felt inside, I knew I would never ever get over it. There was nothing in this world that would make up for their losses. They meant the world to me. And I vowed to make sure Matt felt my pain when I'd be able to meet him face-to-face again.

I sat there in that iron chair for the next thirty minutes and cried my poor heart out. The transit cops thought I was on drugs. But when I told them that I had just come from the hospital and that I had just gotten some bad news, they finally understood why I was acting the way that I was. I was relieved about that considering I was carrying a fucking handgun in my backpack. It hadn't dawned on me until right then that I could've been arrested and booked for this fucking thing. How stupid could I have been to act like that, knowing I had a gun on me?

Thankfully, after everything was said and done, they released me. I even walked out of there without them filing assault charges on me. I apologized to them for my actions and they accepted it. As soon as I opened their office door, the female transit cop held up the jacket that I pulled off the guy's back and said, "Hey, you forgot your jacket."

"That's not my jacket," I told her.

"Are you sure? Because I grabbed it from the bench where you were sitting after we detained you," she replied.

I looked back at the jacket and something inside of me told me to take it with me. So I changed my tune. "Oh yeah, my bad! My mind is all over the place," I played it off, and grabbed the jacket from her.

I thanked them once again and left their office. While I was heading outside the station, a menacing and cold-hearted demon surfaced from my heart. All I could think about was going to war to avenge my family. I wanted Matt's severed head on a platter and vowed to myself that that mission would be accomplished, even if I had to die to it.

I got in the first taxi I saw. "Is everything okay?" the taxi driver asked me in his thick accent. I shot him such a glaring, deadly look that he just turned his little beady eyes back to the road and shut his mouth.

I got the driver to take me back home. I needed to go there so I could regroup. I needed to figure things out. I needed a plan of attack and I needed it right then, because I knew that at any given moment Matt would be getting out of New York as fast he could. I also knew that he wouldn't head back to Virginia. Taking that type of money back to your hometown where people are looking for you would be took risky. Matt would head somewhere he'd least be expected to go. All it would take for me was just a little thought. I used to be with this man. I once loved him so I knew his thought process. And I knew his heart. Unfortunately for me, he had the same advantage, which was how he was able to find me. But he fucked up! Because when he killed my family, he didn't kill me. Big fucking mistake on his part!

During the taxi ride, I went through all the pockets outside the jacket and pulled out a few food receipts. The first receipt was a pizza spot not too far from the hospital where I had my son. The next receipt was from a Chinese restaurant in the same fucking area. My heart rattled in my chest, because I knew this had to be a sign.

I stuffed those receipts back in the same pockets I got them from, shoved my hand down the one inside pocket he had, and pulled out a hotel key card. My heart rattled more and then it dropped into the pit of my stomach. The key card didn't have a name on it. It looked like it was worn off. That led me to believe the hotel was old and run-down.

I leaned forward and asked the cabdriver if he knew which hotel had this type of key card. I held it out so he could get a good look at it. But after he glanced at it, he said, "I can't say. That key could belong to any of these run-down hotels in the city."

Desperation engulfed me. I needed some answers. More importantly, I needed answers that would satisfy me. It had to be something that would bring me closer to where Matt had my family. "Sir, please take another look at it. I need to know which hotel this key belongs to," I pleaded.

"I'm sorry, ma'am. All of the run-down hotels in this city have the same cards. They keep them until they don't work anymore."

Telling me that all the run-down hotels had the same key cards didn't help me at all. I was in total distress. This wasn't the answer I was looking for.

My fists were curled tightly and my toes were bunched up in my shoes as the taxi rounded the corner of the block where my apartment building stood. The closer I got to it the harder my heart drummed against my chest bones. I took a deep breath, but meditation and even a tranquilizer would probably not have calmed me down at that moment. There was definitely a raging wildfire going on in my brain. I couldn't describe the different thoughts and feelings coursing through my mind at that moment. I guess the words that were ringing loud and clear for me were *be-*

trayal and *hurt*. Matt had surely done it now. Everything that he and I ever had had gone out the window. There were no good memories for him and me. Everything had been erased from my mind. And all I could think about was what he'd done to my family. He took the very thing that mattered to me because of some fucking money. I promised I would see to it that he got back everything he deserved, even if it meant a slow and painful death. I was gonna make that nigga wish he never met me. And that was my word!

4

BACK AT SQUARE ONE

With that guy's jacket in hand, I stomped down the carpeted hallway; that much I did know, but I was definitely on cruise control. My legs were pretty much carrying me along because my brain certainly wasn't thinking straight. I guess it was a good thing that my muscle memory knew the direction to my apartment like the back of my hand because as angry as I was, I might've walked right into a damn wall had I not known automatically where to go.

A few of my neighbors gave me some hard stares but none of them dared to question me. They knew I wasn't a very friendly person, even before I lost my family. So after I entered my apartment, I collapsed on my living room sofa. I turned on the TV even though I knew I wasn't going to watch it. I believed I did it so I could hear someone's voice in my apartment other than my own. Thinking about Derek and my baby boy gave me the feeling of not wanting to live anymore. How was I going to go on with my life without Derek and our son? This wasn't how my life was supposed to be. My life was filled with happiness! I was in love and it felt like I finally found someone who loved me back. Now they were both gone. I've heard people say that death was untimely. I guessed I never thought I'd witness it myself. Who would've thought that I was going to wake up that morning with my baby and my man and lose them both? Never in a fucking million years!

I sat there on the sofa with the key card in hand and hoped that God would give me a sign. Then it hit me. I grabbed the food receipts from the pizza spot and Chinese restaurant and noticed that they were only a block away from each other. And the times on the receipts were hours apart, so that led me to believe that the hotel they were staying at couldn't be that far away. I grabbed my cell phone from my handbag and googled hotels near the restaurants. A small list of five run-down hotels popped up. I screenshot all of them and called them one by one. I made the first call to Parkside Hotel on Seventy-Ninth Street. A man answered on the first ring. "Thanks for calling Parkside Hotel, how may I be of service to you?" he said.

"Hi, sir, I'm looking for a guest by the name of Matt Connors. Can you tell me if he checked out yet?" I asked him. I wanted him to believe that I knew Matt was there. This way I'd have a better chance at getting whatever information I needed just in case Matt was actually there.

"Ma'am, I'm looking in our system and I don't see him registered as one of our guests," the man stated.

"Are you sure? I mean, maybe the room is registered under his brother's name. They're both from Virginia."

"Does his brother have the same last name?"

"No, he doesn't. But he'd be registered under a Virginia driver's license," I replied. I knew he heard the desperation in my voice because I heard it myself.

"Ma'am, if you don't have a name then I won't be able to help you."

"Well, would you just tell me if there's someone there registered under a Virginia driver's license?"

"I'm sorry, ma'am. I won't be able to do that."

"Sir, please, this is a very urgent matter," I begged him.

"Ma'am, I'm sorry but what you're asking me to do is against hotel policy."

"Sir, this a life-or-death situation."

"Ma'am, if it's really a life-or-death situation then you need to contact the police," he told me.

Instead of pressing him anymore, I disconnected our call. I was livid that I wasn't able to get the information I needed so I called the next hotel on my list. It was called The Lucerne. It was also located on Seventy-Ninth Street. I crossed my fingers and prayed to God that Matt was at this hotel. *Thanks for calling The Lucerne. Our operator will be with you shortly,"* the recording said.

I waited for a couple of seconds and then I got a live person on the phone. "Thanks for calling The Lucerne, how may I direct your call?" the operator asked me.

"I'm looking for a guest by the name of Matt Connors. Will you please connect me to his room?" I asked the operator.

"Do you have a room number?" she asked me.

"No. He called me and left me a message that he'd be at this hotel and for me to call him back," I lied to her.

"I'm afraid I don't see him as a guest at our hotel."

"Are you sure? I mean, he just left the voice mail for me to call him back at this hotel," I continued to lie.

"Would there be another guest accompanying him?" the operator wanted to know. She was being very thorough with her search.

"You know what? I didn't think about that. He's probably with his friend Kevin," I added, coming up with the first name I could think of.

"What's Kevin's last name?" she asked me.

Once again, I gave her the first name I could come up with. "Ummm, I think it's Brown," I told her, knowing damn well I didn't know a Kevin Brown. Nor did Matt know a guy by the name of Kevin Brown. I knew I only had a small window of opportunity to build a rapport with the woman in hopes that she'd help me locate Matt by any means necessary. I also knew that I needed to sound like she was being very helpful and that I appreciated her time.

I heard her clicking on the keys of her computer keyboard and then the clicking sound stopped. "I'm sorry, ma'am, but I don't see where we have a Kevin Brown as one of our guests."

I let out a long sigh. "This is strange because I just got a message from him saying that he was at this hotel."

"Why don't you call him back?" she suggested.

"Could you tell me if you've had a guest check in with a Virginia driver's license?" I asked while I crossed my fingers.

"I'm afraid I can't say, ma'am. But I'm sure if you call this gentleman back, he'll tell you which room he's registered under."

I sucked my teeth. I was fucking disgusted that I struck out for the second time. I abruptly hung up. "Fucking bitch!" I spat. I was losing patience and time was running out. I needed to find Matt before he and his crew left the city.

Back to the drawing board, I called the third hotel on the list. It was called Hotel Belleclaire. It was on Seventy-Seventh Street and it was only about two blocks from Riverside Park. A female operator answered. "Thank you for calling Hotel Belleclaire. How may I direct your call?"

I took a deep breath and crossed my fingers. "Would you connect me to Mr. Matt Connors's room?" I asked.

"Do you know what room he's in?" she wanted to know.

"No, ma'am, I don't. He just left me a message telling me he was at this hotel and for me to call him back. We're both from Virginia. He came up here yesterday for a business meeting. My plane just landed here at LaGuardia a few minutes ago so I'm very excited and can't wait to see him," I lied, hoping this would help me find out if Matt was there.

"I don't see a Matt Connors registered here. Are you sure he told you that he was at the Hotel Belleclaire?" the lady wondered aloud.

"Yes, ma'am, he did. And now that I think about it, maybe the company he works for has the room registered under their name. The company is out of Virginia. You may also see a few more people from Virginia registered there too. They would be his friends and colleagues. The company my husband works for had a big convention last night. Their formal dinner for the husbands and wives is tonight," I continued to lie. I knew I had to spread this lie on real thick. Plus, I knew I had to keep talking. This would throw her off her game and keep her from realizing that I was trying to get information out of her.

"What's the name of the company your husband works for?" the woman asked.

"East Coast Inc.," I replied. This lying game I was playing was becoming easier by the minute.

I heard a few more clicks. Then she said, "I don't see the name of that company listed in our database, but I do see a Walter Gene from Norfolk, Virginia, registered as a guest."

"Oh, that's his friend of ten years," I blurted out.

"Would you like for me to connect you to that room?" she asked.

"Sure. But what's the room number so I can have it when I get there."

"I'm not at liberty to give you the room number but I can transfer you to the room."

"Well, that's fine," I lied once again. As happy as I was at the beginning of our conversation, now all of that was gone. I felt defeated all over again. I needed a fucking hotel room number. Fuck transferring me to the room. What the hell was I going to say after someone answered the phone? *Hello, this is Lauren and I'm looking for Matt because he just killed my fucking husband and my baby. Can you please put him on the phone?* Yeah, that would be the dumbest shit I could ever do. I guessed I had to take what she gave me and go from there.

"Will you hold on while I connect you?" she asked me, and then I heard a couple of clicks. Seconds later, the line started ringing. Immediately, my mind raced like crazy. I went from being upset that I couldn't get the room number to becoming mentally frazzled. But I knew this was my only chance to find out where Matt was so I gave myself a quick pep talk. *Shake it off, Lauren. You gotta act level-headed. This might be your only chance to find your family. Be smart about it.*

My heart started beating erratically. I couldn't believe that I found out which hotel Matt was staying at. Was this a miracle or what? I thought about what I was going to say when I heard his voice. Was I going to threaten him? Was I going to give him a chance to make things right? Either way, I knew this call wasn't going to be pleasant for me, knowing that my family was dead. And knowing this, I allowed the phone to ring once and then I hung it up. I knew I'd botch my plan of catching Matt if I got him on the phone and asked him where he was. I sat there with the phone in my hands and racked my brain trying to figure out how I was going to execute my plan. Then it hit me. I remembered that Derek and I had a family locator app on our phones. Excited that I could use my GPS and the app to locate him, I turned the feature on and pressed the send button. I waited for the GPS to pinpoint Derek's whereabouts. As soon as the locator beeped, I zoomed in on the location.

Derek's phone was definitely at the Hotel Belleclaire so I was on the right track. Now why hadn't I thought about this before? Fuck! I'd wasted so much time. I could've probably saved my family if I would've thought about using my fucking GPS cell phone locator. "Ugh!" I screeched through clenched teeth. But then I realized that I couldn't beat myself up. I had to get focused. I had to get out of there right then. Knowing this gave me the burst of energy I needed to drag myself off my sofa and out my front door. It only took me several minutes to get back down to the first floor. I grabbed the first cab I saw and instructed the man behind the wheel to take me to Hotel Belleclaire across town.

My adrenaline was pumping while my heart started racing with no plans of stopping. The blood pumping through my veins started boiling at the mere thought of Matt taking their lives. "Can you go a little faster?" I barked at the driver. It just seemed like we were going in slow motion.

"Lady, you want me to speed and get a ticket?" he barked back.

"Look, just get me to the damn hotel!" I spat. My heart was heavy and my mind was going into overload. I didn't know how things were going to go down but I knew I'd figure it out once I was finally at the hotel.

I kept looking down at the GPS tracker on my phone. For the entire drive to this hotel the dot remained still. I couldn't tell if the GPS tracker on my phone was functioning properly, and that scared me. The fear of not knowing began to cripple my mind. Thankfully, I didn't let that deter me from moving forward to find Matt and my family.

As soon as the taxi driver pulled up to the front of the hotel, I wasted no time paying him his fare. "Keep the change," I told him after I tossed thirty dollars at him.

I tried to walk into the hotel lobby as fast as I could without hurting myself. There was no doorman there to let me in so I stepped up to the glass doors. Inside, the lobby was empty. I looked for the desk clerk and there was no one insight. I walked up to the counter and hit the bell placed on top of it. Seconds later, a gentleman who looked like he was from India came forth. "How can I help you?" he asked me in his foreign accent.

"I'm looking for my cousin. I don't know what room he's in but he told me he was at this hotel. So I was wondering if you could call his room and tell him that I am here," I lied.

"What is your cousin's name?"

"Matt Connors," I told him, and then I watched him type Matt's name into his computer.

"I'm sorry, but I don't have any guests by that name registered here at this hotel."

"Well, that can't be right because I just called an hour ago and was transferred to his room," I lied once more.

"Are you sure you've got the right hotel?"

"Of course."

"Maybe he's registered under a different name."

"I'll tell you what, look in your system for an African-American male who checked into this hotel between yesterday and today with a Virginia ID."

"I'm sorry but I can't do that. That's against hotel policy."

"Don't you own the place?"

"No, I am not the owner. And if I were I couldn't do it."

Becoming frustrated by this man's lack of cooperation, I leaned over on the counter as tears filled up my eyes. I knew Matt had to be here. He had Derek's phone. And according to my GPS, Derek's cell phone was somewhere in one of these hotel rooms. "Listen, sir, I am in a severe amount of pain. I just got out of the hospital from having a baby two days ago. So all I'm asking you to do is find out where my family is so I can get off my feet and lie down. Now can you do that for me please? I beg you."

"I'm sorry, ma'am, I can't do that. I told you that's against hotel policy," he said, and stood there as if he wasn't going to budge.

It took everything within me not to take my gun out of my purse and shoot this man right in his head. I figured I really had nothing to lose. But then it dawned on me that I was going to find out where Matt was one way or another.

I changed my tune and told the hotel clerk that I appreciated his time. This allowed me to put him in a mind frame of letting his guard down. And guess what? It worked. As soon as he turned to walk back to the room from which he came, I pulled my gun out of my purse as I rushed toward him. Before he could fully turn around, I had the gun pointed in his back. "Turn your motherfucking ass around and walk back to that fucking computer," I snapped.

"Please don't hurt me! I will do anything you want," he whined like a little bitch.

"Shut the fuck up! I ain't gonna hurt you. I just wanna find my fucking family like I told you the first time," I barked as I pushed him toward the counter.

He started hitting the computer keys without me asking. When I looked at the monitor, I noticed that he was signing back into the system with his ID number.

"Who am I looking for?" he uttered, barely audible.

"Just find anyone in the system who registered under a Virginia driver's license," I instructed him.

There was a long list of people who had checked in the hotel between yesterday and today. He went from floor to floor as he searched his database. I stood behind him and peered over his shoulder as we both read all the names on the list. Then my heart stopped. I couldn't believe my eyes. There in black-and-white was Derek's full name. "Oh my God! He used Derek's name to get the fucking room." I panicked. My heart began to race at an uncontrollable speed. Now why the fuck hadn't I thought of that? I felt an influx of sweat pouring from the pores of my hands. I searched the screen for the room number. And there it was listed at the bottom. Room 318. "Get a key card for Room Three-Eighteen now," I instructed him while I buried the gun deeper into his back.

The hotel clerk scrambled to make a key card for Room 318. "Hurry up before somebody comes in here!" I ordered him while I kept my eyes on him plus the front entrance.

"I'm doing it as fast as I can," he replied.

"Well, do it faster." I ground my teeth. I found myself looking toward the entryway the guests used to get back and forth to their rooms. I could never be too careful. Matt and his boys could've easily come down while I was holding the hotel clerk at gunpoint.

After I nudged him in the back a couple of times, he made a copy of the key card and handed it to me. I snatched it from his hands and grabbed him by his right arm. "Come on, let's go," I said. I was ready to go and face these niggas head-on.

"No! No! I must stay down here just in case someone comes walking through the front door," he protested. He didn't want to budge.

"Nah, fuck that! You gotta go with me. You won't fuck around and call the cops on me," I said, and then I pushed him in front of me.

"No, I promise I won't call the cops," he pleaded.

"I know you ain't, now walk faster before you get one of these bullets in the back," I threatened him. I was serious as hell. The way I was feeling, I'd shoot anyone who got in my way of finding my family. It didn't matter if they were dead or alive. I just needed to find them.

The guy picked up his pace and headed toward the elevator. I crossed my fingers and prayed that no one was on the elevator when the doors opened. I was able to exhale after the doors opened and saw that no one was inside. I immediately nudged him in the back and said, "What are you waiting for? Get on." He stumbled into the elevator, finally catching his balance while the doors were closing. I pressed the button for the third floor and waited while the elevator moved.

"Don't try to do anything stupid when we get off this elevator. All I wanna do is see who's inside of Room Three-Eighteen. So as soon as we get to the door I want you to open it. But before you do that, I wanna stand outside the door very quietly and see if I can hear any movement."

"Lady, I don't wanna get hurt."

"And you won't if you do everything I tell you to."

"Well, will you please tell me what's going on?" he begged.

"I'm sorry but I can't get into that right now. Just do what I tell you to do and you'll be fine," I replied, as anguish washed over me. But simultaneously I wondered if I was about to go to war with Matt and the niggas he brought with him from Virginia. I finally shoved my phone down into my pocket as the elevator door opened. I took a deep breath and exhaled. "Let's go," I instructed him, and nudged him in the back once more.

He walked off the elevator and I followed him. There wasn't a soul visible in that hallway. But I looked up and down the hallway twice just to make sure my eyes and ears weren't deceiving me. It was completely silent. With my heart still racing painfully in my chest, I tiptoed behind the Indian guy as he led the way.

Please. Please. Please. Let this whole thing go right, I was chanting in my head. It didn't help that my mind raced with a million thoughts about how this situation was going to go down. Too bad I couldn't tell the Indian guy that he might get murked in the crossfire. I figured he'd be all right if his life was right with his maker. He walked ahead of me while I tailed him closely.

"Remember what I told you to do. And don't try to be a hero," I uttered quietly.

"Yes, of course," he replied. It was barely audible.

Shaking like a leaf, the Indian guy walked a total of ten steps and then stopped in front of Room 318. It was on the left side of the hallway. I grabbed his arm and motioned for him to stand still while I listened for any movement in the room. Then I took my eyes off the door and looked down each end of the hallway. I noticed that there were two exits on the floor. One for the elevator and the other one was the staircase. I looked at the Indian guy and asked him how many guests were staying on this floor. After he told me that there was only one guest, I asked him if the other guests were a couple and he confirmed that they were a white young couple from Pennsylvania.

"A'ight, well, get close to the door and slide the key in the lock real slow," I instructed him in a whisper-like tone as I moved away from the door. I stood alongside the wall just in case someone was inside the room and they started firing shots at the door.

"If someone is in there, act like you opened the wrong door," I continued whispering.

I watched as he slid the key card inside the lock slowly and pulled it out. After the green light flashed he pushed the door in very carefully. "Hello, I'm here to fix the thermostat," he yelled out. I swear, I was about to jump out of my fucking skin when he made that loud outburst. I didn't tell him to announce himself until he saw someone. Fucking idiot! That shit wasn't a part of the plan. He was supposed to open the door and remain quiet. But no! This crazy-ass cat yelled out like he was the fucking handyman. I almost lost all my composure. I rushed down behind him and rammed the barrel of my gun directly into his spine. "What the fuck are you doing?" I huffed as we stood in the foyer of the room.

"It's okay. It's okay. No one is here," he spoke quietly as

he pointed to the lights being shut off all over the room. I stood there for a second to take it all in. Was he right? I asked myself. Couple of seconds after hearing no noise or movement, I pushed the Indian guy farther into the room. As he walked toward the main area where the bed was, I checked the closet and bathroom to make sure I wasn't walking into a trap. Once I realized that everything was clear, we moved into the main area. The moment we walked onto the open floor, the Indian guy stopped in his tracks, causing me to stumble into him. "What the fuck are you doing?" I snapped. Before he could open his mouth, I peered over his shoulders and saw a man lying facedown on white sheets soaked in his blood. I looked at his shoes first and that's when I knew that it was Derek's lifeless body lying on the bed. Horror and rage shot through me like lightning as I took off toward my dead husband.

Once I was within arm's reach of Derek's body I realized that Matt had hog-tied him, laid a pillow over his head, and shot him point-blank. Derek hadn't had a fighting chance. My heart was broken looking down at my husband. I stood there and cried like a baby while I watched my man lie in his own blood. My body felt weak while my legs began to buckle. I thought I was going to be strong, but my body proved otherwise.

My legs finally gave out and I collapsed back onto the chair next to the bed and my gun fell to the floor. That's when the Indian guy made a run for it. "I'm calling the cops!" he yelled as he fled on foot.

Hearing the word *cops* made me gather my senses. I knew I couldn't be there when the cops came, so I got up on my feet and searched around on the bed for my baby. I pulled every sheet and pillow off the bed but there was still no sign of my son anywhere. I crawled down onto the floor and looked under the bed, and there was still no sign of my baby. "Where the fuck is my baby?!" I screamed as I dragged myself back up on my feet. I picked my gun up off the floor after I stood up. Once I felt like I could stand up completely, I looked into the nearby closet once again and then back into the bathroom, but there was no sign of him. I swear, it felt like my heart was about to be ripped out of my chest. I couldn't for the life of me figure out where my baby could be. I knew I couldn't stand in that room any longer if I didn't want to get arrested for holding the hotel clerk hostage so I got out as soon as I could.

Instead of taking the elevator down to the first floor, I took the staircase, hoping I could get out of the hotel before the police got there. Unfortunately for me, that didn't happen. As soon as I entered onto the first floor, I saw five cops rushing toward the elevator. "Oh my God! If they catch me with this gun, I'm leaving out of here in handcuffs," I said aloud, but only for me to hear it. *Lauren, you can't let that happen*, I thought to myself. So without hesitation, I slid back into the staircase and took the stairs down to the basement floor. I had no idea where I was going. But I knew I had to get as far away from the cops as I possibly could.

I damn near tripped going down the steps to get to the bottom floor. There was a door to my right. The sign on it read PARKING GARAGE, so I opened it and went through it. I closed the door behind me very quietly to avoid being heard just in case the cops decided to take the flight of stairs going up to the third floor.

My heart was pounding like I had run miles and miles at top speed. It beat so hard that I could even feel it throbbing in my throat. Sweat poured down the sides of my face while I quickly managed to maneuver my way through a few tight spots behind parked cars that allowed me to avoid being seen on the garage surveillance cameras. It took me about three minutes to get out of there and back on the streets without being detected and that was all that mattered.

Out of breath, I flagged down a taxi and instructed the

driver to take me to my apartment. En route, my heart and mind raced with uncertainty. I had no fucking idea what I was going to do next. But I knew I needed to go back to my apartment, get a few things, and leave before the cops got there. After they ran the surveillance footage back from the hotel cameras, they were going to find out who I was and it would be matter of time before they came kicking down my fucking apartment door. "Come on, Lauren, think," I mumbled to myself.

"You say something?" the female taxi cabdriver asked.

"No, I'm talking to myself," I said, brushing her off.

"You don't look too good. Are you all right?" she wondered aloud as she looked at me through her rearview mirror.

"Yes, I'm fine. Just please get me to my apartment as soon as you can," I begged.

"Honey, if you are having man problems, you better get rid of him," she advised me in a casual but friendly manner.

"Ma'am, listen, I appreciate the advice. But right now is not the time for it," I brushed her off once again.

"Okay, I get the picture. You don't have to tell me twice. I know how to close my mouth," she commented, and turned her attention toward the cars in front of her.

While I watched the female cabdriver dip in and out of traffic, my head swirled with a mixture of anger, heartbreak, and betrayal. I mumbled to myself because the thoughts going through my head were just too much to keep inside. Confusion was the biggest thing for me at that moment. *How could he? How the fuck could he shoot Derek in cold blood like that? Matt killed my husband execution-style. What the hell did Derek do to warrant that type of execution? Was it because Matt believed he was a fucking threat?* I couldn't answer that question but I was going to sure as hell find out after I finally tracked that mother-fucker down.

I tried to focus on what was before me and what I

needed to do to find out where Matt was. I knew that if I found him, I'd find my baby. The thought of my baby pained me. Not knowing where he was became unfathomable to me. How was it that Derek's body was lying in a pool of his own blood and our baby was nowhere to be found? Had Matt really killed my son? Or had he taken my baby with him? I swore, I wished I knew the answers to those questions because it was killing me inside not knowing.

The drive to my apartment took thirty minutes. When the cabdriver pulled up in front of the building, she told me my fare was thirty-two dollars, so I handed her two fifty-dollar bills and asked her to wait for me. "I sure will, honey. But if you ain't out here before your hundred dollars runs out, I'm gonna have to leave you here," she warned me.

"Don't worry, I will be back in five minutes," I assured her, and got out of the car.

My doorman opened the door for me, "Ms. Lauren, put a smile on that beautiful face," he said as he held the door open for me.

I ignored him of course and headed up to my apartment. The moment I walked through the door, I made a beeline to my bedroom. I grabbed my Louis Vuitton travel bag and stuffed it with every piece of clothing I could get in it. I threw a few toiletries into the bag as well as a pair of comfortable sneakers. Once I saw that I gathered all I could carry, I grabbed Derek's checkbook from his desk in our home office. I figured the only way I could get some money was to write a check to myself from his account. I also knew that if I didn't hurry up and get to the bank, the cops would shut down his account. Now, I couldn't let that happen until I took care of my business first. Shit, I needed every dime I could get because deep down in my heart I knew I was going to have to take a trip back to Virginia. Matt wasn't built to live in this city. He'd gone back to a place he was all too familiar with—I knew that for sure. And I was going to meet him there on his home turf. I just had to make sure that he didn't see me coming. Catching him off guard would be the best way to take him down. Because I knew I would be able to go toe to toe with him. He lived for that type of shit. That's why when I went after him, I'd have to do it right. That way I wouldn't have to worry about him ever again.

5

WHERE IS MY BABY?

Like I had asked, the female cabdriver was still awaiting my return when I walked out of my apartment building. She saw me struggling with my travel bag and jumped out of the car to help me. "I got this, sweetie. Just climb in the backseat and I'll handle the rest," she said.

Immediately after I sat down in the backseat, she handed me my LV bag and closed the back door right after. "Where are you headed to now?" she asked.

"Take me by Bank of America."

"Is that your final stop?"

"No, all I need to do is run in there for a moment. I will be right back."

"You know that I have to keep the meter running?"

"Yes, I know."

"All right, sounds good to me," she commented, and sped away from a building.

Thankfully, Bank of America was only a few blocks away. I don't know how I did it, but I mustered up enough strength to walk inside the bank and cash a $1,500 check I wrote to myself, but of course I forged Derek's name on the signature line. I wanted to write a larger amount on the check but I knew if I did, there was a chance the bank would try to call Derek's phone to get the approval to release the funds to me. Having that happen would be too risky, so I settled for the next best thing.

"May I help you?" the young Caucasian woman asked me. I swear she looked like the UK singer Adele. She looked like her fucking twin. Her strong similarities caught me off guard. She smiled at me. I smiled back even though I was still on edge. I needed to cash this check or I'd be in another fucking jam. "I wanna cash this check," I told her as I placed the check down on the counter in front of her. I had to play it cool. Act relaxed.

"Do you bank with us?" she asked me.

"No, I don't."

"Since you don't have an account with us, I will have to charge you a fee to cash this check."

"That's no problem." I told her. "Here's my ID," I continued, and handed it to her.

She took it, looked at it, and then she looked at me. I almost had a fucking heart attack when she looked over my ID thoroughly. "Has anyone told you that you look like the singer Adele?" I asked her. I figured I needed to say something to distract her just a bit. Get her mind off my ID and more on cashing the damn check.

She smiled at me again. "Yes, I get that all the time," she replied.

"You could probably make a lot of money acting as her body double," I suggested, trying to carry on a brief conversation.

"That would be great. Anything that would take me away from this place," she commented, and then she chuckled while she hit the computer keys. A few seconds later she wrote on the front of the check, pulled out her cash drawer, counted the money on the counter in front of me, and then handed it to me. "Here you go, one thousand five hundred dollars."

After I took the money into my hands, I felt a huge burden off my shoulders. I almost wished that I'd written the check for more money. But then again, I figured, why press my luck? Besides, I now had money to leave town to go after Matt's ass. This was only a small victory, but at least it was one. I thanked the teller for her assistance and made my way back out of the bank.

As soon as I got back inside the cab I instructed the cabdriver to take me to the Asian bus station on Forty-Second Street.

"As you wish," she replied, and pulled back into the road.

I decided to take the Chinese bus down south to Virginia because it was less risky to travel on the Asian charter bus. The Asian folks who ran the bus transit business never asked you for ID. All they wanted was for you to tell them where you wanted to go and hand over the money to complete the process to print you a ticket. So it was that easy to get out of town undetected. This way was perfect because I didn't want the authorities in New York to know where I was headed.

While we were driving across town, I thought about my baby boy, how I was going to move on with my life without Derek. And then all of a sudden, I thought about his cell phone and the fact that I didn't bother to search for it after I got inside the hotel room. So, out of curiosity, I pulled my cell phone from my pocket, zeroed in on the GPS tracker, and noticed the signal was completely gone. That led me to believe that the cops must've found it and turned the phone off.

A sharp pain shot through my heart. Did I just get a reality check or what? Was Derek really dead? Was he really gone out of my life forever? He didn't deserve to die like that. And I didn't know what Matt had done with my baby, but I knew I would soon find out, whether it killed me or not. It would be revealed to me.

"We're here," the cabdriver announced.

He looked out the window and saw a ton of people boarding another bus with the marquee saying that it was heading to DC. So when I realized that that wasn't the bus I was going to be traveling on, I paid the driver an extra twenty dollars for being my chauffeur for the past hour or so.

"You take care of yourself, you hear?" she said.

"Yes, I hear you," I replied, giving her a half smile.

"Need some help carrying your bag?"

"No, I'm good. The ticket booth is only a few feet away."

"Okay, well, you be safe," she mentioned.

"I will. And thanks," I replied, and walked away.

I got in line to purchase my ticket and watched the cab as it sped off into the congested city streets. There were about eleven people in front of me so it didn't take that long to get my ticket. I shoved it down into my purse and sat down on a nearby row of metal seats. I watched as men, women, and children walked throughout this little waiting area. And when I saw this young lady carrying a baby girl who looked to be at least one year old, I thought about my baby.

I began to wonder if he was still alive. Because why wasn't I able to find his body? Unless Matt dumped the body in a nearby Dumpster. Oh my God! Just the thought of my baby being thrown into a garbage Dumpster made me sick to my stomach. I mean, how fucking wicked could someone be? Matt knew he fucked up when he took my family from me. So I knew that finding him wasn't going to be easy. It was definitely going to be a daunting task, but I was up for it. But my quest for revenge weighed on me far heavier than thinking about the task itself. That was what I needed to focus on.

I dried up my tears and tried to focus on that task. For many years, I had taken from people and had not cared how my actions affected them. But as of today, I felt a tremendous blow that would affect my life forever. And I knew that in order for me to get payback, and execute it in proper fashion, I was going to have to take my heart out of the equation and deal with things with my head.

I couldn't tell you how this would all end, but I knew that no one would be able to walk around and speak about what they'd done to me. I promised Derek and my son, wherever he was, that I would have the last say.

During the bus ride, I planned to drum up some ideas about how I was going to track Matt down if he was back in Virginia, but I found myself sitting next to this very talkative young guy by the name of Quincy. He was a very handsome guy. He kind of reminded me of a younger version of the rapper T.I. He sparked up a conversation with me only a couple of minutes after he sat next to me. My seat was by the window, so I was looking out of it and minding my business when he introduced himself. From the intense look he gave me, I could tell that he sensed my troubles. But he didn't ask me any questions. Instead, he told me he was a college student from Norfolk State and that he was visiting a friend in New York while he was on spring break. I said hi, and then I told him my name was Chantel and that I was on my way to Virginia to visit my grandmother, hoping that would be enough, but it wasn't. This guy kept talking.

I did I manage to tell him that I was tired and that I wanted to get some rest, but it went in one ear and out the other. He rambled on about how his girlfriend left him for another guy and that he was cool because the night before spring break started he met another young lady, who was really nice, so he was looking forward to getting to know her.

This whole puppy love situation he had going on was a little too cheesy for me. I had to admit that he seemed like a nice guy, but naïve for the most part. To hear him talk about his life made me look at my own. This guy was a college student and it seemed like he had a bright future ahead of him. I'm talking lucrative career, a wife, kids, and maybe a home on a lakefront property. But here I was, living a life of chaos. I stole people's identities and took everything that they'd worked so hard for. I literally turned people's lives upside down in the blink of an eye. Because of it, I became this vengeful and greedy person. And that alone caused the death of my family. But what was really screwed up about my life was that I couldn't change it. I was stuck in this bottomless pit forever, while this guy here could live a normal life. Whether he knew it or not, he had it good.

Fortunately for me, he finally noticed how tired I was and left me alone after he ran down his whole life story. I dozed off to sleep for a few hours, but that was short-lived once Quincy told me that we had made it to our destination. I was a bit groggy but I managed to gather my thoughts together and muster up enough energy to grab my travel bag and exit the bus. "No, wait, let me carry that for you," Quincy insisted as he took my LV bag from my hands.

"Thank you," I said, and then I led the way to the front of the bus.

It was night, and I was still in a bit of pain from having just delivered my baby two days ago. In essence, I tried to take it easy as I put one foot in front of the other.

"Do you have someone here waiting to pick you up?" he wondered.

"No, I don't. I was going to take a cab," I told him.

"Oh no, that's nonsense. My roommate from my dorm is here so I'm gonna get him to take you wherever you need to go. Now, is that all right? Are you cool with that?"

"Yes, I guess so," I replied.

"Well, let's go. He's parked just a few feet away in that black Wrangler Jeep."

Quincy escorted me to his friend's Jeep. As soon as he opened the passenger-side door, he introduced me to the guy. "Trevor, this is Chantel and Chantel this is Trevor," Quincy said.

"Nice to meet you," Trevor and I said simultaneously.

"She's pretty, Q. What, you have a girlfriend now?" Trevor joked.

I got a quick look at Trevor and he was handsome like Quincy. Trevor kind of resembled Chris Brown. He wasn't as cute as Chris Brown, but he was close enough.

"No, man. I met her on the bus and I told her that you'll give her a ride so she wouldn't have to take a cab."

"Oh sure, get in. Where are you headed?" Trevor wanted to know.

My mind went totally blank. I honestly didn't know where the hell I was going. But I knew I had to think of something fast, so while I was climbing in the backseat of the Jeep, I said, "Take me to the Hilton Hotel on the corner of Military Highway and North Hampton Boulevard."

"But I thought you were going to see your grandmother," Quincy interjected.

"Oh, I am. Just not tonight. I need to get some rest and then I'll be refreshed to surprise her in the morning," I lied.

"Okay, well, cool," Trevor said, and then he started up and drove out of the bus station parking lot.

I watched Quincy and Trevor interact with each other while they listened to Drake's latest CD. The brotherly love these two guys had for each other was priceless. They both looked like they came from wealthy families. They even seemed innocent and unaware of how life really was. For their sake, I hoped they'd stay in their little bubble because it was safer in there. These harsh streets would swallow them whole and spit them out to be devoured by stray dogs. Boy, would that be a fucked-up way to go.

When Quincy's friend pulled up in front of the hotel, I thanked him for dropping me off, and then I told him that I'd return the favor one day. Quincy helped me out of the

Jeep and escorted me into the hotel while he carried my bag. I thanked him at least three times before he left. He gave me his cell phone number and told me to call him if I needed anything. I assured him that I would.

I checked into the hotel using a fake ID. I got it from my Maryland connect before I left Virginia and hightailed it to New York. I only used it a few times while I was in New York. But after Matt was arrested, Derek convinced me to throw it away. I didn't, of course. I put it in a safe place for a time such as this. Now I was Chantel West. I was a twenty-five-year-old New Yorker. And if anyone asked why I was in town? My answer would be that I was visiting a friend. But I was here to find Matthew and that motherfucker who took my money from me and ran off. And I vowed to die doing it.

6

THE DIRTY SOUTH

My travels back to Virginia were a bit bumpy, but safe. I was tempted to call a few people I knew to find out if Matt had reared his ugly face around them, but I decided against it. The people he and I knew together were more loyal to him than me. I couldn't chance blowing my cover just to make my search a little easier. So I turned on the TV and lay back on the queen-size hotel bed. I tried to watch it but I couldn't stop thinking about my baby. Thinking about Derek's lifeless body lying in that hotel bed consumed my mind too. The way his body looked made me sick to my stomach. I almost vomited at the sight of his blood. It was still dark and gory-looking. I could only imagine how his brain and other living organs in his head looked underneath the pillow. If I wasn't worried about the police coming to the hotel and catching me there, I would've stayed with my husband a little longer. I hated that I had to leave him. I hated that I couldn't do anything to stop his murder. I was to blame for his demise. And now I'd have to live with it.

I also knew that if I would've stayed at that hotel for just a few more minutes, I could've found something that would've linked Matt to Derek's murder. New York has homicides every day, so it wouldn't surprise me if Matt never got charged with my husband's death.

Now that I thought about it, my fingerprints were at the scene, so I would be on the list of suspects after the cops went through the room with a fine-tooth comb.

I sat back and thought about how I had gotten there. I thought I had everything under control but I didn't. I thought I was going to move away start a fresh new life and live happily ever after. But that didn't happen. Instead, I got the opposite. I was a widow. I didn't know where my son was. I was broke. And I was gonna be homeless once the cops identified Derek's body and found out I was his wife and that I was wanted in the state of Virginia for numerous counts of identity theft, fraud, forgery, and grand larceny. You might as well have said that my life was completely FUCKED!

I thought to myself, *Even after I find Matt and he tells me that he killed my baby, too, how am I going to come back from that? I won't have any choice but to turn myself in to the cops. I mean, it's not like I can move forward and try to put my life back together. That will be impossible after losing everything that I've held dearly to my heart. I believe prison would be better suited for me. There I can waste my life away. Maybe find a correctional officer to fuck my brains out from time to time to get a few special privileges and a couple of meals from the outside world. Because I promise that when I see Matt and everyone he had working for him to pull off the kidnapping of my family, I'm going to make sure I end their lives on-site.*

While I was in thinking about the events that led up to this very moment, the eleven o'clock nightly news broadcast, so I tuned in. I listened intently to what was going on around the Tidewater area. It had been over a year since I had walked these streets, so to be able to learn firsthand what was happening around town made me feel right at home. It also revealed to me that I wasn't missing much. It was always the same shit, but on a different day.

First the news journalist talked about how the unemployment rate had gone down and how things were looking up for the Tidewater area. Then she talked about a serial bank robber who had been hitting up a few of the local banks in the area. And of course, if anyone had any information about the suspect to call 1-888-LOCKUUP. From there the news station changed anchors and switched it to a young white reporter who was covering the story of a local gang. I continued to listen intently. *"We're out here in the Huntersville section of Norfolk, where two young black men in their early twenties have been shot and killed doing a drug deal gone bad. I've talked to several witnesses, who were afraid to go on camera, but they say that this incident was inevitable. They even mentioned that the two young men were brothers who had just gotten out of jail stemming from other drug charges. No names will be released until the families are notified first,"* the woman reported. I turned the volume down on the TV when the news station switched their camera back to headquarters. It was time for the weather segment and I wasn't interested in that.

There was nothing new under the sun in the Tidewater area. Someone dies every day. It was the way of life. Dysfunction was normalcy around here. If men weren't raping children and women, or prostitutes weren't selling their bodies, and junkies weren't stealing from loved ones to get their next fix, or guys weren't selling drugs to support their weed habit, or buy hot cars, designer labels, and diamond chains, something was wrong. This was the only way the people around here knew how to live. I hated this place all my life. And I won't say New York is better. But it was a change of pace and I had finally found someone who loved me. And on top of that, he gave me a baby. There was nothing else in this world that I could have possibly wanted. But now, my happiness was gone. It's funny how life will change, without giving you notice. It's a dogg-eat-dog world out here. So you gotta learn to adapt, at any cost. Whether it be a life or not. You gotta learn how to survive or you'll get swallowed up. No questions asked.

I was feeling a little hungry from that long bus ride, so I called and ordered some Chinese food from a menu I found in the desk drawer near the TV. I ordered a small box of shrimp pancit and two shrimp egg rolls. Immediately after I placed my order, I lay back in the bed and thought about my two-day-old baby boy. Anxiety washed over me while I thought about whether he was safe or not. I prayed to God that Matt had some good left in his heart not to harm a baby.

And even though it hadn't been twenty-four hours since I'd seen my son, I could still smell his scent on my clothes and my skin from when I was breast-feeding him. He was so precious to me. He was innocent and the joy of my life. So I couldn't imagine not seeing him ever again.

I knew one thing. It didn't matter how long it took, I was going to find out what happened to my baby. And if I survived this ordeal I would redeem myself. Going through all of this heartache had taken at least ten years off my life. My body was aching. My head hurt. Everything was wrong with me. And right then I didn't see a light at the end of my tunnel. But I would, even if I did it before I took my last breath.

Approximately thirty-five minutes passed before the hotel telephone rang. It startled the hell out of me. At first I wasn't going to answer it, but when I figured that it could be the delivery person from the Chinese restaurant, I picked up the phone and said, "Hello."

"Hi, this is Sharon from the front desk. I have a gentleman standing here with an order you placed at a Chinese restaurant. Would you like for me to send him up? Or would you prefer to meet him in the lobby?"

I thought for a moment about the chances of me running into someone who knew me from this area. And when I came to the conclusion that I could possibly run into one of Matt's homeboys from the streets, I declined and asked the young lady to send the delivery guy up to my room.

"Sure, that would be no problem. I will send him up right now," she assured me, and then I hung up.

The Asian guy arrived at my hotel room in less than two minutes flat. After I paid him, I told him "thank you" and closed my door. When I sat back down, I found myself only eating a few bites of my food. I had just lost my appetite that fast. I think it was because I thought to myself, *How could I be eating at a time like this? How could I enjoy a meal knowing that my husband and son were taken away from me just hours ago?* For moment, I was really starting to feel ashamed. *I shouldn't be lying around here relaxed. I should be out there looking for Matt so I can avenge my husband and hopefully find my baby.* I guessed now was the time for me to switch gears. I knew I couldn't do anything that night. But I would start searching for my son bright and early in the morning.

I tossed and turned all night. I knew I wasn't going to get any sleep, especially with everything weighing heavily on my mind. But what really had my stomach turning knots was what Matt had done with my baby. For the life of me, I couldn't figure out why he didn't murder him and leave him in the hotel room lying on the bed alongside of Derek? But then what if he killed my baby and dumped him off on the side of the fucking highway? I swore, if I found out he killed my baby there was going to be an all-out war. I'd be dropping bodies everywhere. Innocent bystanders and all. Everybody who had any dealings with Matt and his crew would have a funeral in the coming days. I didn't care who it was. It could be the mothers, grandmothers, sisters, cousins, uncles, aunts, nieces, and nephews, because everyone would go straight to hell. I meant that from the bottom of my heart.

Instead of trying to go back to sleep, I got out of bed, walked down to the first-floor lobby, and bought a few packs of ibuprofen to help me with the pain I was experiencing since I'd just had a baby. I had no other choice in the matter. It was either stay in my room to avoid being seen or go and get a pack of painkillers. This was the only way my pain was going to subside.

Lucky for me, I hadn't had a C-section birth because if I had, I wouldn't be able to do any of the stuff that I'd done to get where I was at that point. It just wouldn't have been feasible. Before going back up to my room, I got a box of maxi pads because the box I had taken from my apartment in New York wasn't enough. This childbirth thing had me bleeding heavy.

On my way back upstairs, I noticed the hotel had a security guard who looked very familiar to me. I walked to the elevator and stood there, waiting for the elevator door to open just as the guy walked by me. In my mind, I was trying to figure out where I had seen him before. It didn't click until he spoke. "Hey, what's your name?" he asked right after he stood beside me. I turned my face to the right just enough to give him eye contact. "Chantel," I lied while I tried to sound like I was from up north. "Why you ask?" I inquired.

"Well, because you look like this young lady I know named Lauren. She used to go to high school with me and my brother Kevin. I wanted to go out with her but my brother got to her first. I always wondered what happened to her." He smiled.

"I'm sorry but what's your name?"

"Rick."

"Well no, I'm sorry. I'm not Lauren," I lied once again, and turned my focus back to the elevator.

"Well, that's too bad because I would love to tell Lauren

how I was crazy in love with her and that I would've treated her way better than my brother did."

"I'm sure she would've loved to hear that," I assured him, keeping my eyes on the elevator. Thankfully, the doors opened a few seconds later.

"Talk to you later," I said, and walked onto the elevator.

"Okay," he replied as the doors closed.

I let out a long sigh after the doors closed completely. I couldn't believe how I almost blew my fucking cover. To run into someone I went to school with over ten years ago was risky as hell. Just imagine if I'd run into someone I hadn't seen in a little over a year. I'd be messed up for real. I couldn't let that happened again.

Knowing in my mind and my heart that the security guard recognized me had me on edge. I definitely remembered him trying to talk to me a few times after school when I had detention and he had band practice. He was a really nice guy. But he wasn't my type. He was one of those charming guys who would open the car door for you, bring you flowers when he picks you up for a date, and write you poems expressing his love for you. I wasn't into that corny stuff. To me, it showed me a guy's weakness. Any sign of weakness was a turnoff for me, which was why I was attracted to his brother. His brother was a thug. He stayed in group homes for boys for grand theft auto, snatching old ladies' pocketbooks, and pickpocketing teachers' wallets in school. His brother was off the chain. But he was exciting. Kevin was the first guy I dated who had a long rap sheet. Essentially it was puppy love, because after he carjacked an old man's car, he was arrested, charged as an adult, and sent away to prison for ten years. He should have been home by this point. Who knew?

After Kevin left to do his time, I fell in love with Matt. He was much older so my attraction for him grew much faster. He was a petty thief like Kevin. Matt was a drug dealer making major moves in the streets and everyone knew him. He was the man. And being with a man made me feel good about myself. It made me feel like I was the woman. His main chick. But look at me now. If I would've gotten with Kevin's brother, I probably wouldn't have been in any of this mess. Yeah, we would've been living off a security guard's salary, but I'd probably have a lot of peace. You can't put a price on that. But hey, I didn't go that route, so now I had to clean up my mess before things got any worse.

I just hoped that guy didn't get on the phone and call Kevin and tell him he saw me. Or call someone else who knew I was on the run. I just prayed to God that he didn't. Hopefully, he'd buy my story that I wasn't who he thought I was. If not, then I'd be shit out of luck!

The window in the hotel room had a front and side view of the parking lot. As long as everyone who came to the hotel drove into the parking lot from this angle, I'd be able to see them. If they came from the opposite direction, then I could get blindsided. So again, this all boiled down to the security guard and if he'd open his mouth. Besides praying, I knew I needed to keep my fingers crossed. Having an escape plan to get out of this hotel if someone came looking for me would be in my best interest too. Time would tell, though.

7

CHECKING OUT THE SCENERY

The very next morning my body felt a lot better from the ibuprofen I had taken the night before, so it wasn't hard for me to get up, shower, and dress. I knew I had to go out on the streets and do some surveillance work that day, so I picked up the hotel phone and called a cab. Besides killing Matt and anyone who got in my way, finding my baby was all I could think about.

The cab arrived at the hotel less than fifteen minutes later. The driver was an older black man with long dreadlocks. He looked like he was in his fifties. There was no doubt in my mind that he was a Rasta. He didn't have a West Indian accent but he dressed the part with the dreadlock hair covering the green, black, and red jacket. The long-ass hair growing from his beard looked disgusting as hell. I couldn't deal with a man with all that hair on his head and all over his face. That's not attractive to me. He even had a mild body odor. I let down the back window a bit just so the air could circulate. He greeted me as soon as I sat down in the backseat and asked me where I was headed. "How much would you charge me to run me around to a couple of places?" I asked him boldly.

"Are we staying in the area?"

"Yeah."

"Where exactly do you want to go?"

"I need to ride through a couple spots in Norfolk. Huntersville is the first place I wanna go and then I'm gonna need to check out a few places in Park Place."

"Where in Huntersville you trying to go?"

"Lexington Avenue and B Avenue."

"You ain't going out there to buy drugs, are you?"

"Of course not. Do I look like I'm on drugs?" I replied sarcastically.

"You can never tell these days," he commented, and then he said, "So, where are we headed to after that?"

"I just want you to ride down West Thirty-Seventh Street and then I'm done. So tell me how much is that gonna cost me."

The cabdriver thought for a moment. I could see the dollar signs circling around in his head. "I'll tell you what, give me a hundred dollars," he finally said.

"Come on now, a hundred dollars is a lot. You're gonna have to come at me a little better than that," I barked. I knew he was trying to get one over on me.

"Okay, give me seventy-five dollars and you've got yourself a driver."

I thought about his offer for a second and then I said, "Okay."

The driver held his hand out for me to pay him. I looked at him like he'd lost his damn mind. "I'm not paying you up front," I huffed. "I'll give you half now and half when we get back to the hotel."

"Deal!" he said. So I pulled forty from my purse and handed to him. Immediately after he put the money in his pocket he turned on his meter and pulled out of the hotel parking lot.

"Wait, I thought I was paying you a flat fee?" I asked.

"You are. But I'm still required to monitor my mileage and fares. So, you're good," he explained.

"All right," I replied, and then I laid my head back on the headrest.

"What's your name?" he asked as he pulled his car onto Military Highway.

"Chantel," I told him.

"Hi, Chantel, my name is Sam. You from around here?" he questioned me again. I knew this was about to be a long and drawn out Q & A session so I mentally prepared myself to go with the floor.

"No, I'm not from around here. I'm just here visiting." My web of lies continued.

"You must be here visiting your man," he indirectly asked.

I gave him a half smile. "Something like that," I said, and then I looked out the back window at the passing traffic.

"Does he know you're here?"

"Yeah, he knows."

"So, why isn't he with you now?"

"It's kind of complicated," I answered while I kept my attention on the cars we passed by.

"I hope you ain't mixed up in no love triangle. You're too pretty to be playing second base."

I let out a long sigh. "I know, I know," I replied, playing the role of a side chick.

"So, where you from?"

"New York."

"I knew I heard a Northern accent in there somewhere."

I smiled.

"So, how long have you been in this love triangle?"

"A little over a year now."

"Does the other woman know about you?"

"I'm sure she does. What woman doesn't know when her

man is cheating? I mean, it's not like y'all are the best liars. All you have to do is change your routine a few times and there's your evidence," I schooled him.

"That's not all the way true. See, the men you're talking about don't know how to be a player. Now if you were my old lady, I'd treat you so good that you wouldn't be thinking about if I'm messing around on you. The young guys these days don't know how to handle their business. And that's why they get caught with their pants down."

I chuckled. "So, you're a pimp, huh?" I joked.

"Nah, I ain't no pimp. But I do know how to handle my women."

"Are you married?"

"Yep. Been married twenty years."

"So what's your secret?" I inquired, thinking about how Derek and I could've lasted twenty years if he was still alive. But Matt took him away from me and he would pay for it.

"Let's just say that she knows her place and I know mine."

"That doesn't sound hard to do."

"It's not. But a lot of people aren't able to do it."

"You're right," I commented, and peered back out of the side window. I couldn't get my mind off what could've been if Derek was still alive. Anger and rage began to mount up inside of me like never before. The hurt I was feeling began to spread through my entire body. It would bring me sweet satisfaction to kill Matt with my bare hands. I wanted him to suffer the same way he made my husband suffer, maybe even worse. Tears started welling up in my eyes. I tried to hold it back but I couldn't. And before I knew it, the floodgates opened and tears streamed down my face. I wiped them away with the backs of my hands, but that didn't help. The tears kept coming. "Are you okay?" the cabdriver asked me as he looked at me through this rearview mirror. I used my hands to wipe away the constant flow of tears falling from my eyes and then I lied, saying, "Yes, I'm fine."

The cabdriver pressed the issue. "Are you sure? Because you're crying up a storm back there."

"I'm just going through something right now. I'll be all right," I told him while I continued to wipe the tears away from my eyes and face.

"If you wanna talk about it, I can lend you my ears."

"No, I'm good."

The cabdriver took his eyes off the rearview mirror and put them on the road before him. He made a couple left turns and made a right turn and we were finally at our destination. "We're on Lexington Avenue. Is there anywhere you would like for me to park?" he asked me.

"No, just ride by the gray house on the right," I instructed.

I slid down in the backseat so I wouldn't be noticed around the scene. All I needed was for Matt or one of his street snitches to see me pulling up, because I'd be screwed. I felt the cabdriver slow the car down in front of a two-story house covered in dark gray vinyl siding where Matt hung out to gamble. No one knew about this spot but a handful of people. Not even the cops knew about it. This spot was run by his cousin Otis. Otis was an old-school cat who was in his late forties. He was always known to be a street hustler, whether it was selling weed, selling shots of liquor, or running a gambling spot. He never sold anything that would give him a lot of time in prison. He also ruled with an iron fist. No one ever tried to rob him nor had anyone ever called the cops on him. He was well respected in this area, to say the least.

The cabdriver did as I told him and drove by Matt's cousin's gambling spot without looking suspicious. There were only a couple of cars parked outside. Otis's Cadillac Escalade was parked in the driveway and I also saw a dark blue F-150, along with a silver Chevy Tahoe. I had no idea who those other trucks belonged to, but I knew they weren't anything that Matt would be in because none of the windows were tinted. Matt never rode around in a car without tint on the windows. He liked to move around undetected. And he'd never compromised that rule.

"Do you wanna head to A Avenue now?" the cabdriver asked me.

"Yeah, let's go," I told him as I sat back up in the backseat.

My mind started racing while en route to A Avenue. Where in the hell was this asshole at? Did he come back to Virginia? And if so, where could he be?

"I'm about to turn onto A Avenue," the driver announced. So I slid back down into the seat, lifting my head up just enough so I could see all the movement on this block.

"Slow down as we pass that brick duplex on the left," I said.

"Are you sure? I mean, there's a lot of people standing outside of it."

"I know. But they can't see me. I just need to see who they are, that's all."

"As you wish," he replied as he pressed down on this brakes and looked forward.

The blood through my veins started pumping and the hair on my arms started standing up when I looked into all the faces of the people who stood around on the porch of the duplex. There were a total of four guys and a woman. Right off the bat, I knew that three of those guys were street dealers and the other guy and lady were junkies. I watched how the female junkie handed one of the dope boys her money and he gave her something white in exchange for it. Immediately after she got what she wanted, the male and female junkie walked off. By this time, the cabdriver had gotten within a few feet of the three guys so

I was able to get a bird's-eye view of their faces. But after I looked at them, I realized that I didn't know any of them. They must've been new to this spot as I had never seen their faces before. I let out a loud sigh of frustration as I turned and faced the back of the cabdriver's head.

But then I saw movement through my peripheral vision, so I yanked my head back into that direction, and that's when I saw a familiar face. The nerves in my stomach started rumbling. I swear, I couldn't believe my fucking eyes when I realized that this was the same guy who Matt had sent to pick the money up from me at Grand Central Station. He had just walked out of the door of the duplex and got the attention of all three guys standing out front. I watched him talk to them as I stared out the back window, and I figured that if he was in fact back in Virginia, then so was Matt. At this very moment, I wanted to jump out of the fucking cab and bust a couple shots at his ass. I wanted to kill him on the spot but I knew I was outnumbered. I also knew that would be a dumb move on my part. I needed to find out where Matt was. So I needed to be smart about everything I did.

I stared at the guy until I was no longer able to see him. The cabdriver drove for about a half a block up Church Street before I told him to stop the car. "Pull over for a minute," I instructed him.

He did as I said and pulled into the parking lot of a warehouse that looked abandoned. I got out of the car and took a short walk away from the cab. I started crying instantly and began to swing my fists in the air like I was in a brawl. I thought the cabdriver would intervene and try to stop me but he didn't. I wasn't sure how long it took me to go through my meltdown, but when it was over I got back into the cab and asked him to take me back to the hotel.

"Are you sure? I thought you wanted to go to Park Place?"

"No, I've seen all I needed to see. Take me back to my hotel," I snapped. He knew my mood had changed. He knew I saw something that got me upset. I wasn't the nice lady anymore. I was more irritated now than anything.

"As you wish," he said, and turned his cab around and headed back in the direction of the hotel.

Before I got out of the cab the old driver handed me his business card and told me to call him anytime I needed to get around. I assured him I would as I shoved his card into my purse. When I turned to walk about he said, "I don't know what you saw today that made you so mad. But whatever it was, don't let it consume you. If you do then you're allowing that thing or person to have power over you. And that's not good."

"It's far deeper than you could ever imagine, sir," I assured him, and then I walked away from the cab.

8

TIME TO REGROUP

Ithought I'd be able to go back to the hotel and get a clear head so I could figure out my next move, but I couldn't. My mind wouldn't let me focus. For the life of me, I couldn't figure out my next step because all I wanted to do was see that guy's face bloody. Fuck all the politics! I wanted that motherfucker dead right then! He was one of Matt's flunkies! He took my money from me and in exchange I didn't get shit. So he would get dealt with. He would feel my fucking pain.

I can't tell you how many times I paced the floor in my hotel room, but I can say that when my cell phone rang it stopped me in my tracks. I rushed over to my purse and grabbed it from inside. I looked down at the caller ID and saw that it was the college kid I'd met on the bus. "Hello," I spoke after I pressed the send button.

"You up?"

"Of course I'm up."

"Have you seen your family yet?"

"No, not yet."

"Have you even left the hotel yet?"

"What's up with you asking all these damn questions?" I spat. I was not in the mood for his shit. Not right now.

"Because me and my roommate don't have class today and we wanna take you to get something to eat and hang out."

"I'm not in the mood to eat anything right now," I told him.

"What's wrong?"

"I just got a lot on my mind."

"Well, I'll tell you what, if you come and hang out with us, my roommate and I will help you take your mind off your problems."

"Nah, I don't think so," I replied in a nonchalant manner.

"Ahh, come on now. It'll be fun."

I thought for a moment before I answered him. What were the odds of him and his friend helping me to relieve some of this stress I had? I was dealing with some serious shit. My husband was dead and my baby boy was missing. Now how in the hell were they going to help ease that kind of pain? "Look, let me take a rain check," I finally told him.

"No, Chantel, we are not taking no for an answer so get your butt up," he replied, pressing the issue.

"Okay, I'll tell you what. I'll hang out with you guys for a couple of hours and that's it," I said, thinking about how I could use them to spy on that spot in Huntersville. I figured if that guy was there, then Matt couldn't be far.

"Cool, be ready in an hour and we'll be right over," he told me.

"All right," I said, and disconnected the call. I thought for a moment about the level of persistence Quincy had when he was persuading me to hang out him and his friend Trevor. He was giving me the impression that he was developing a crush on me. I hoped he wasn't crushing on me because I didn't have the time to deal with being hit on.

But I wouldn't mind using his interest to get him to help me with my search.

Quincy called my cell phone after he and Trevor had pulled up in front of the hotel. I told them I'd be down in a few minutes. I grabbed my gun from underneath the pillow on the bed, stuffed it inside my purse, and walked out of the room.

The sun had just set, but the moment the double doors slid open and I walked through them, I could see both guys' faces light up like I was the fucking Queen of England. Quincy got out of the passenger seat and held the door open for me. "No, I'll prefer to sit in the back," I told him.

"A'ight," he said, and turned around and opened up the back door. After I got inside he closed the door behind me and hopped back in the front passenger seat.

Trevor greeted me with a smile and said, "Hello."

"Hi, Trevor."

Quincy turned around in his seat. "So whatcha been doing since we dropped you off last night?" he questioned me. He seemed overly excited that I was in his company.

"I went out for a few hours this morning. Saw a few things that I needed to see and then I came back to the hotel."

"So you did get a chance to see your grandmother?" Quincy asked.

"No, I didn't."

"Have you at least called her?"

"Listen, Quincy, I'm not here to see my grandmother. I'm here because my boyfriend came to New York, took my newborn baby, and brought him here to Virginia. So I'm here to get my baby back from him and go back to New York."

"Are you serious?" Quincy blurted out. His facial expression changed drastically.

"Yo, that's fucked up!" Trevor interjected. His facial expression wasn't as dramatic as Quincy's.

"Why don't you call the police?" Quincy suggested.

"It's not that simple."

"What, y'all got joint custody or something?" Trevor asked.

To avoid telling these guys the truth, I went along with the joint custody story because it sounded more plausible than for me to say that my baby was being held by my ex-boyfriend for ransom. Besides that, they wouldn't be able to wrap their minds around the fact that I was a bona fide white-collar criminal and I'd just lost my husband in a murder behind a score I did a year ago. These guys were babies. They were wet behind the ears, so they wouldn't understand if I told them that my ex-boyfriend was a sociopath and that he'd kill them just for being around me. I also knew that I couldn't tell them that type of information because I needed them to help me get my baby back. I figured that as long as they believed it was a custody issue with Matt, then they'd feel like they could handle it. But then I thought to myself, what if they helped me and we found out that my baby was in fact dead? That would be a devastating blow to me as well as them, and it would change the dynamic of this entire scenario. So I needed to be careful with everything I did around these guys. It was the only way.

"So where are we going?" Trevor asked.

"To Huntersville," I told him.

"Where is that?" he asked aloud.

"It's a run-down neighborhood in Norfolk."

"Is it off Church Street?" Quincy asked.

"Yep, that's the one," I confirmed.

"To Church Street we go," Trevor announced, and then he sped out of the parking lot of the hotel.

"Slow down, man," Quincy whined.

"You can't take this horsepower, huh?" Trevor joked.

"Just slow down. We want to make the ride to Huntersville as peaceful as possible," Quincy instructed Trevor.

I sat in the backseat and stared out the back window. I couldn't get my mind off my baby. I hoped and prayed that he was really still alive. I mean, he had to be. Matt didn't leave him in the hotel room after he killed Derek. So where else could my baby be? He had to be alive and he had to be with Matt. I felt it in my gut.

"Are you okay back there?" Quincy wanted to know.

"Yes, I'm fine."

"Thought about what you're gonna do once you see your ex-boyfriend?" Quincy's questions continued.

"Good question. I was about to ask her the same thing," Trevor chimed in.

"I'm just gonna ask him for my baby," I replied nonchalantly.

"Do you think that's going to work?" Quincy asked.

"I don't know. But we'll find out."

"Does he hang around a lot of guys?" Trevor chimed back in.

"Yes, he does. But don't worry, you guys are going to be fine," I lied, hoping that nothing jumped off during our surveillance.

"Is he like violent?" Trevor asked.

"Yeah, is he in a gang or something?"

"No, he's not in a gang. And the guys that he hangs around with are simply just his friends he grew up with. I told you that you guys are going to be fine."

"Well, I hope so. I would hate to have to jump out of my Jeep and pistol-whip somebody."

"Oh, shut up, Trevor! You don't even own a gun."

"So what!? She didn't have to know that. Now you got her thinking that I'm some type of fraud!"

"Listen, you guys. I don't want you to do anything. I don't even want you getting out of the car. I will deal with my ex on my own when I see him."

"But what if he tries to put his hands on you?" Quincy shot the next question at me.

"He's not," I lied.

"Have you thought about what you're gonna do if he doesn't give you your baby back?" Trevor asked. I could see him looking at me through the rearview mirror.

"Yes, I've thought about it."

"So what's your plan?" Quincy chimed back in.

"Let me just try to get my baby back first. Now, if he wants to start acting crazy, then we'll go to plan B."

"What's plan B?" Trevor asked.

"When we cross that bridge, I'll let you know," I told them both, and then I turned my focus to the cars and buildings we passed by.

For ten minutes, we rode in total silence. That all ended when Trevor made a right turn onto Church Street. We were officially in the Huntersville neighborhood. My mind started racing while a massive amount of fear crept into my heart. My palms started sweating profusely. I rubbed them across my pant leg to alleviate some of the wetness. It felt like I was about to have a panic attack. "Make a right turn on the next street and drive until I tell you to stop," I instructed Trevor while I shook my head left to right, trying to get my thoughts together. Thinking about getting caught out here during the day was making me too weak-minded to carry out the mission I had at hand. I gave myself a quick pep talk. *You can't get weak now Lauren. Stay on point.* I felt slightly better and then it was time for me to instruct Trevor on his next move.

As instructed Trevor turned onto the next street, which was A Avenue, and as soon as I got within a bird's-eye view of the duplex, I zoomed in. This time around there was no one in sight. None of the guys who were standing in front of the house earlier were there. This blow hit me hard. "Fuck!" I roared, and hit the back of Quincy's seat.

Startled, Trevor looked back at me and said, "Yo, you all right?"

"Yeah, what happened?" Quincy interjected.

"There's no one standing outside. They're all gone."

"Who are you talking about?" Quincy asked.

"The guys who hang out with my ex."

"Which house is it?" Trevor chimed in.

"The duplex on the right?"

"Hey, wait, I see two people sitting in the car parked in front of the house," Trevor announced as he drove toward it.

I tried to zoom in on the car parked in front of the duplex. I couldn't see anything because it was too dark outside.

"Can you see if it's a man or woman?" I wanted to know.

"No, I can only see the backs of their heads," Trevor said.

"Yeah, me too," said Quincy.

"They're getting ready to leave. The driver just put their feet on the brake light," Quincy continued.

"Trevor, slow down so they can go before you," I instructed.

Trevor slowed down his Jeep just in time for the car to pull out in front of them. "What kind of car is that?" I wondered aloud.

"It looks like a brand-new Maxima."

"Nah, that's a Nissan Ultima," Quincy corrected.

I sat on the edge of the backseat. "Look, I don't care what kind of car it is, just follow it."

"What if they notice that I'm following them?" Trevor sounded skeptical.

"They won't if you stay back far enough."

"Are you sure about this?"

"Look, Trev, stop being a little bitch and do like she said," Quincy scolded Trevor.

"A'ight, but if my Jeep gets shot up, then I'm putting all of this shit on you. You're going to take the weight when my parents ask me what happened to my truck."

"Trevor, calm down. No one is going to shoot up your Jeep. Just listen to me and I promise that everything will be fine," I assured him.

"Well, I'm telling you right now, if those people in that car noticed that we are following them, I'm gonna back off and go in another direction," Trevor warned.

"Would you stop the whining, please?" Quincy joked.

"Fuck you, man!" Trevor snapped.

Quincy chuckled. "You know, I've never seen you so freaked out before. This is hilarious!"

"Please be quiet so I can concentrate."

"You heard her, you little drama queen. Stop bitching!"

Before Trevor could make another comment, I became alarmed and said, "Shhh, why are they stopping?"

"I don't know," Trevor answered.

"Want him to go around them?" Quincy suggested.

"We are on a one-way street, Einstein, and they are in the middle of it, so I couldn't go around them even if I wanted to," Trevor acknowledged.

"Shhh, you guys! They are moving again," I blurted out.

"Do you still want me to follow them?" Trevor wanted to know.

"Yes, but take your time. We cannot let on that they are being followed," I said.

Nervously, Trevor continued to follow the car in front of us. Thankfully, there were a lot of one-way streets in this neighborhood, so tailing a car for a few blocks really wouldn't seem obvious to someone who knew this area.

But then again, when you're a crook and you have a long list of people you've fucked over, you're going to always look over your shoulder.

We ended up following the car to the next street over, which was Lexington Avenue. The car pulled right up in front of Matt's uncle's gambling spot. An alarm set off in my head. I knew Trevor couldn't pull the Jeep over and park, because it would seem really obvious that we were following them, so I instructed Trevor to keep driving, but to slow down as we passed the car so I could try to get a look at the people inside.

Trevor followed my instructions to a T. But I wasn't pre-pared when the passenger-side door opened at the same time as the Jeep and the car were side by side. I gasped when their interior car light showed me the face of the guy who took my fucking money. I quickly turned my face in the opposite direction just in case he could see inside the Jeep. As soon as the Jeep passed him, I quickly looked out the back window and noticed there was a woman in the driver's seat. I couldn't see if I recognized her because the interior light of the car turned off immediately after Matt's flunky closed the passenger-side door.

"Is that him?" Quincy asked me.

"No, that's not him. But this guy knows where my ex is," I replied as I watched the guy walk up to Matt's uncle's place. Before he was able to knock on the door, someone opened it and let him inside. I couldn't see who the person was, but from the silhouette radiating from the light coming from inside the house, I could tell that it was a guy.

"We're coming to a stop sign, do you want me to make a turn or keep straight?" Trevor asked.

"Circle back around the block," I told him.

"Are you going to knock on the door?" Quincy inquired.

"No."

"But what if your ex is in there?" Quincy asked.

"When I confront my ex, I wanna be in an open environment. Not behind closed doors," I explained. But I wasn't telling the truth. I couldn't tell them the truth because I knew that they couldn't handle it. So I continued to play the victim-of-domestic-abuse ex-girlfriend trying to get my baby back. Saying anything other than that would be suicide to my mission to murder Matt's ass and take my baby back.

After Trevor circled the block, I instructed him to park his Jeep seven houses before Matt's uncle's house. I got him to park behind a white utility van. This spot was perfect because the van was larger than the Jeep, so we were hidden very well.

"Trevor, you may wanna turn your Jeep off."

"Nah, I'm sorry. I'm not doing that. Not in this fucking neighborhood. We already look like sitting ducks out this bitch," Trevor replied sarcastically. It seemed like his attitude went from jovial and carefree to that of a madman. He even snapped on Quincy after Quincy told him to apologize for cursing at me. "Come on, Trevor, don't talk to her like that. She's only trying to make moves so she can figure out a way to get her fucking baby back," Quincy said, jumping to my defense.

"I understand all of that. But do you see where we're at?" Trevor started off.

Quincy jumped to my defense once again. "Yeah, I see where we at. But that doesn't give you the right to talk to her like that. We're dealing with an asshole, so you can't blame her if she wants to be careful."

"Well, I'm trying to figure out why she won't call the cops and let them deal with it."

"Didn't she say they were having some custody issues?"

"She can tell us anything."

"Look, Trevor, I don't know what you're insinuating, but I do know that whatever it is, it's just a figment of your imagination. You really and truly don't know shit about me so keep your comments to yourself. Now, it's quite obvious that you don't want to be out here, and I understand your position. But acting out like you're doing now is not helping the situation. So you can just take me back to the hotel. I'll deal with my ex later," I told him.

"I thought you'd never ask," Trevor said, and then he put his clutch in first gear. He sped off down a one-way street in an instant. We were out of the Huntersville neighborhood in less than thirty seconds. As badly as I wanted to stay out there and watch Matt's uncle's spot for any traces of Matt's whereabouts, I knew I couldn't do it while I was with Quincy's friend Trevor. This guy was acting like a pure bitch! I couldn't believe it. When I met him yesterday, he was cool as hell. But tonight he showed me a different side of him. A side I wouldn't tolerate under normal circumstances. The next day I was gonna head back out there to Huntersville and do my own surveillance. And it was going to be on my own terms.

Trevor and Quincy argued the entire ride back to my hotel. I had already had a headache from the drama looming over my head. So to be in the middle of these two clowns fussing over me was a little more than I could handle. "You fucked up my entire night," Quincy argued.

"And I'm the one who fucked it up, huh?" Trevor asked sarcastically.

"You fucking right, Trev. The way you talk to her was foul, homie," Quincy replied.

"Yo, dude, did you see where the fuck we were? We were scoping out a house in the hood. Do you know what could've happened to us if one of those guys out there saw us and decided that they wanted to rob us?" Trevor pointed out.

"Man, let's just kill it right there because you're exaggerating."

"I'm not exaggerating. Do you watch the news? The crime rate in Norfolk is at an all-time high. Niggas is getting robbed every day. So who do you think will be next?" Trevor continued to make his point.

"Yo, Trev, I'm done with the conversation. You're being a dickhead and you're really not making any sense right now," Quincy said, and then he fell silent.

Trevor rambled on a little bit more. But when he realized that no one was going to keep feeding into his antics, he ended up closing his mouth. I was glad of that. The old me would've told that nigga to kiss my ass. But I was in a different headspace right then. I had bigger fish to fry so in the end, he would not have been worth the argument.

The moment Trevor stopped his Jeep in the hotel parking lot, I got out of the backseat without saying a word. I closed the door and headed toward the entryway of the hotel. I heard the car door slam behind me as I entered into the hotel lobby. "Hey, Chantel, wait a minute," Quincy said.

I stopped and turned around. "What's up?" I asked nonchalantly. And even though it wasn't his fault, that his friend acted like an asshole, I was still a little frustrated with him being in my presence. He noticed it.

"Look, I'm so sorry that my friend acted like that toward you," Quincy apologized.

"Don't worry about it. It's okay. I knew I shouldn't have taken you guys out there anyway. I knew it was a bad move from the start. So technically, I gotta take the blame for this," I pointed out.

"Nah, is not your fault. It's that nigga's fault and I'm going to talk to him about it again as soon as I get back into the Jeep," Quincy assured me.

"Listen, Quincy, you don't have to do that. You said enough on the way here. So I'm good. I made a bad judgment call, and I paid for it. So that's it. End of story," I told him, and then I tapped his arm. "I'm gonna go to my room now. Call me tomorrow," I continued, and then I walked off.

"A'ight. But make sure you answer your phone," he yelled.

"I will," I replied. I heard my voice echo as I continued toward the elevator.

9

WHAT THE F*@K JUST HAPPENED?

When I thought I was this close to finding out where my baby was, a fucking monkey wrench got thrown in the freaking mix. I couldn't believe how Quincy's friend snapped on me like he did. I swear, I was so close to taking my pistol out and scaring his ass with it. Fucking punk! Got me out there looking for my baby, but then in the middle of things, he pulled the plug on me. Was this guy on drugs or something? Whatever issues he was dealing with, I hoped he got help for it. Because if he ever tried some bullshit like that again, I was gonna shove the barrel of my gun down his throat until he choked on it. Fucking bastard!

I found the elevator and took it to my floor, and as soon as I walked off, I bumped into the same freaking security guard from the night before. He looked me straight in the eye. "How you doing?" he asked me.

"I'm just great. And you?" I politely asked, knowing full well that I wasn't feeling him snooping around on my fucking floor. I knew he was the security guard and he was supposed to patrol the inside and the outside of the hotel, but this constantly bumping into me had to stop. Better yet, let's call it stalking because in my opinion that's what that nigga was doing.

"I'm okay. Thanks for asking," he replied, and then stepped by me to get on the elevator.

I turned my back to him and headed straight to my hotel room. But then I heard a dinging sound coming from the elevator. A couple seconds later, I heard the security guard's voice. "Hey, Chantel, excuse me," he said.

I stopped in my tracks and turned around, but I didn't say one word. The security guard stood there, pressing his weight against the sliding doors to prevent them from closing on him. "Yes?" I finally replied.

"If I bring you a picture of the girl my brother used to date from high school, will you look at it? 'Cause I swear, if you got a chance to see her, you'd see exactly why I thought you were her," he explained.

"You don't have to bring me any pictures. I'll take your word for it," I told him, and then I said, "Good night!"

Before he could utter another word, I turned back around and continued on to my hotel room. "You have a good night too," I heard him say.

Immediately after I entered my room, I fell down on the bed because I felt an anxiety attack coming on. I dropped everything in my hands and sat up on the edge of the bed. "I want my fucking baby!" I screamed. I could tell that I was about to have a nervous breakdown. I was also growing cold down to my core and I wanted revenge on everyone who had done something to me. Trevor was now added to the list of niggas I wanted to torture to death. The way I was feeling right then, all the motherfuckers who caused me heartache were going to either die or suffer when I was done exacting swift moral justice on their asses.

Going on another day without getting any closer to my baby boy had started to take a tremendous toll on me. I couldn't keep living under this mental stress. I didn't know how much longer I was going to be able to endure all of the anxiety. It seemed like it was mounting more and more by the day.

I did know that from that moment forward, every day I was out there searching would have to count. I had to make some type of progress or else.

Once I came to terms with what I had to do, I got up, showered, and then I lay down on the bed and tried to get some rest. But of course that didn't work. Instead, I found myself getting back out of the bed. I started pacing my hotel room floor for the next twenty minutes trying to figure out my next move. Walking around with this upsetting feeling that either my baby was dead or being taken care of by a total stranger tormented my mind. Next thing I knew, I was balled up in a fetal position on my hotel bed crying my poor little heart out because my heart was heavy. I was going through this ordeal all alone. I was fighting this battle by myself. I had no help or no one's shoulder to cry on. So how was I going to get through this? Who was going to save me if Matt caught me off guard and killed me before I could get revenge on him? Nobody! "Why me, God?" I cried out. My tears were running down my face like a faucet. "God, my son is an innocent baby, so why did he have to get pulled into my drama? He had nothing to do with any of my past transgressions, so why has he been taken from me? God, please give me some answers," I begged.

I didn't realize that I cried myself asleep until I got up really early the following morning. It was four AM, to be exact. I couldn't sleep because I wanted to get back to Huntersville. I figured I would've probably found Matt by now if I hadn't gone with Quincy and his little buddy Trevor yesterday. Trevor fucked up my entire trip. Now I needed to make up some ground. So I pulled out my cabdriver friend's business card and called him to see if he'd be able to help me. "Hello," he said.

I really didn't expect him to answer the phone this time of the morning, so I was kind of shocked. "Hi, is this . . . ?" I said, and fell silent as I looked down at the business card to find out what his name was. ". . . Sam?" I finally said.

"Yes, it is. And who am I speaking to?" he asked.

"This is Chantel from the hotel. You took me around yesterday."

"Oh yeah, how are you?"

"I'm good. I didn't expect you to answer the phone this early in the morning. I was waiting for your voice mail so I could leave a message."

"Oh no, I'm up. I'm actually working right now. Just dropped off my last fare."

"So you work all night, too?"

"I work several different shifts. There is a quota I must meet on a weekly basis. So if I can't do it in an eight-hour shift, then I'll do a double."

"What time do you get off?"

"I'm clocking out around eight o'clock."

"Do you have to pick up another fare right now?"

"No, why? Do you need me to come by and take you somewhere?"

"Yes. If you can?"

"Of course I can. Are you ready now?"

"I can be ready in like fifteen to twenty minutes."

"Well, I'll see you then," he told me, and then we both disconnected the call.

When Mr. Sam drove up to the valet area of the hotel, I was there front and center and I wasted no time getting in the backseat of the car. He greeted me with a huge smile. "Hi there, little lady."

"Hi, Mr. Sam," I replied, giving him a half smile.

"So where are we going this time of the morning?" he wanted to know.

"I need you to take me back to Huntersville."

"Are you sure? Because you were pretty upset when I took you there yesterday."

"Yeah, I know. I'm okay now."

"Are we going to the same two places?"

"Yes."

"Okay. Let's go," he said, and turned on the meter.

10

DIDN'T SEE THIS COMING

It didn't take Mr. Sam long to bring me back to Huntersville. I swear, it seemed like as soon as I blinked my eyes, we were there. As we turned onto Church Street, he wanted to know exactly how I was going to proceed. I instructed him to drive me down Lexington Avenue first so I could see if there was any foot traffic. "Just drive by the same house like you did yesterday," I told him.

"Am I going to stop this time?"

"No. I just wanna see if those guys we saw yesterday are outside."

"Roger that," he replied, and proceeded through the neighborhood.

Mr. Sam drove down two one-way streets that led us to A Avenue. And as soon as he was about to make the turn onto the street, he announced it. I sat up in the backseat and zoomed directly in on the duplex from the corner. "Doesn't seem like anyone is out this time of the morning," he mentioned.

"Yeah, I see that," I commented.

"Do you wanna drive by that other house on Lexington Avenue?"

"Yes, please."

Matt's cousin's house was one block over in the opposite direction. And just like the duplex on A Avenue, this place looked deserted too. "Where the hell is everyone?" I asked out loud.

"Beats me," Mr. Sam said. "Is there anywhere else you're trying to go?" he continued.

"Yeah, take me back over by A Avenue. But instead of driving down A Avenue, drop me off on Washington Street and I'll walk from there."

"You want me to drop you off?" He sounded alarmed.

"Yes, I need to check out something," I told him.

"Please don't tell me you're out here trying to buy drugs."

I chuckled. "No, Mr. Sam, I am not out here to buy drugs. I'm looking for someone. And I see that I'm not going to be able to find them if I don't do some further investigating of my own. So, pull over right here and I'll be right back," I said after he pulled up onto Washington Street.

"This is a dangerous neighborhood so I hope you know what you are doing."

"I'm gonna be just fine," I assured him as I opened up the back door.

"Don't take too long because then I'll have to leave you," he warned me.

Before I closed the back door, I promised him I'd only be gone for five minutes. I couldn't risk being seen by anyone who could pose a threat to me, so I cut through the backyard of a known crack spot and made my way through the backyard of an abandoned trap house. Luckily for me, the metal fences that marked off each backyard were low enough for me to climb over the top of them. After the first two fences, it seemed easy. But when I got to the third one, my strength was tested. Remember, I had just had a baby three days ago, so I was really doing too much strenuous stuff to my body.

Thankfully, four backyards and four metal fences later, I had come upon the backyard of the duplex. I was tired as hell. I was also scared to death. I was breathing so hard that it sounded really loud to me, so I held my breath for a second, just to make sure no one heard me.

With my heart still racing painfully in my chest, I exhaled and finally got the nerve up to move forward toward the duplex. I tiptoed up the brick steps. Just as I got about two steps up, I paused. It was very quiet in the back of this house so I wanted to make sure I wasn't making any noise at all.

I continued tiptoeing up on the back porch of the duplex very quietly. Every curtain and mini blind on all the back windows was closed shut but one. I couldn't believe that there was one small tear in one of the mini blinds in the kitchen window. I squinted one eye and peered into the kitchen. Someone walked by the window and it scared the shit out of me. I jumped back from the window. "Fuck!" I whispered after I exhaled. "Come on, Lauren, let's focus," I said to myself, to root myself on.

"Are y'all done bagging that shit up?" I heard a male voice say.

"Yeah, we almost done," I heard another guy say. So I leaned forward and peered through that damaged mini blind again. My eye went from left to right trying to get a look at something inside of that kitchen. And bingo, it happened. Standing there clear as day was the same guy who took my money from me. He was standing over two guys at a kitchen table. I couldn't see the faces of the other guys but I could see their hands bagging up dope. "Kanan, you know we're gonna sell out of this shit as soon as we go outside, right?" one guy said.

It seemed like I held my breath waiting to see who was going to respond to the name Kanan. It had to be the guy standing up because he looked like he ran the spot.

THE MARK 85

"Yeah, I know. And that's why Matt said he's gon' make sure we get the re-up pack before tonight," the guy standing up finally said. I swear it felt like a victory when I found out what this guy's name was. But to hear him mentioning that he'd spoken to Matt about a re-up was like music to my ears. One of my questions had been answered. Matt was indeed somewhere around. Now I needed to find out where he was.

"Are you sure we gon' get enough dope to carry us through the night?" he asked.

"Yeah, I was wondering the same thing. Remember, it was dead around here for a week because we didn't have any dope. Now that we got some more, I just wanna know how long we gon' be good because I need this money," I heard the other guy say.

"Let me tell y'all niggas something. That nigga Matt came up on a gold mine so we ain't gon' run out of dope no time soon," I heard Kanan explain with excitement.

"Damn right! We are about to be paid in motherfucking full!" one of the guys said, and then they all chuckled.

Hearing these guys get excited over a package of drugs Matt bought with the ransom money they stole from me made me want to vomit. These simple-ass niggas were celebrating at the expense of my husband's blood. How fucking sick was that? I swear I wanted to kick the door down and shoot and kill everybody in this fucking house because of the pain I was now suffering. Just last week these niggas were around here scrambling to get a drug package they could flip for a profit. Now they had all the drugs they could possibly need.

It didn't shock me to hear what Matt did with the money once he returned to Virginia. Buying and selling drugs was all Matt knew. He'd never go out and invest in a legal business. No. He'd rather spend all of his money on massive amounts of cocaine and heroin so he could continue to reign as the king of the streets. It's always been about appearances with Matt. He didn't like my check fraud hustle when I first introduced it to him after he came home from jail. I saw it in his eyes. But he dealt with it for a while because he knew the Feds were watching him for the first few months after he was released. He had no other choice. And I think that killed him inside too. He didn't like me running things. He wanted to be the man and when I stripped him of that, it ate away at his pride. I guess that forced him to cheat on me with that desperate-ass bitch Yancy. But it's all good, though. My day would come.

While I was eavesdropping on the guys in the kitchen, I was startled by the light that was turned on in a bedroom next to the kitchen. I didn't know if the person in the bedroom heard me outside or what. All I knew was that I needed to get off of that back porch before someone saw me.

I walked off the back porch very quietly. I started to head back to the cab but the possibility of finding out who else was in the house convinced me to stay a little longer. I couldn't see any movement from where I was standing so I walked on the opposite side of the duplex where there was another window that belonged to that room. The grass in the backyard was at least two feet high so I had to be careful when I walked through it. Syringes, beer bottles, and broken glass were just a few things a person could step on while walking through this mess. Didn't want to hurt myself or trip over anything and bring unnecessary noise. Cats like the ones bagging up that dope in the kitchen stay on high alert when it comes to the cops and other cats that wanna rob them. So you see, I had to be extra careful while I was hanging around this spot.

I traveled a few feet around the side of the duplex to see if I could get a look through the window since it didn't have a mini blind covering it. But as I approached, I realized that the window was too high off the ground. I looked around the yard for something to stand on. Thankfully, there was a plastic crate by a nearby tree. I dragged the crate to the window because it was too big to pick up. It took me about a minute or two to get it close enough so that I could stand up on it. After I got it close to the house, I climbed on top of it and looked through the sheer curtains. I couldn't see anything but a bed and a small television. Nothing else. "Fuck! I took too long," I hissed. I immediately became frustrated because I knew that whoever turned on the bathroom light had already gone out of the room.

I stood there for a couple more seconds and waited, but there was still no movement. But as I turned to step down from the crate, someone turned on the television. I quickly turned back around. My heart started racing rapidly. And then out of the corner of my eye came movement. I couldn't see the person's face. But from the silhouette of the person's body, I could tell she was a woman. I could see her hourglass figure very clearly. I can also see that all she was wearing was a T-shirt. There was no doubt in my mind that she was there for Kanan. She must've been one of his side chicks. She had to be. No classy woman would allow a man to fuck her in a trap house when there were a dozen hotels nearby.

"Whatcha turn the TV on for?" a male's voice came out of nowhere.

"Because I wanna watch TV," the woman replied.

"Well, you gon' have to do that at home. 'Cause I got some shit I gotta take care of and you can't be here when I do it," the same male voice said. This time I knew the voice belonged to Kanan.

"So you just gon' fuck me and kick me out?" she spat. I could tell that she was pissed off.

"Look, I don't care to hear all of that. Just put on your clothes and get the fuck out," Kanan roared. He was getting more irritated with her by the second.

"You know what? Fuck you!" she yelled. And then I saw

her grabbing her things from a nearby dresser. I couldn't see exactly what she was grabbing but I saw a lot of movement. "Are you still gonna let me take this box of Pampers with me?" she asked sarcastically.

"Fuck, nah! They belong to somebody else," his voice boomed, and then he said, "You taking too long. Now let's go!"

"Don't you see I'm trying to put my fucking clothes on?" she yelled at him once more.

That apparently didn't sit well with Kanan, because I didn't hear him say another word. I did hear some scuffling in the bedroom. And then I heard her screaming, "Get off me." Before I knew it, I heard her voice again, but it was coming from the front of the house. I jumped off the crate and hid behind the nearby tree just in case Kanan decided to come outside and walk the perimeter.

"You ain't shit, nigga!" she yelled as she walked away from the house.

"Since I ain't shit, don't bring your ass back over here," he yelled back at her.

"Fuck you!" she yelled once more.

I thought Kanan would have more to say, but I didn't hear him say another word. I realized he had gone back into the house because a few minutes later the light and TV in that room were turned off. This was my cue to leave and head back to the cab before Mr. Sam left me stranded out here in this freaking jungle.

On my way back to the cab, I thought about everything I'd heard. From Matt making sure the spot received their re-up of dope, down to there being a bag of Pampers in that bedroom. Were those Pampers for my baby? Had he been there? I swore I needed some answers because I wasn't getting them fast enough.

Luckily for me, I had gotten back to the cab when I did because as soon as I walked onto the next block over, Mr. Sam had started driving very slowly down the street. I had to run down behind the car. He stopped when he saw me through the rearview mirror. "You weren't lying when you said you'd leave if I took too long," I said after I got back inside the car.

"Whatcha didn't believe me?" he asked as he continued down the block.

"I thought you were joking."

"Oh no, I don't do no joking around when I come out to neighborhoods like this."

"Hey, do me a favor," I blurted out, unfazed by what he was saying. All I could think about was that chick who Kanan kicked out of the spot.

"What is it?"

"Drive down A Avenue, then go up Lexington Avenue, and then circle around and drive down B Avenue. I'm looking for this young lady who just got kicked out of that duplex we drove by earlier."

"What do you mean she was kicked out?"

"One of the guys from the duplex kicked this girl out of the house. And she was not happy at all. She cursed that guy out really bad."

"And what did he do?"

"Nothing. He told her not to come over there no more and closed the front door."

"And where were you when all this was going on?"

"Hiding behind a tree," I told him.

"Is this the young lady I'm pulling up to now?"

I looked through the front windshield of the cab and saw the same woman Mr. Sam saw. I zoomed in on her attire and realized that it was the same girl. "Yeah, that's her. Pull up next to her," I insisted.

"You better hold your head outside the window and announce yourself so she doesn't pull a gun out on us," he warned me.

So out of respect, I rolled down the window, leaned my head out a bit, and yelled out, "Hey, excuse me."

The woman turned around at the sound of my voice and asked if I was talking to her. She looked really scared. I had to assure her that I was no threat to her. "Look, I'm not here to cause you any harm. I just saw Kanan kicked you out of the house so I wanna know if I could talk to you for a minute?" I asked her.

"Whatcha want to talk to me about?" she asked as she stood there with a jacket in her hands.

I got out of the cab and walked over to her because I didn't feel comfortable with Mr. Sam hearing my conversation. The moment I approached her she looked at me from head to toe and wanted to know who I was. "My name is Chantel," I lied to her. "And yours?"

"Eva," she replied. I looked at her from head to toe. She was definitely a bargain-basement chick. She had to be dealing with some low self-esteem issues too because what woman would allow a man to fuck her brains out and then kick her out of the house at five o'clock in the morning? She was either desperate for a piece of dick, or she was mentally retarded.

"Hi, Eva, well the reason why I stopped you is because when I was pulling up to the house I noticed Kanan had let you out."

"And what does that have to do with you? Whatcha, his bitch?" she asked sarcastically.

Now my first reaction was to curse her the fuck out, but I figured why be ignorant like her? And besides, I knew I wouldn't get any information from her if I let her have it. "Eva, listen, I'm not Kanan's bitch! I'm his baby mama. Now when I saw you leave the house, I approached him and asked him who you were and he lied and said that you were there for the other two guys, and that they ran the train on you. Now, I'm not stupid because you don't look like you'd let two cats fuck you at the same time. But if I'm wrong you can correct me right now."

"Hell, nah! I ain't into that shit!" she spat. "I wouldn't let two niggas run a train on me. Kanan's ass is lying! I was there with him the whole night until we got into an argument and that's when I left," she explained.

"I knew that bastard was lying. I'm so tired of his no-good ass! It's over. He can't ever bring his black ass back to my house," I said, trying to create a scene for her. I needed her to believe that I was Kanan's baby mama and that I was on her side.

"He sure is."

"How long have y'all been messing around?" I questioned her.

"I've been fucking with him for about two months now," she replied confidently. She wanted me to know that she'd been in that nigga's life for a while, so I could feel even more betrayed. Little did she know, I never fucked this guy and I couldn't care less about his pathetic ass. And as soon as I got my hands on him, I was going to put a fucking slug in his heart!

"Oh really?" I said, trying to sound surprised.

"Did you know he had a baby?"

"Nope."

"So he didn't tell you that he had a baby mama and that I was on my way there to get a box of Pampers for our baby?"

"No, he sure didn't. As a matter of fact, when I first saw the box of Pampers in the bedroom I asked him who the Pampers belong to and he told me that I could have them because I have a three-month-old baby."

"When was the last time you were over there before this time?"

"I was over there two nights ago."

"Were those Pampers there?"

"Nope. Last night was my first time I seen them."

"What size were the Pampers?"

"They were for a size one."

"How can a three-month-old baby fit in a size one Pamper?" I inquired. Her answers weren't adding up.

"My baby was a two-and-a-half-pound preemie when she was born. She's almost nine pounds now."

"Oh, I am so sorry to hear that."

"Don't be, because she getting big now. And the doctor said that as long as she's growing at this steady pace, she's going to be fine."

"That's good to hear," I said. I changed the subject. "Do you live around here?"

"Yeah, I live on the next block."

"So, you're fine to walk the rest of the way home?"

"Yeah, I'm good. But I'm more concerned about you."

"Why you say that?" I asked. I was definitely alarmed.

"Because your baby daddy ain't shit! Trust me, I ain't the only bitch that's been in there fucking him. So tell him to stop lying on them other niggas and be a man about his shit! He has different bitches over there all the time. I caught one of his bitches leaving his spot last week before he left to go to New York. He tried to act like they was there dropping off his re-up package. But I knew that was some bullshit."

"Do you know who else went to New York with him?"

"Yeah, all them niggas in that house went to New York with Kanan. They had to help bring the dope back in a different car."

"Oh, wow! You know about everything, huh?"

"I only know what I hear when I'm in there. Those young niggas in there are dumb as a brick. They tell all their fucking business. If I was a snitch, I could rat their ass out and they wouldn't even know it."

I was amazed at how much information this chick knew. My first thought was to get her number so I could pick her brain a little more. But I decided against it. I figured if she was this loose with her mouth about their business, then she'd definitely throw my ass underneath the bus if I gave her the opportunity. Besides, I needed to keep my identity a secret. I couldn't afford to blow my cover.

I thanked her for her time and wished her luck. "Keep your head up!" I told her.

"Oh, don't worry about me. I'm a trouper 'round here. Niggas know I'm a loyal bitch, that's why they fuck with me like they do," she said proudly.

"Well then, hold it down, sis!" I said as I looked up into the sky. I could see the sun was about to rise, which meant I needed to be heading back to the hotel.

"Yeah, you do the same," she said, and then she turned around and walked off.

I got back inside the cab. "Take me back to my hotel," I instructed Mr. Sam.

"Got all the information you needed?"

"Yep. I sure did," I said.

"She sure did a lot of cursing."

"Yeah, she did," I agreed.

"I hope you don't talk like that."

"Trust me, I don't," I assured him, and then I laid my head back against the headrest.

While I rested my head, I couldn't help but think about how Matt took my family, killed my husband, took my money and bought drugs with it. Knowing him, he bought at least two kilos of dope. Being able to buy that amount of drugs makes a man like him feel powerful. But once again, he did this at the expense of my husband. Now I take some blame too, but Matt pulled the trigger. And to now know that Kanan and the rest of those niggas that work for Matt accompanied him to New York. They didn't know they had just signed their own death certificate. Everything Matt had coming to him, they would be greeted with the same fate. They'd better hope the police kicked up in that crib before I got my hands on them. Because I wasn't play-ing, especially with all the anger and hurt I had built up inside of me. I would have their heads. To get someone in their families would sweeten the deal. I just wanted those niggas to feel the pain I was feeling right then. This shit hurt me to the core. And being away from my son all that time was tearing me down even more. I swear I didn't know how I'd been able to live from day to day. It had to be God.

11

BACK TO THE BASICS

I thought I'd be tired when I walked back into my hotel room but I wasn't. Just the thought of my baby still being alive made me feel like I was completely wired up on drugs or something. The feeling was becoming overwhelming. All I needed to figure out was how I was going to find out where my baby was. I knew Kanan was expecting another shipment of drugs tonight, but that didn't mean that Matt was going to drop it off himself. Matt was many things, but he wasn't dumb. When he went to prison before this last time, it wasn't because the cops caught him with a huge supply of drugs in his car. He vowed never to carry drugs in his possession again. So I knew that sitting out there on the block, waiting for him to bring Kanan more drugs, would be a waste of time. However, I did believe that whoever brought those drugs would pick up Matt's money in the process and deliver it right back to him after the drugs were dropped off. Now all I needed to do was be out there when it happened.

To pass the time, I turned on the TV and watched a few back-to-back episodes of *Law & Order*. The first one was about a man who killed his wife and made it look like his mistress did it. I thought that was very interesting. The second episode was about a pedophile's obsession for little kids, and while children were coming up missing the police thought the pedophile was the one combing the streets for these kids, but later found out that his mother was the one feeding them to him. I swear, I could not have written that story if someone told me to. It was pretty sick. Which of course led me to thinking about my son. My heart started aching at that very moment, thinking about the possibility that Matt could be hurting him. People who mistreat children are monsters. Sickos, to say the least. I just prayed that my little one was safe and sound.

An hour passed by and I got an unexpected knock on the door. It startled the crap out of me. Who the hell could be at the door? No one here knew that I was staying at this hotel except my little friends Quincy and Trevor. And they didn't even know which room I was in. With my heart pounding uncontrollably, I slid off the bed and tiptoed to the door. I looked through the peephole and saw no one. I stood there for a second, just in case the person decided to knock on the door again. This time I would see them.

After sixty seconds passed, I backed away from the door slowly. I was very careful because I didn't want to be heard. I couldn't blow my cover. I was too close to finding my baby. Once I had him, I couldn't care less what happened after that.

Instead of climbing back onto the bed, I walked over to the window and peeked out the side of the curtains. I made sure the curtains didn't move; I couldn't afford to bring any attention to this room. For all I knew, anyone could be outside watching me.

Once I scanned the parking lot area three times, I backed away from the window and took a seat on the chair next to the small table right by the bed. Trying to figure out who was at that door was worrying me. I couldn't stop thinking of the many possibilities of who it could have been. I wanted to call the front desk, but I decided against it for fear that the cops were there waiting for my call. So I sat there.

Thirty minutes turned into one hour and then one hour turned into two. I was going crazy. My mind couldn't take it. I had to get out of there. But where was I to go? And how was I going to get there? I had a lot of shit to think about. But whatever my decision was, I needed one now.

I stood up from the chair and as I was about to go into the bathroom, someone started knocking on the door again. My heart completely jumped out of my chest and I instantly froze.

"Ms. Chantel, it's the security guy," the voice yelled through the door.

As much as I wanted to scream, after hearing the security guy's voice, I let out a sigh of relief. Knowing it was him and no one else was like music to my ears. I rushed to the door and opened it up. Standing there with a smile from ear to ear, the security guy held out a book that very much resembled a high school yearbook. I looked down at it and then I looked back at him and said, "Please don't tell me you brought me a picture of that young lady after I told you not to bother."

"I know. I know. But I just had to bring it here and show you," he insisted.

"Did you just knock on my door about two hours ago?" I asked him.

"Yeah, that was me. I thought you'd be up. That's why I came earlier," he explained. "So, can I show you this picture now?"

I exhaled. "Yeah, go ahead," I said reluctantly.

Without hesitation, the security guy opened the yearbook and went straight to the page where my picture was. It was my senior picture. I had on the whole cap-and-gown ensemble, holding my diploma in hand. I looked at that picture really hard and saw a young woman who could've had a bright future if she hadn't run into Matt a few months later. All of my dreams and ambitions and my 4.0 GPA went right out the window. Now look at me, I thought, hiding out in a hotel with less than $1,100 to my name and a prayer that I would get my baby back. My life was in ruins and this picture proved it.

I couldn't believe I was starting to get filled up with emotions as I stared at my picture. I had to catch myself because I realized that the security guy was watching me. I held back the tears, but I couldn't hide my glassy eyes. "Are you okay?" he asked me.

I quickly wiped both of my eyes with the backs of my hands. "Oh yeah, fine. I have allergies really bad," I lied. It was the quickest excuse I could come up with that seemed plausible. But I could tell he wasn't buying it.

"Tell the truth, you two look like twins, right?" he insisted.

I smiled. "Yeah, we you do," I agreed, because I knew he wasn't going to let it go.

"I told you," he burst with excitement.

"Well, now that you proved your point, let me go so I can get dressed. Got a long day ahead of me," I replied.

"Well, if you need anything, let me know."

"That's really nice of you. Thank you," I told him, and I closed the door.

While I headed to the bathroom, my cell phone started ringing. I rushed over to it and looked down at the caller ID. The call was coming from Quincy. I answered it to see what he wanted. "Hi, Quincy," I greeted him.

"Hey, Chantel, how are you?"

"I'm okay. What's going on?"

"I'm calling you because Trevor wants to speak with you."

"About?" I asked, even though I kind of knew what it was in reference to.

"He wants to apologize to you for being a dickhead last night."

"He doesn't have to do that," I responded nonchalantly. At this point, I couldn't care less to hear his voice or his apology. I was in another space and wanted to be left alone.

"Chantel," I heard Trevor's voice ring in my ear with a little bit of crackling sounds. It was obvious that Quincy forced him on the phone.

"Yes, what can I do for you?" I forced myself to say.

"This is Trevor and I want you to know how sorry I am for acting like an asshole last night. I was being very inconsiderate," he said.

"It's okay. I'm good. No hard feelings."

"Well, Quincy and I wanna still help you get your baby back if you don't mind."

"No, you guys don't have to do that. I'm gonna handle everything myself."

"She doesn't want our help," I heard Trevor say to Quincy as he moved his mouth away from the phone. I heard a shuffling sound and then Quincy started speaking into the phone.

"Hey, Chantel, we're not taking no for an answer. Trevor and I have decided that you shouldn't be doing this alone. So we're gonna come by there in another hour or so. Now be ready."

Before I could utter one word, Quincy disconnected our call. I shook my head because this kid had no freaking idea what we were up against. I just found out that all of those niggas had something to do with my husband's murder. Those guys were actual fucking killers. I knew I was treading on dangerous ground bringing these two young guys into his atmosphere. But I had to think with my head not my heart. I had to be focused on my son. I couldn't put anyone else before him. Not Quincy nor Trevor.

12

EMPTY APOLOGIES

Quincy and Trevor showed up an hour and a half later. They were both all smiles. Quincy helped me get in the backseat and closed the door once I was inside. Trevor turned around in his seat. He gave me the most apologetic expression he could muster up. "Listen, Chantel, I am really sorry about last night. I was being an insensitive jerk. So I wanna make it up to you."

"Look, Trevor, I told you I was good," I tried to reassure him.

"No, you're not. So stop saying that," Quincy interjected.

"Look, you guys, I know everything you're saying is coming from a good place but you don't owe me anything."

"We know that," Quincy said, "so, just sit back and relax and let us handle everything from here."

"You hungry?" Trevor asked.

"Yes, I can stand to put something on my stomach," I told him.

"Good, because we know this really nice spot in downtown Norfolk. They have the best Caribbean food ever," Quincy chimed in.

"Oh yeah, that place has some great food. You're gonna love it," Trevor agreed, and then he turned around in his seat and drove out of the hotel parking lot.

Quincy made small talk with me during the course of the drive to the restaurant. "Have you been able to get in contact with him?" he asked me.

"No, I haven't."

"I know you don't want to go to the cops, but they might be your best bet," Trevor stated.

"I told you that the cops won't get involved because he and I have custody issues," I lied once again. My best course of action for these guys was to act like I had no other recourse to get my baby back. And that they were the only ones who'd be able to help me. This tactic needed to be reiterated as much as possible.

"Oh yeah, you did mention that," Trevor agreed.

Trevor said nothing else until we arrived at the restaurant. He seemed really excited about dining at this restaurant. Quincy did too. After we were shown our table, we ordered our food. While we sat around the table waiting for our meals, I searched the room, looking at everyone's face to see if anyone looked familiar. Thankfully, I didn't recognize anyone and vice versa. Trevor and Quincy had their eyes set on four women sitting at a table not too far from us. I could tell that they were much older women, but these guys didn't care. "Instead of looking at them, why don't you guys go over to their table and introduce yourselves?" I suggested.

"Oh no, I'm not going to play myself," Trevor spoke first.

"What are you afraid of?" I asked.

"He's afraid of rejection," Quincy blurted out.

"No, I'm not. That's what you are," Trevor joked.

"I'm not afraid of rejection," Quincy said confidently.

"Well, go over there and introduce yourself to them," Trevor dared Quincy.

"I'm not gonna go over there just to prove a point to you," Quincy replied.

"You two are so funny." I smiled. It was kind of comical to see these two go back and forth about a group of women. This was my first time witnessing men being intimidated by gorgeous women. I mean, those four women were very successful-looking. They all possessed this air about them that they were no-nonsense and they were about their business. I take it that's why these two college guys were too intimidated to approach them.

Trevor and Quincy finally let each other off the hook concerning those women after we got our food. I had to admit that our meals were looking very tasty. I got the steamed red snapper with cabbage while Trevor and Quincy got oxtails with rice and peas. They dug into their food without saying grace. I said a silent prayer to bless my food, but I reminded God that I needed Him more than ever concerning my baby. I told Him how I needed Him to cover me and the guys when we went back to Huntersville. And after I told God how thankful I was for His grace and mercy, I ended my prayer.

Unlike Quincy and Trevor, I couldn't devour my food. My stomach was completely empty, but I really hadn't had an appetite since everything went down. So in all, I ate a couple of spoonfuls of cabbage and a little bit of the fish. I was ready to go before Trevor and Quincy finished their food. "You're not gonna eat the rest of your food?" Quincy wanted to know.

"No, I'm done," I told him.

"Well, I'll take it," he said, and pulled the plate over to

his side of the table. I sat there and watched him eat my food up right along with his. I watched in amazement while he fed his face. He had not a care in the world. Damn! I envied him. I figured after I got my baby back I could also go back to a life of peace and not have a care in the world.

On our way out of the restaurant, I made a detour to the bathroom and told them I'd meet them at the car. I had to pee really bad so I was kind of upset when I rushed into the bathroom and there was one person in front of me for a two-stall bathroom. "Is there something wrong with the other stall?" I asked.

"Yes, it's stopped up," the black woman replied.

"Shit!" I mumbled.

"You can go in front of me if you like," the lady offered.

"Oh, thank you so much."

A few minutes later a full-figured woman exited the bathroom stall and held the door open for me to go inside. But the smell coming from it pushed me back a couple of feet. I couldn't do it. I wasn't going in there. Not now. Not later. So I turned around and made my way out of the bathroom.

As soon as the door closed behind me I noticed that the men's bathroom was right in front of me so I knocked on the door twice, asked if anyone was in there, and when I got no response, I went inside. Luckily for me, the men's restroom was empty and it didn't have a foul smell to it. It couldn't get better than this. I rushed into the stall and squatted over the toilet. Immediately after I was done, I wiped myself with a little bit of tissue that was left on the roll and then got up and flushed the toilet. While I was exiting the bathroom stall, the bathroom door opened. "Someone's in here," I announced. But it was too late; the

gentleman had already entered halfway into the bathroom. Our eyes connected instantly. Then I looked down
at his police uniform. I swear I wanted to run out of there
as fast as I could but I knew that wouldn't be a very smart
thing to do so I remained calm.

"I'm sorry!" he said.

"It's okay. I'm on my way out anyway," I told him as I
walked over to the sink. My heart was racing uncontrollably. I felt my hands shaking too.

"I take it the women's restroom was occupied?" he
asked as he stood there with the door open.

"You're absolutely right," I replied, as I proceeded to
wash my hands. I watched him closely through my peripheral vision. I watched his every move as he watched me.

"You live around here?" he asked me.

I immediately caught a lump in my throat. Was this a
trick question? I didn't know whether to lie or tell the truth.
So I did what came naturally and that was a lie. "No, I'm
not from around here," I finally answered, avoiding eye
contact with him.

"So, where are you from?"

I turned the water off in the sink, grabbed two paper
towels from the dispenser next to the mirror, and said,
"I'm from up north."

"What brings you here to Virginia?"

I dried my hands and threw the paper towels into the
trash next to the door. "I'm just passing through," I told
him as I approached the doorway.

"Well, may you have safe travels to wherever you're
going," he said, and then he stepped to the side so I could
exit the bathroom.

"Thank you, officer!" I replied, and left.

I tried to control my breathing on my way out of the
restaurant, but it seemed like I couldn't get it together.

What were the odds of me walking into a freaking cop? Thank God he didn't recognize me or else I'd be in hand-cuffs right now.

Back at Trevor's Jeep, the guys were talking to each other about the exams they had to take the following week. Trevor seemed stressed out while Quincy acted like he had his exam in the bag. "You guys ready to go?" I asked them after I opened the door and climbed into the backseat.

"As ready as we will be," Trevor commented, and started up the ignition.

"So, which house are we going to?" Trevor wanted to know.

"We're going to the duplex on A Avenue," I told him.

A Avenue was saturated with crackheads. Normally, when fiends wanted to get high, they'd buy their drugs and then leave. So seeing this type of foot traffic led me to believe that Matt's spot had run out of drugs like it was predicted. None of Kanan's dope boys were outside. I figured they were either inside bagging the dope up or they were wait-ing to get their supply.

"Park right here at the corner," I instructed Trevor. After he parked his Jeep, he turned off the motor without me even asking him to.

"Why are all these people out here?" Quincy asked.

"They're looking for drugs," I told him.

"All of these people?"

"Yep."

"Wow! That's a lot of people," Quincy commented.

"That's what happens when you're either around the wrong crowd or something drastic happens to you and you let it destroy you," I explained.

"Do you know any of these people?" Trevor asked.

"No, I don't."

"Lucky you," Quincy said.

"Who are they waiting for?" Trevor wanted to know.

"The dope man," I said.

"She's talking about a drug dealer," Quincy added.

"I knew what a dope man was," Trevor replied sarcastically.

"Shhhh, you two," I said when I saw the front door of the duplex open. I wanted them both to be quiet so I could focus on what was about to happen.

Moments later one of Kanan's workers walked out on the front porch first while another one followed suit. And almost instantly the crowd of drug addicts swarmed them. "Yo, do you see that shit?" Trevor asked. He seemed amazed.

"So I guess those guys would be the dope man, huh?" Quincy assumed.

"Bingo," I said.

"So that's a drug house?" Quincy asked.

"That's one name to call it," I replied nonchalantly.

"So your ex sells drugs?" Quincy's questions continued.

"He used to."

"But he hangs out with guys who do?" Quincy pressed the issue.

"Shhh, be quiet," I instructed him as I rolled down the back window. I saw the first guy motion his hands toward the drug addicts so I wanted to hear what he was saying. "Y'all gotta get the fuck back! Or we ain't serving you," he yelled.

"Fuck!" I huffed as I banged my fist on the side of the back door.

"What's wrong?" Quincy asked.

"Yeah, what happened?" Trevor wanted to know.

"We're too late," I uttered, not even realizing what I was saying.

"Too late for what?" Trevor asked.

"Fuck!" I roared. I knew my window of opportunity had come and gone. If only we had gotten here sooner, I would've been able to see who dropped off the dope package to the morons and would've been able to follow them back to Matt. But no. We had to stop at a fucking restaurant first. Now I didn't know when I was gonna be given a chance to find out where Matt was. This day could not have been more fucked up for me.

Quincy turned around in his seat. "What's wrong?" he asked with concern.

"I found out that Matt was going to be here around this time but he wasn't going to be here long. So I was hoping we'd catch him before he left and possibly follow him back to where my baby was," I lied. I had to make up something. I couldn't tell them that Matt was going to have someone drop off drugs to his spot and when they left we were going to follow them. That would not have gone well with them. So I did the second-best thing and that was to tell them something they'd believe.

"Look, I believe you when you said that your ex was an asshole but wouldn't it be easier if you go up to the house and tell one of them to tell you where he is?" Trevor suggested.

"No, it wouldn't, dummy! Everyone isn't as civilized as you," Quincy interjected.

"Man, shut up! I'm only trying to help her figure this thing out," Trevor tried to reason.

"Look, I know you guys are trying to help, but will you just be quiet for a moment while I think this thing out?"

"Yeah, butthead, you heard what she said, be quiet," Quincy clowned Trevor.

Trevor stuck his middle finger up at Quincy, and then he turned his attention back on the dope fiends hanging around the duplex. We all sat there in silence while the guys traded money for drugs. And once the drugs were in the drug addicts' hands, they left the scene. Before we knew it, there was no more crowd. All of the drug addicts had disappeared. A few minutes later, so did the two guys who had the drugs.

"How much money do you think those guys just made?" Quincy asked.

"I'm thinking about maybe a thousand dollars," Trevor guessed.

"Nah, man, it had to be double that amount. There was a lot of people out there," Quincy stated.

"Yeah, you might be right," Trevor replied, and then they both fell silent.

About five minutes later, Trevor made an outlandish suggestion. "Look, I think one of us should go to the door and ask one of the guys where we can find Matt."

"No, that wouldn't be a good idea," I interjected.

"Yeah, it sure wouldn't. And speak for yourself," Quincy commented.

"Well, I think it would be. I mean, how else are you going to find her baby? Sitting outside in a car and watching the same house every day isn't going to get you closer to finding your son," Trevor explained.

"I understand what you're saying. But these guys aren't the type you could just walk up to and ask questions. They aren't friendly," I explained to Trevor.

"So what is your plan then? I mean, it seems like I'm the only one who's speaking with some logic," Trevor replied.

"I think we should just wait," I said flatly.

"For how long?" Trevor asked me.

"For however long it takes," Quincy jumped to my defense.

"I'm not going to sit out here for the rest of the night,

especially since I have an eight o'clock class in the morning," Trevor huffed.

"Hey, Trevor, just give me a few more minutes of your time and then you can take me back to the hotel. Agreed?"

"A'ight," he said, and then the car went silent.

Even though Trevor agreed to stick around for a few more minutes, he started getting a little antsy. He'd make little innuendos about how could someone could live or even a nap in this area. Then he started playing his music loud. Quincy and I both had to tell him to turn the volume down a few times. He was really getting on my nerves. But I held my tongue, to prevent me from screaming at him. And besides, I needed to stay out here as long as I possibly could. I figured if I left too soon, I'd miss another window of opportunity to find my baby boy.

During Trevor's little tantrum, a couple of drug addicts walked by his Jeep after they scored some dope from one of Matt's boys. They looked like they were in a hurry but that didn't stop Trevor from getting their attention. He rolled down his window and said, "Could y'all ladies please tell me what y'all are doing out here?" Both of the women looked at each other and then they looked back at Trevor.

"Whatcha mean what we doing out here? We live out here," one of the women said as they continued to walk in the direction they were already going.

"You sound like you're proud of it," he commented. Before he could say another word, Quincy grabbed his arm.

"Man, what the fuck is wrong with you? Why are you even talking to those ladies? Can't you see that they're in a rush to go and get high?" Quincy pointed out. He seemed agitated too. But I was more aggravated than he was. Why was Trevor trying to bring attention to us? We weren't out there to interview drug addicts. We were out there looking for Matt. That was it.

Trevor laughed it off like it was some big joke. But I wasn't buying it. He was being an asshole and Quincy made him aware of it. After they went back and forth for a few more minutes, Trevor finally closed his mouth.

13

MORE TRACES OF EVIDENCE

All three of us sat in Trevor's Jeep and we watched Matt's boys for about thirty minutes as they ran in and out of the house selling drugs to the local drug addicts hand over foot. We even noticed a couple of the drug addicts trade stolen clothes and electronic equipment in exchange for drugs. But what caught my eye as well as Trevor's and Quincy's was when a woman walked up with two bags of Pampers. She handed both bags to one of the guys, and he handed her drugs as payment for them. My heart sunk into the pit of my stomach. "Did you see that?" Quincy asked.

"Yes" was all I said because I really didn't have any words. I was more shocked at how this was the third bag of Pampers I saw at this spot. This was no coincidence.

"I betcha your baby is in that house," Trevor blurted out.

"No, he's not. My ex wouldn't have my baby in that type of environment. It would be too risky. And besides, he knows that this would be the first place I'd come look," I reasoned.

"Well, why did that guy just take two bags of diapers

from that lady if there wasn't a baby there?" Trevor tried to point out.

"Listen, Trevor, that guy only traded dope for those Pampers because that's what street hustlers do. They buy stuff if they need it. So in this case Matt probably told them to get some of the dope fiends to go out and boost some Pampers just so he wouldn't be spotted doing it himself," I replied.

"I understand what you're saying but I still say there's a chance that your baby could be in there," Trevor pressed.

"Well, I'm telling you that he's not," I said, getting frustrated with this whole conversation.

"Wanna put a wager on it?" Trevor suggested.

"What? A wager? What are you talking about?" I questioned him, trying to figure out where he was going with this.

"Yeah, Trevor, what are you talking about?" Quincy asked him.

"Well, since I believe there's a chance that her baby is in that house, I want to make a bet."

"How are we going to find out otherwise?" Quincy wanted to know.

"Yeah, how are we going to find out if you're right?" I chimed in. I really was curious to hear what this fool had to say.

"Because I am going up to the house, knock on the door, and act like I'm looking for someone else. And by the time one of the guys tells me that I have the wrong address, I would have had enough time to listen for a baby's cry."

"I don't think that'll be a good idea," I disagreed. This fool was crazier than I thought. He had no fucking idea who these guys really were.

"I think it is," Quincy agreed with Trevor.

"So what happens if he doesn't hear my baby cry?" I asked.

"Then I'll just leave. We'll just have to come up with another plan," Trevor said.

"Yeah, he's right, Chantel. Because at least if he did that, then we wouldn't have to waste any more time out here," Quincy explained.

I hesitated for a moment before I opened my mouth and gave these guys a rebuttal. I had to weigh the pros and cons of Trevor's plan. I figured the likelihood that the guys wouldn't suspect anything unusual if Trevor knocked on their door and asked for someone who didn't live there was slim to none. Guys who sold drugs out of trap houses are always suspicious. So this time wouldn't be any different. "Trevor, I don't think you should do it," I warned him.

"Why not?" he asked me.

"Because I just don't."

"You gotta give me a better reason than that." Trevor wouldn't let up.

"Because it may not work," I told him.

"Well, we'll just see about that," Trevor said, and then he abruptly got out of the front seat of his Jeep.

"Wait, where are you going?" I yelled, but it was too late. Trevor had already closed the car door.

"Let him go, Chantel. If one of those niggas swing on him and whip his ass, just remember that he brought this on himself," Quincy spoke up.

I moved to the middle of the backseat and watched Trevor through the front windshield as he approached the duplex. No one was standing outside so I held my breath as he walked up toward the front door. Seconds later, Trevor knocked on the door. He looked back at Quincy and me while he waited for someone to answer. A few moments later, the front door of the duplex opened. One of Kanan's workers stood in the doorway and looked at Trevor from head to toe. Trevor's mouth started moving, so I assumed that he said hello, and gave the spiel he'd run by Quincy and me. Immediately after his mouth stopped moving, the guy standing in the doorway said something to Trevor. For the next five to ten seconds, words transpired between the two of them. I even saw the guy at the door crack a smile. I swear, I couldn't believe what was going on. "I guess his plan is working out after all," Quincy stated.

"It sure looks that way, huh?" I agreed.

Three seconds later, the guy turned around to close the door. Trevor turned around too like he was getting ready to leave but he doubled back and looked over his shoulder before the guy could close the front door. The guy saw what Trevor did, and instead of closing the door he opened it wider and motioned for Trevor to come to him. Trevor turned back around, walked up to the entryway, and without warning, the guy looked to his left and then to the right, and then he grabbed Trevor by the collar of his shirt and yanked his entire body into the house. The front door slammed shut. I gasped. "Fuck! Did you see that?" Quincy gasped. He almost seemed spooked.

"Yes, I saw," I said, panicking. My first reaction was to jump behind the driver's seat of the Jeep and pull off. But I knew it wouldn't be right to do that so I took a deep breath and exhaled.

"What are we going to do?" Quincy wanted to know.

"I don't know," I replied, because in reality I didn't know. Okay, I was strapped with my gun. But that was only one gun compared the countless ones those niggas may have had in the house. So how was I gonna go to war with them? Those guys outnumbered Quincy and me. We were no match for them.

"Why do you think he snatched him in the house like that?" Quincy's questions continued.

"I don't know."

"I'm calling the police," Quincy said as he pulled his cell phone from his pocket.

"No, we can't do that. Not right now." I knew that if he

called the cops, shit was going to get worse before it got better.

"Well, we can't just leave him in there," Quincy pointed out.

"I know we can't," I said as my heart began to race at a rapid speed. My mind was scrambling to come up with a logical enough plan for getting Trevor out of the situation he had just put himself in.

"We need to figure something out now," Quincy said.

"I know, I know. That's what I am trying to do."

"This can't be happening right now," Quincy mumbled. "What if they hurt him? Or worse, what if they kill him?"

"Quincy, please stop talking. I can't hear myself think."

"Look, somebody is looking out the window," Quincy yelled as he pointed toward the house.

I looked up at the first-floor window on the side of the house and realized that he was being paranoid. "Quincy, I'm going to need you to calm down because no one is looking out the window," I told him calmly.

"But there is. You don't see that black curtain moving?"

"Okay, listen, you acting crazy like this isn't going to help the situation. We've got to remain calm. We won't be able to help him if we're carrying on like this, Quincy."

"How do you want me to act? My roommate is in that fucking house with those drug dealers. They could be hurting him right now and you want me to be calm!" he spat.

"Look, I'm gonna handle this," I said, trying to calm him down. But it didn't work. Quincy wasn't trying to hear anything I had to say. He was dead-set on getting Trevor out of the house right then. And I understood him completely but we weren't dealing with your average guys. We were dealing with street cats who would kill you if you looked at them wrong. Those guys played no games, especially when it came to their territory and their money.

"If you don't figure out a way to get my friend out of that house right now, then I have no other choice but to call the cops," he replied.

I sat there in silence for a moment trying to figure out the best way to handle this without any one of us getting hurt. Once again, I began to weigh the pros and the cons of me bringing out my gun, knowing I was going to be outnumbered. This shit wasn't going to work at all. It wouldn't be a fair fight at all. And as much as I wanted Quincy to know that I would fight for him, he also needed to know that it had to be on my terms.

I was wanted by the cops for questioning in New York, and here in Virginia, so seeing them right now wouldn't be a good time. I had to get my baby back first. Everything else was secondary and Quincy needed to know this.

"Hey Quincy, listen, I'm gonna go around the back of the house and see if I can see or hear anything. Because if I can, then I'll be able to figure out a way to get Trevor out of there without him getting hurt. All right?" I asked. I needed him to assure me that he wouldn't do anything stupid while I was trying to check things out.

He hesitated for a moment, and then he said, "Yeah, I'll wait for you to check the house out. But if you come back and tell me that they're beating my friend up, then I ain't gonna have no choice but to call the cops."

"All right, that's fair," I said, knowing I didn't agree with anything he'd just said. Did he really think that I was going to come back and tell him that Trevor was getting beat up, even if I saw it firsthand? No. That wasn't going to happen. I warned Trevor not to go up to that house. But he wouldn't listen, so now I had to take matters into my own hands.

"Stay right here, and I will be right back," I told him.

"Okay. But you better hurry."

"I will. So don't call the cops," I instructed him as I slid out the backseat of the Jeep. Before Quincy could utter another word, I held my purse close to me with my gun inside and shut the door.

I was on pins and needles, dreading that I had to face this unnecessary bullshit Trevor threw at me. All he had to do was shut the fuck up and stay his ass in the car. But no, he had to get his dumb ass out of the car and walk up to these niggas' trap house like he was a fucking insurance man or something. Now he was probably tied up, getting the shit beat out of him. I swore if I came out of this thing unscathed, I was gonna beat Trevor's ass myself.

14

THE WRONG MOVE

Instead of walking up the sidewalk toward the duplex, I cut between the two houses where the Jeep was parked and circled around to a dark path that led to the back of the duplex. I climbed over the fence and crept up to the rear of the house. Lights were on everywhere. I approached the back door as I walked up the steps quietly. I knew I had to be extra careful not to be heard. I stuck my hand inside my purse and grabbed ahold of my gun just in case I had to pull it out in a hurry. But before I could get close enough to the window located in the kitchen, a hand grabbed my shirt. I screamed, "Ahh!" and spun around in a flash.

"Shh, it's me, Quincy," Quincy whispered.

"What are you doing here? You scared the shit out of me!"

"I came to see if you needed any help," he continued to whisper.

With my back turned toward the window and the kitchen door, the lights went out and the door swung open. Two guns were pointed directly at Quincy's head and mine. "Get'cha motherfucking asses in here," a masculine voice boomed.

"Please don't shoot!" I begged as I began to turn my body around.

"Nah, don't turn around. Back your ass up and walk backward," the guy instructed as he grabbed ahold of the back of my shirt.

I took one step backward and then I took another one while I was still holding on to my gun. I couldn't see anything but the silhouette of Quincy's body. I couldn't see his face because the lights in the house had been turned off. But I could see Quincy's body shivering with each step he took along with me. I tried to get his attention so I could hand him my gun but he wouldn't look at me. His eyes were fixed on the two guys pointing their guns at us. I knew I couldn't make any sudden moves because I'd risk getting shot in my back. And I didn't want that. I wanted to live. I had my baby to think about.

By the time I had stepped into the house one of the guys had pushed me off to the side and I stumbled and fell to the floor. In an attempt to break my fall, I pulled my hand out of my purse without letting the gun go, and it slid out of my hand onto the floor. It made a loud THUMP the same time I hit the floor. I heard it slide a few feet away from me. But it was dark, so I couldn't see it. Simultaneously, both of the guys took their attention off Quincy for a mere second to see where I had fallen since it was dark, and Quincy bolted off the back porch and away from them like a flash of lightning.

"He's getting away!" one of the guys yelled.

"Juice, get 'em!" another male's voice boomed. I knew that voice instantly. It was coming from Kanan. Just like that, the other guy holding his gun bolted out the back door behind Quincy. I heard one gunshot and then I heard another one. By the time I heard the fourth gunshot, Kanan had me at gunpoint in the kitchen and slammed the back door shut. I lay on the floor in the fetal position. I swear I couldn't take another man's blood on my hands right now. I was still reeling from Derek's death.

Without warning, Kanan flipped on the light switch. It blinded me for a few seconds, so I covered my face with my arm.

"Get the fuck up!" he roared as he stood over me.

I removed my arms from my face slowly because I knew that at any moment he was going to know who I was, and my plans to get my baby would go out the window if Matt instructed him to get rid of me. *Lord, please let Quincy get away alive,* I prayed in my mind.

"Get up, I said!" Kanan's voice boomed even louder. I turned around on the floor and used both of my hands to push myself up. While I was doing so, I noticed my gun had slid underneath the kitchen table. I wished like hell that I could get it. I just hoped no one else would see it.

"Who is it?" another voice spoke. It was coming from behind me. When I stood up completely on my feet, I turned around and faced Kanan and the other guy head-on. Kanan's eyes grew twice the normal size. Shocked, Kanan kept his gun pointed at me but looked at the other guy and said, "Yo, Preech, that nigga in there wasn't lying. This is the bitch with the baby. She was the one I took the dough from while I was in New York with Matt."

"That's Matt's ex-girl?" Preech asked as if he wanted clarification. He seemed more shocked than Kanan.

"Yeah, and I can't wait to tell Matt this shit," he continued as he pulled his cell phone from his front pants pocket with his free hand.

I stood there while Kanan dialed Matt's number. Meanwhile, the other guy, Juice, tapped on the back door a couple times and then announced himself. "Yo, it's me coming in," he said, and then he opened the back door.

One part of me wanted to run, but the other part of me knew that I probably wouldn't get out the back door. So I decided against it.

"Did you get 'em?" Kanan asked Juice.

"Nah . . . that . . . nigga got away. He was . . . fast as shit!" the Juice guy replied, panting between each word.

"Well, did you pop 'em?" Kanan wanted to know.

"Yeah, I think I popped him twice before he hopped the fence but as soon as he got on the path and turned the corner of the first house, he sprinted off like a fucking horse. That nigga gotta be running track or something. But who the fuck is this?" Juice continued.

"This is Matt's ex-bitch!" Preech spoke up.

"You bullshitting!" Juice commented, and then he looked at Kanan. "This is Matt's ex-bitch, for real?" he asked him.

"Yep."

"I'm not a fucking bitch!" I hissed. I gritted on all three of these niggas, thinking to myself about the fact that every last one of them had something to do with the kidnapping of my family. And now I was standing in front of them with so much hatred built up inside of me. If I hadn't dropped my gun on the floor when I fell, I would've put a bullet in each one of their fucking heads like they did my husband. The sight of them repulsed me. Damn, I wished the shoe was on the other foot. I wanted to do these bastards in right then.

"A yo, Matt, you ain't gon' believe this but I got'cha bitch standing in front of me right now," Kanan announced into the phone.

"Ask him where the fuck is my son?!" I spat as loud as I could. I wanted Matt to hear my voice. I wasn't there for an introduction to a family reunion. I was there to get my son back.

"Shut the fuck up before I smack your ass!" Kanan threatened me as he lunged at me. But I wasn't afraid because I knew Matt wouldn't let Kanan touch me. If anything would be done to me, it would be by Matt's hands only. So I sucked my teeth and gave him a look that said *I dare you.*

I couldn't hear what Matt was saying, so I tried to read Kanan's facial expression but he didn't give me anything to work with. "We caught her snooping around the spot on A Avenue. She came with two other niggas. We got one of them in the other room but the other one got away," Kanan explained to Matt, then fell silent again.

Seconds later he continued, "A'ight. We gon' pack up and get out of here now. But whatcha want me to do with that other nigga, 'cause we beat him up pretty bad."

Hearing bits and pieces of Kanan's conversation about Trevor immediately got me sick to my stomach. I could only imagine how he looked, especially after hearing that he'd been beaten up. I stood there horrified, listening to Kanan give Matt details. "The nigga tried to act like he knocked on the wrong door, but when we caught him trying to peep in the crib Preech snatched that nigga inside the house. As soon as we got 'em in here, he started crying like a little bitch, talking about he with this girl that his roommate met on the bus coming back from New York who said her ex-boyfriend took her baby and that she was looking for him to get her baby back," Kanan explained, and then he fell silent.

"The other nigga they was wit' got away," Kanan spoke again, and then he fell silent once more. Kanan said a few more things to Matt and then he ended the call. He summoned Preech to go and get Trevor. "Hurry up because we gotta get out of here before the other guy bring the cops back here," Kanan said.

"What we gon' do?" Juice wanted to know.

"Matt want us to clean the crib and bring her to him."

"What we gon' do with homeboy in the other room?" Juice continued.

"We gon' get rid of him on the way to the other spot. So go upstairs and get all our shit and meet me in the car in two minutes," Kanan explained, and when Juice walked out of the kitchen, he turned his attention toward me.

"You just wouldn't leave well enough alone. All you had to do was get lost and move on with your life. Start a new fucking family or something. But nah, you had to come back to VA looking for trouble."

"Nigga, fuck you! I came to VA to find my fucking son! I gave y'all all the money I had to get my family back but y'all took it and didn't give me shit. You took my fucking husband away from me and now I can't find my baby. So tell me, where is he? Tell me where Matt has my son!" I roared. I wasn't backing down. I came here to get my baby. Point blank.

"Bitch, don't be talking to me like I owe you something. If you would've gave Matt all his fucking money back your husband would be alive right now, you dumb-ass ho!"

"Fuck you! You piece of shit! You think you're doing something big because you work for Matt? Let me tell you something about your boss," I said, and then I paused before continuing. "As soon as that nigga works the dog piss out of you and uses you up until he can't use you no more, you're gonna be history. Don't fuck around and get locked up selling his dope because you're gonna be done. He's gonna turn his back on you and the rest of these damn idiots quicker than you can blink your eyes. He's out for himself. He doesn't give a fuck about me or you, Mr. Big Shot!" I continued. I was in rare form. At this point, I figured I had nothing else to lose. I waited for Kanan to curse me out, but instead, he burst into laughter. "Yo, you're funny as shit! You gotta big fucking mouth too. I see why Matt wants me to handle you himself. But I'll tell you what, if you talk to me like that again, I'm gonna make you wish you'd never met me," he said in a menacing tone.

Before I could give that nigga a rebuttal, my attention was directed to Preech as he walked into the kitchen with Trevor on his arm. I blinked a few times to be certain that my eyes were not deceiving me while Trevor was being dragged before me with his wrists tied behind him in zip ties. I felt like my entire world had crashed in on me. *This can't be! No! No!* My mind raced at the speed of light. This person didn't look like Trevor at all. His mouth was bound and gagged. His entire face had been beaten. Blood poured from the wounds around his eyes and nose. "What the fuck have they done to you?" I said, my voice cracking. I tried to force back the tears but it didn't happen. I took a step toward Trevor but Kanan and Preech blocked me. Kanan pushed me backward. I stumbled a bit.

"What the fuck is wrong with you people?" I screamed at Kanan after I caught my balance.

"Shut the fuck up!" Kanan's voice boomed. "Preech, throw that nigga in the backseat of the car. And Juice, hurry up with that shit! We gotta go," Kanan yelled. "And you come with me," he said, and grabbed my arm really hard.

"Get off of me!" I screeched so loudly my throat itched while I tried to break away from his grip. I needed to get to my gun now or never.

"Where the fuck you think you're going?" Kanan roared as he grabbed me by my hair.

"Fuck you! Get the fuck off me!" I boomed, feeling blood rushing to places on my body that I didn't know even existed. I bucked my body wildly, but all of my fighting efforts were to no avail. Of course Kanan was stronger than me. Of course I wasn't going to be able to break free, but it just made me feel slightly better inside to try. I never dreamed of going out of this life on my feet. I had always been a fighter, so today wasn't any different. I planned to live up to that name before I died.

Kanan wrapped a handful of my hair around his fist and started tugging on it really hard. I caught an instant migraine and I couldn't shake him for the life of me.

"Let my hair go," I screamed, while I continued to buck wildly and we both fell down to the floor. And when I looked in the direction where my gun was, I realized that I was only a few feet away from it. But that didn't matter, because as soon as we hit the floor, Kanan had regained control by getting back on his feet. Without notice, he began dragging me toward the back door of the kitchen.

I started kicking my feet at him like I had completely lost my mind. I struck him a few times by kicking him in his leg. That didn't sit well with him and he made it known.

"Bitch, you better bring your ass on out of here," he hissed through clenched teeth as he dragged me roughly out of the house. He held a tight grip on my hair and I felt something at the base of my skull come loose. I was dazed for a few seconds, but not for long. I was brought back to reality when I felt a boot slam into my ribs before he threw me in the backseat of a truck. The force was so great that I spurted out a mouthful of blood.

I could barely see through the tears pouring from my eyes. But I was able to make out Juice's silhouette scurrying by us with a shoe box of things in his hands. I knew what was inside when I first looked at it. Niggas always kept money, drugs, paraphernalia, and guns in shoe boxes. Shoe boxes were like their safes.

"Help me put this bitch in the truck," Kanan instructed Juice, referring to an old, dark blue Ford Expedition SUV that was parked on the side of the duplex. Juice sat the shoe box on the front seat of the truck and helped Kanan lift me in the air and toss me into the backseat. Kanan slammed the door, rushed around the truck, and climbed in from the other side. Juice climbed in the front passenger seat and placed the shoe box on his lap.

While Kanan was patting his pockets to make sure he hadn't dropped anything on the way out of the house, I looked around for Trevor. He was nowhere to be found. "What did you do with Trevor?" I asked the guy named Preech. He was sitting in the driver's seat.

"He's all the way in the fucking back," Preech spat.

"You got him thrown back there like he's fucking trash," I screamed. My body was racked with the shakes.

"I ain't gon' tell you to shut up again!" Kanan warned me.

"Whatcha gon' throw me in the back of the truck too?" I snapped. I wasn't backing down.

WHAM! The force and pain from Kanan's fist slammed into the side of my face. I fell back against the window on the opposite side of the truck. "Didn't I say shut the fuck up?!" he roared.

I couldn't react in any manner whatsoever after Kanan struck me with his fist. I sat up in the seat and eased as close as I could to the passenger-side door. I held my face with my hand, hoping it would ease my pain while I turned to look out the window. I watched as we drove away from the duplex. I even got a chance to look in the direction where Trevor's Jeep was but it was gone. I exhaled with a sense of relief, knowing that Quincy was somehow able to get away.

We drove out of the Huntersville neighborhood and headed up Tidewater Drive toward I-264. Before Preech could take the ramp onto the highway, Kanan instructed him to go around the loop and take the underpass. I was on high alert after Preech took the detour. I sat up even more in the seat. I braced myself for what was about to happen. If only I had my freaking gun.

"Pull over here right here," Kanan told Preech.

"I thought you were taking me to Matt," I blurted out while Preech drove us through the dimly lit underpass.

"I am," he replied.

"So why are we coming here?" I continued questioning, while I tried to collect my thoughts. It seemed like everything in my head was going in a circular motion. I couldn't get things to make sense. And when the truck came to a complete stop, my heart collapsed. It felt like I was no longer breathing.

"Juice, help Preech get that nigga outta here. And when y'all done, Preech, finish him off," Kanan said, cold and calculating.

Knowing Kanan had just instructed Preech to take Trevor's life sent a shock wave through my entire body. It felt like I was about to hyperventilate. I wanted to scream but I knew that it could possibly cost me my life, so I sat there and screamed in my head while I watched Preech and Juice carry out Kanan's orders.

When the hatchback of the SUV opened, I turned around in my seat and watched as they dragged Trevor by his arms and legs like he was a bag of dirty laundry and dropped him down on the ground. Preech pulled his pistol from his waist, aimed it at Trevor's head, and then he pulled the trigger. BOOM! BOOM!

Tears sprang to my eyes immediately and I could feel my heart crumbling to a million little pieces in my chest. My head started pounding like somebody was using it for a drum. My stomach swirled with nausea. Before I knew it, Juice had closed the hatchback and they were both back inside the truck. The darkness of the night nearly made it impossible for me to see Trevor's lifeless body as Preech sped off. The orange shirt he wore illuminated the dark. The images of how badly he was beaten stuck in my head while we were leaving him behind. He didn't deserve to be beaten and killed like that. I didn't give a damn what he did. These motherfuckers I was with were some cold-hearted bastards and I would make it my mission to end their pathetic-ass lives.

"I wonder how long it's gonna take for someone to find his ass?" Juice joked.

"Probably a day or so. 'Cause you know homeless people be hanging down there underneath that underpass," Preech assumed.

"And I say, who gives a fuck?! That nigga got what he was looking for coming up to our spot, knocking on the fucking door like he was looking for somebody. Because of him, we had to shut shop down. Do you know how much money we lost tonight because of that fucking maggot?" Kanan complained.

"At least ten grand," Juice said.

"Nah, probably more like fifteen," Preech chimed in.

"Yeah, fifteen grand is the number I was thinking too. And that's gon' hurt us, being that this is the weekend and a lot of people got their checks. We gon' have to set up shop somewhere else since we ain't gon' be able to go back to that spot for a while," Kanan said.

"They got a couple spots on C Avenue that we can set up in. They know the chick that lives there. She'll let us work out of there for little or nothing," Preech suggested.

"You must be talking about that bitch Trina," Juice blurted out.

"Yeah, I've been dying to get over there with her. She could make us a lot of fucking money because she knows all the dope fiends," Preech continued.

"Well, I'll talk to Matt about it when we get to the house and see what he says," Kanan said.

I couldn't fucking believe it. All these niggas could talk about is how much dope they could've made if Trevor and I hadn't come by and rained on their parade. Well, these niggas rained on *my* fucking parade when they came to New York and disrupted my world. Fuck their drug-making money ambitions, I thought to myself. Shutting down trap houses and setting up new ones came with the fucking territory. These motherfuckers had just killed an innocent human being. So this karma shit would be coming back to greet these ungrateful motherfuckers!

While these dumb-ass niggas continued to talk about frivolous shit, I tried to convince myself that this was all a dream. But when Kanan opened his mouth and told Preech to head over to where Matt was, I knew that everything going on around me was real. And it was all my fault. Damn! I shouldn't have brought those kids into this. And now I'd have to wear his blood on my hands. Thankfully,

Quincy got away. Because if he hadn't, I'd be really feeling fucked up.

I fumed the entire drive to where Matt was hiding out. Halfway there, Kanan threw a pillowcase over my head and dared me to take it off. "Take it off and you gon' end up like your homeboy back under the underpass," he threatened me.

I sat there with the satchel-like pillowcase over my head as my imagination ran wild. I knew I was on my way to see Matt but how the meeting would go was beyond me. I mean, what could we talk about? I was outnumbered and I had no protection, so how was I going to get out of this? I surmised that I would be joining Trevor and my husband, Derek, soon enough.

15

THE MEETING

Preech drove the SUV across the crunch of the gravel that popped under the tires until he came to a complete stop. Everyone inside the truck was quiet until Kanan spoke first. "Preech, help me with her while Juice go up to the front door."

My teeth began chattering uncontrollably. My body trembled as well because I knew that they knew the fate that awaited me. I immediately started praying in my head but the words weren't really that clear to me. I knew then that I had started losing touch with reality.

I couldn't see anything but I knew that Kanan had gotten out of the truck first, after I heard the other back door close. So when the door on my side opened I got a burst of courage, snatched the pillowcase from my head, and started attacking Kanan and Preech. I had to send a message that I wouldn't lie down easily for no one. I swung at Preech first because he was the closet to me. My fist connected the top of his left eyebrow and he wasn't a happy camper at all. "This fucking bitch!" he huffed. He grabbed hold of my wrists and squeezed them so hard it made me buckle over at the waist. It felt like he shattered every bone in my wrist. "Ahhh," I screamed, but I didn't stop fighting. I couldn't move my arms but I sure kicked and bucked my body like a wild animal being carried to slaughter after Preech and Kanan both snatched me from the backseat. "Grab her fucking legs," Kanan demanded.

"Get off of me! Agh! Get the fuck off of me!" I screamed at the top of my lungs as I looked around me. It was dark and I saw nothing but we were deep in the middle of a freaking cornfield. I couldn't make out my location but I knew today was going to be the last day of my life if I didn't try to get away from these guys now.

I jutted my foot out forcefully and kicked Preech in his side. He made a noise but he kept trying to contain me. My kick didn't faze him but it sure did infuriate him.

"Yo, I swear, I'm gonna kill this bitch myself!" Preech roared, pulling his gun from his waist.

"No! Let Matt deal with her shit!" Kanan barked. Preech sucked his teeth and slowly put his gun away.

"You're one lucky bitch!" Preech boomed as he gritted on me.

"Fuck you, nigga!" I spat.

"Let's get her the fuck inside so Matt can take this headache off our hands," Kanan spoke as he dragged me through the tall grass toward an old, run-down house surrounded by a cornfield. I frantically looked around for landmarks that I could file away in my memory for later use.

Immediately after I was carried inside the old house, the smell of old wood and cigars quickly assailed my nose and hit me in the gut. It felt like little people were standing in my stomach mixing up a witch's brew. My stomach made a loud growling noise that could've awoken the dead. I guess that was the first time I realized I was starving.

A few seconds later, I was led into the den area and dropped down onto the floor. I hit the floorboards hard. BOOM! I tried to scramble to the nearby run-down sofa but I was stopped in my tracks.

A foot appeared out of nowhere. And when I looked up and saw that the foot belonged to Matt, I lost my train of thought. "I've been expecting you." He smiled. It looked sinister. I couldn't believe that I used to find him attractive. Now I saw him as this angry, bitter nigga with a bunch of fucking gray hairs growing out of his beard and the top of his head. He looked like a monster now. Correction, he *was* a monster now.

My mind went totally blank until I heard a baby crying from a nearby room. I looked in the direction of the room and then I looked back at Matt. "Is that my baby?" I asked. Hearing my son's voice was like music to my ears. Everything that I had gone through up until this point no longer mattered to me. All I wanted the whole time was to find out if my baby was alive, and now I knew that he was.

I tried to stand up but Matt pushed me back down to the floor. "Where the fuck you think you going?" he huffed.

"I wanna see my baby," I told him.

"Not until after we talk," Matt continued.

My mind raced in a zillion directions and my body felt tense and rigid as I looked around the room at Kanan, Preech, and Juice, who were standing nearby. I could tell that they were itching to do something to me. All they needed was for Matt to give them the word. "What is it?" I wondered aloud.

"Help her up to that chair, right there," Matt instructed Juice.

When Juice reached for my arm, I snatched it back from him. "I got it," I gritted.

It took me less than three seconds to stand up from the floor and have a seat on the nearby sofa. "Comfortable?" he asked me.

I let out a long sigh. "I'm good. Just tell me what you want. I wanna see my baby," I spat.

Matt took a metal chair from the other side of the room

and placed it directly in front of me. He took a seat on it and looked directly into my eyes. "You know you short me a substantial amount of money, right?" he started off.

"I had been gone for almost a year. What did you expect me to live on?" I tried to reason with him.

"But that was my money," he pointed out.

"It was our money," I reiterated.

He got straight to the point. "Do you wanna walk out of here with your baby?"

"You fucking right I do."

"Well, you're gonna have to give me the rest of my money."

"How am I going to do that when I've given you everything I had?"

"You're gonna have to do another *score*," he told me. His facial expression was so serious that it was almost scary.

"How do you expect me to do that?" I wondered aloud, more frustrated than anything.

"You're gonna have to pull off a bank heist."

"You want me to rob a damn bank? Are you out of your fucking mind?" I shrieked. It just came out of nowhere. It had bubbled up from the pit of my soul. The scream zapped all of my energy. How the hell was I going to do that? I knew this city would be crawling with cops looking for Trevor and me, especially since Quincy had gotten away. For all I knew, my face could be plastered all over the freaking news, and this moron wanted me to rob a fucking bank. Was he trying to set me up to go to jail and lose my baby altogether? Or was he just plain fucking stupid?

"Nah, bitch, I ain't out of my fucking mind. You were out of your mind when you ran off with my motherfucking bread. Do you want your son back?" he barked.

"You fucking right!" I barked back. Was this a trick question or something?

"Well, I want my money. So if I don't get my money then you ain't gon' get your son," he warned me.

I wanted to tell Matt to go straight to hell but I knew that wouldn't help me get any closer to getting my son back, or even getting a chance to see him. But before I agreed to his outlandish demand, I asked him what exactly I had to do. "You and Preech are going to go inside First Union Bank while Juice stays in the car. I want you to grab the bank manager and take her ass to the back of the bank and take as much money as you can while Preech watch all the tellers behind the counters. And when you're done filling up the backpack, knock the bitch out, grab Preech, and then y'all get out of there."

"So we're not taking any money from the tellers?" I asked. I needed clarity.

"No. They don't carry enough dough in their drawers. The only thing I want Preech to do is to make them hoes get on the floor as soon as y'all get in there so they don't get a chance to hit the alarm."

"And you don't think that we need a third man to help out. Preech isn't going to be to watch everyone in the front of the bank. I mean, what if someone tries to come inside?" I asked. I was putting my life and my freedom on the line behind another fucking score. I needed all the inside information I could get, especially since it was only going to be a two-man job. Normally, for a job of this magnitude, it required you to have at least three to four people watching every angle so that the heist could be executed perfectly. But this nutcase standing in front of me had these unrealistic expectations that could get us railroaded for sure.

Right before he answered me, my baby started crying like he had been struck at that very moment. As soon as I jumped to my feet, Matt blocked me from moving any farther. "I'm not done talking to you," Matt said through clenched teeth. My eyes went wide.

"I'm only trying to see what's wrong with my son. Don't you hear him crying?" I spat.

Matt grabbed me by the neck and pushed me headfirst into the sofa. I crashed into it with my head and shoulders but I managed to catch my balance and turn around.

By the time I was able to sit straight up on the sofa, Matt was standing over me, holding my face roughly and forcing me to look at him. "You better stop fucking wit' me before I kill you right here on the spot!" he said, snarling at me. I had come to the quick conclusion that he was at his wit's end with me.

I locked eyes with him. Matt's eyes were black and icy. I swear I had never seen him like this. He had this intimidating look and it was scary. And I knew at that very moment that he meant business. He was more concerned about this last score than anything. He could care less that my baby was in that other room crying his poor little heart out. He didn't give a fuck about me or my baby, for that matter. So I knew that if I didn't agree to help him get that money, then I could kiss me and my baby good-bye.

"How much are we trying to score from this job?" I asked him, trying to act like I still had some control.

"My inside contact told me that we can make out with half a million if we get in the back safe. And make it out of there with a clean getaway."

"How much is in it for me?" I quizzed him. I knew he had no intentions of giving me shit. But it didn't hurt to test the waters.

"I shouldn't give you shit since you and those punk-ass niggas you were with brought heat to my trap house and my boys had to close down shop because of it. But since I'm a nice guy I'll give you ten percent of what you bring out," he answered quickly. I didn't believe him, though. He said it too fast. Matt was never a person who wanted to give away money that easily. He was bullshitting me and he knew I knew it. But at this point in the game it didn't matter so I agreed to do the last score for him.

"When are we hitting this bank?" I asked him.

"Tomorrow after the lunch traffic dies down. That's the best time to make the mark."

"How long have you planned to rob this bank?" I wanted to know. It sounded like he just thought this shit up. I mean, didn't he have enough money? He used some of the money I gave him back to get a couple of kilos of dope. And I was sure he was making a profit off that.

"After I found out that you didn't have all of my money. You owe me."

"I don't owe you anything. Your crew can handle this robbery."

"No, I need you to pull it off," he began to explain. "I knew once I took your baby, you'd come looking for him. So I figured when you got here, I'd put you to work."

"If you knew this, then why kill my fucking husband?"

"Because I didn't like the nigga for one. And two, I had to make an example out of him. Do you think I was gonna keep having that nigga around me looking in my face, knowing that he was fucking my ex-girl? And he gave you a baby on top of that? Fuck, nah! I wasn't having that."

"That's fucked up. You're a heartless nigga! You know that?" I spat. Just thinking about my husband lying dead in that hotel room back in New York made me even sadder. I still couldn't believe that he was gone.

"I've been called worse," he commented, and then he chuckled.

I shook my head with disgust because I had no other words for him. "Can I see my baby now?" I changed the subject.

"Yes, you may," he said, and then he turned around and motioned Juice to go in the other room. A minute later Juice walked back into the room with a woman in tow. It was the same woman I saw with Kanan the other night, dropping him off at Matt's cousin's spot on Lexington Avenue. The way she cradled my son in her arms sent me the message that I could easily be replaced. This made me sick to my stomach. But then I quickly reminded myself that I couldn't be replaced. As a matter of fact, I refused to be replaced. I'd die before I let anyone take my son from me.

I erased the notion that my son could be taken from me and preceded toward the young lady. She held him out for me to take me into my arms. After I grabbed him, I looked down at his face and saw how he was sound asleep. He looked so peaceful.

"I missed you so much, Lil D," I whispered loud enough for only him and me to hear. "I love you so much," I continued as tears began to fall from my eyes. I stood there sobbing, but it was tears of joy. I was so happy to finally have my baby in my arms. The relief that I felt inside of me was so overwhelming that I could hardly catch my breath. I could only think that it had to be God's will for me to find him.

"Did you just say that his name was Little D?" Matt asked me.

I ignored him, hoping he'd think that I didn't hear him. But that didn't stop him from repeating his question. "Did you say that his name was Little D?" he asked me once more.

"Yeah," I replied, and then I used my right hand to wipe away the tears falling from my eyes. I was having a moment.

The young lady stepped backward, and then she left the room.

"What does 'Little D' mean?" Matt pressed the issue.

"Damon," I lied. I knew I couldn't dare tell Matt I named my baby after his father, Derek. Things were going smoothly right now; I couldn't afford to turn the tables.

"Why didn't you name him after his daddy? I mean, he is dead. And that way that lil nigga can carry on his pop's name," Matt commented sarcastically.

Listening to Matt mock me with Derek's death was a hard pill to swallow. I wanted to curse the day he was born but I decided against it. Instead, I continued to admire my son's face as I walked over to the love seat not far from where I was standing and sat down.

"I see you've become really good at ignoring me." He wouldn't let up as he walked in my direction. I tried to keep my eyes on my baby, but the closer Matt got to me, the more uneasy I felt. I looked up at him as he approached me.

"I'm not ignoring you," I told him while I cradled my son closer to my chest.

"Well, it sure seemed like it," he said, and then he looked down at my baby. "You know that should've been my son, right?"

Instead of commenting, I smiled.

Matt knelt down in front of me. "Since he ain't gotta daddy no more, think I can be his stepdaddy?" Matt asked in a sinister type of way.

"Think you're up for it?" I asked him, tossing the question right back at him. I refused to give him the impression that he could be my son's stepfather. He was fucking disgusting. The sight of him made me cringe. He was like a bottom feeder and I would never see myself getting back with him again.

"Of course I am," he replied, and then he stood up and turned around toward the other guys in the room. "Don't y'all think I'll be a good daddy?" Matt asked them.

"Yeah," Kanan said.

"Damn right!" Preech agreed.

"Of course," Juice added.

Matt turned back around toward me. "See, even my boys know that I'll hold shit down," he mentioned proudly.

I smiled at him once more. But on the inside my blood was boiling. I knew I once loved this man, but he turned into someone else. This guy I was in front of was a maniac. He was a cold-blooded murderer with no compassion. I could literally see the terror in his eyes and it was all directed at me. He'd already murdered my husband. So I knew he wouldn't hesitate to kill me and my baby, especially since we meant nothing to him. Matt always wanted to have a baby with me. And as much as I had loved him, I knew that I couldn't have a future with him. Not with the lifestyle we lived, which was why I aborted both of my pregnancies with him. It hurt him to his heart when I told him what I had done while he was in prison and after he came back on the streets. It broke his heart. So I guess that was why he fucked Yancy and got her pregnant. I thought it was fucked up that he'd betray me like that, but hey, that is what men do, right? Cheat!

"Let me hold 'em," Matt said as he leaned forward with his arms extended toward me.

I knew he was testing me. He knew I didn't want him touching my son, but I had no other choice. I had to do what he said, or else! My stomach started doing somersaults. And my body was so tense it felt like I was coming down with the flu. I guess that was what stress could do to you.

A flash of heat came over me and I quickly averted my eyes back down to my arm, where my son lay. As bad as I wanted to lift my head up and tell Matt to kiss my ass, I was too afraid that he might kill me on the spot. I swallowed the lump that had formed in the back of my throat and fought the urge to spaz out on him. Instead, I lifted my baby away from my chest and held him out for Matt to grab him. I cringed when he took my son from my hands. I forced myself to smile the whole while.

Matt looked down at my son, cradled him close to his

chest, and then turned around toward the other guys. "What y'all think? I look like daddy of the year, huh?" he boasted.

"Yeah man, that's a good look on you," Preech spoke.

"Yeah, you good," Kanan chimed in.

Juice nodded his head.

"Think we can be a family again?" Matt asked me after he turned back around and faced me.

I forced myself to say, "If you want to."

Matt turned away from me and turned his attention back to the guys. "Y'all hear that? Me and Lauren getting back together," Matt announced.

The guys smiled, but I could clearly see how uninterested they were. They saw my facial expression. They knew I wasn't feeling Matt, but they dared not express that to Matt. Matt looked down and smiled at my son and then he looked up at me. "I want you to change his first and last name to mine," he demanded.

"Are you serious?" I asked him, knowing that he was.

"You fucking right I'm serious. You think I'm gonna be taking care of this little nigga while he got another nigga's name?" Matt chuckled in a menacing way.

"All right, then," I reluctantly replied.

Matt continued to walk around the room with my son in his arms. The sight of it sickened me, but what could I do about it? He had transformed into someone I didn't even recognize. He was like a sadistic goon all of a sudden. Certainly not the man I grew to love all those years ago.

Just hold on, Lauren, this will be over soon, I tried to convince myself. All the while my stomach was churning over and over, I was sweating, and my head was pounding like someone was hitting it with a huge sledgehammer. Watching Matt rocking my son in his arms rattled me. I would've taken anything at that moment that would've calmed my raggedy nerves.

Matt's little charade lasted almost an hour. I couldn't believe I lasted through it. And when it was time to call it a night, Matt instructed me to go with him to his room. "Y'all hold shit down out here while I go handle business in the other room," Matt told them, and then he led me out of the den. I had no idea what kind of business he was talking about and I didn't want to know. I just prayed his business had nothing to do with me.

On my way to the room, I walked by the bathroom and got a glimpse of the woman again. She was standing in the mirror brushing her hair. She looked back at me and gave me this ugly stare. I was taken aback by it but I brushed it off and figured that maybe she was having a bad day. That fucking place looked like a fucking war zone, a trap house in the backwoods.

16

THE FINAL SEDUCTION

I was taken to a bedroom on the other side of the house. It was dank, dimly lit, cold, and smelled like mildew and incense. I don't ever remember being in a place so dark and dreary in my entire life. In all of the trap houses I had ever been in, this one was by far the worst.

I surveyed the bedroom to see if there was a way to escape. No such luck. The windows were covered with metal bars on the outside of them. I figured my chances of getting out of there were slim to none. Even if I were small enough to fit between the bars, I would have to break the glass to slide through it. Yep, it would be impossible.

Matt locked the bedroom door behind us and laid my baby boy down on what looked like a queen-size bed. Of course the bed wasn't made up. There were piles of clothes everywhere. The room was a fucking mess. That didn't stop him from trying to seduce me, though. "Come here," he demanded as he pulled me into him. I cringed immediately. My worst fear had come to a reality. That nasty motherfucker groped me while he tried to force his tongue down my face. He started saying nasty things to me and licking my neck and the side of my face. I was disgusted down to the core of my soul. Several times I was tempted to push him away from me, but then I stopped. I knew it would be a very bad idea, considering the position I was in.

"Come on, and give me some of this good ole pussy for old times' sake?" Matt huffed into my ear. He wasted no time going back to putting his hands up my shirt.

My nostrils were flaring and I clamped my legs together on his hand. He grabbed my face with both of his hands and pulled it directly into his. Our noses practically touched while he zeroed in on my eyes. His face was crumpled into an evil snarl and his icy blue eyes were glinting with hints of malice.

"Why is your body so stiff? Don't you love me anymore?" he questioned me.

I knew not to dare answer this question wrong. I knew I had to play the role or else. "You know I love you, Matt. You are my first love," I told him, trying to sound pretty convincing.

"I can't tell. You act like you're not enjoying what I'm doing."

"I'm tired. And I would really like to lie down and get some rest before I do that score for you tomorrow. And besides, you know I just had my baby a couple days ago. I'm still bleeding," I replied, hoping this would turn him off.

"I don't give a fuck about that. Your pussy belongs to me and I want some of it now," he spat as he let go of my face and pulled my body in closer to his. He whirled me around and pressed his groin against my butt. The fact that he was touching me made me sick to my stomach. But I kept my cool.

"Open your legs," he grumbled, moving his hand down inside of my pants. I tried my best to relax. I closed my eyes, eased the muscles in my legs, and allowed him to thrust his hands up into my crotch. I murmured my disapproval and I turned my head to the side so he wouldn't see the tears rimming my eyes. I wasn't going to give him the satisfaction of knowing he was dominating me. That's what Matt's plan was all about. He hated the fact that I left him and started a new life with another man. Not to mention, that I took his share of the last score we did too. Everything he was doing now was his way of getting revenge.

Matt kissed me on my lips, licked my neck, and fondled my breasts. I was dying inside, but I wanted to stay in Matt's good graces so I played along. One by one, Matt took off all of my clothes. I was stripped down to nothing.

As I stood there, butt naked, waiting for him to do whatever he was going to do to me, there was a volcano of emotions exploding inside of me. It was a mixture of pure hatred, sorrow, fear, and most of all the desire for revenge.

At first he started kissing me on the back of my neck. I closed my eyes and bit the inside of my jaw. It was all I could do to keep myself from screaming out or from turning around and punching him in the face. Next, Matt reached around to the front of me and fondled my bare breasts from behind. He started off soft, but I could feel his touch getting rougher and more forceful with each passing minute. He was breathing hard—an animalistic pant that also made me sick to my stomach.

"You feel like magic. I miss you so fucking much!" he panted into my ear as he unzipped his pants and pulled out his dick. My eyes shot open. *You disgusting piece of shit! I don't love you anymore. I hate you and everything you stand for.* I was screaming in my head, but I didn't dare say a word. Matt continued to have his way with me.

A few minutes later, he grabbed a handful of my hair and forcefully yanked it until he succeeded in pulling me down to the floor. I was too shocked at his sudden abuse to even put up a defense or break my fall. My knees went crashing to the hardwood floor and pain shot through my legs. I felt my teeth click in the back from hitting together.

The pain in my scalp from him pulling gave me an instant headache.

"Ahhh!" I screamed out. I tried to put my hands on top of his to ease the pain shooting through my scalp, but Matt was too fast and too strong.

"Suck this dick good, baby! You know how daddy likes it," he said.

I was about to go completely insane. How the hell was I going to suck his dick and restrain myself from biting it off? The sight of this fucking maniac repulsed me. The smell of his musty dick made my stomach even sicker. "Put it in your mouth," he instructed me.

I reluctantly opened my mouth, allowing Matt to push his manhood inside it. "Grab it and put it in your mouth," he demanded.

Semi-paralyzed, I reached up and grabbed ahold of Matt's penis and put it in my mouth very slow. "Stroke it," he continued.

I began to stroke it like he instructed me to do and I tried my best to pretend I was enjoying it but I started gagging. This pissed Matt off.

Breathing like a raging bull, he grabbed my hair again and stopped me from blowing him. "What the fuck are you doing?" he boomed.

I removed his dick from my mouth so I could speak. "What do you mean?" I asked.

"Don't fucking play games with me!" he hissed, and lifted me up to my feet and tossed me onto the bed. I hit the bed hard. I thought I had awakened my baby, but when I looked over at him, he stretched out his little body, then curled right back up and continued to lie in the fetal position.

Matt would not have cared if my son had awakened or not because within seconds he was straddling my stomach with his body and pinning my arms to the bed with his knees. His weight felt like it was crushing my chest. I had always hated being held down. Fear of suffocation had started taking over my senses.

"Ouch! You're hurting me!" I struggled, trying to buck my body and at least kick my legs. I was no match for Matt's body.

"You better shut the fuck up before you piss me off really bad. I'm trying to have patience with you," he said in a tone that sounded more maniacal than he had earlier. His dick was mushy against my chest. I felt vomit creeping up from the pit of my stomach to my throat. I was afraid that if it came up I would choke to death so I fought hard to swallow it back down. It was hot and acidy. I started coughing.

"Can you please move down from my chest?" I begged. But my words fell on deaf ears. Matt's mind was made up. He knew he was going to fuck me no matter if I wanted it or not. I could tell that he was taking great pleasure, too.

For the rest of the time in that room with Matt, I closed my eyes and tried to block out the horrible act he was inflicting on me. The sounds of his moans and the thrusts he made while he was inside me sickened me. I could feel the blood flowing out of me. The whole thing felt messy and disgusting. And when it was finally over, it felt like he was still on me. When I asked him could I go in the bathroom to wash up, he gave me the green light to do so, but he escorted me in there. I guess he thought I was going to try to escape or something. I couldn't believe how he sat on the toilet and watched me shower the entire time I was in the bathroom. He made the young lady watch my baby while we were in the bathroom. "Lisa, go in the room and watch her baby while she takes a shower," Matt yelled. That was the first time I found out what her name was. I noticed she jumped every time he asked her to do something. I wondered why Kanan allowed this. It was all too weird for me.

While I was showering, Matt made a few comments

about my body. Talking about how good I looked. I ignored him for the most part. I swore, the way I felt right
then, I'd kill him and then kill myself. But when I thought
about how I'd be leaving my son on earth all alone, I got a
grip on myself. I knew I had to get out of this jam for the
both of us.

17

THE NEXT MORNING

My baby woke up at three AM for a bottle and then again at six AM. I wanted to make his bottles both times myself but Matt wouldn't let me out of his sight. While he and I lay in bed, he demanded, "Lisa, go in the kitchen and make another bottle." She looked so pitiful as she dragged herself from the kitchen and into the bedroom where we were both times and I felt extremely bad for her. She seemed so nice. I thanked her both times. But for some reason she wasn't feeling me. It almost felt like she didn't like me because I was with Matt. Was she fucking him and I didn't know anything about it? Whatever it was, I could tell that she wasn't too happy.

A few hours later, Kanan knocked on the door in an alarming manner. "Yo, Matt, we need to talk," he yelled through the door. It startled the hell out of me.

Matt got up and opened the door. I was already sitting up on the bed with my back against the headboard, cradling my baby in my arms. "What's up?" Matt asked him while they both stood at the entryway of the bedroom door.

"I just got a call from Ant out the way and he said the cops is crawling all over the spot and the streets of Huntersville looking for her and that nigga that we got rid of last night," Kanan said. He looked really spooked. And for the first time I saw that nigga shook. He acted like he had just seen a fucking ghost.

"Did they go inside the house?" Matt wanted to know.

"Yeah, Ant said they went in that joint in the middle of the night and they been roaming the streets asking questions about who own the place and who be in there," Kanan continued.

"Say word!" Matt commented. He started looking worried too. I was getting a kick out of this. Both of these niggas supposed to be hard-nosed criminals, and one mention of cops looking for them got them running around with their tails tucked between their legs.

"Yo, Matt, but that ain't it. Ant said they got the newspeople out there filming and asking questions so you know it's about to be on TV," Kanan said.

"Turn the TV on and listen out for that shit. I'll be out there in a minute," Matt instructed Kanan.

Immediately after Kanan walked away from the door, Matt closed the door and instructed me to get up, grab the baby and follow him into the den area. Since I already had on my clothes, I was ready to leave the room when Matt made his exit. The only problem I felt I had was that I didn't have a spare of clothes to change into, but when I thought about it that was the least of my worries. I was going to rob a bank in a few hours. That was what I really needed to be concerned with. Not fucking spare clothes. I needed to figure out how I was going to get in there, get the money, and get out without getting caught. That was it. Everything else was secondary.

When Matt and I entered into the den, I sat on the same love seat I sat on the night before. Juice and Kanan were in attendance but Preech and that chick Lisa weren't. I wanted so badly to ask where they were but I knew that was a no-no. So I left well enough alone. I figured I'd find out sooner than later.

Kanan had turned on the TV like Matt had instructed him to do. It was on the local news station too but a commercial was being televised. But about three minutes later, Kanan's cell phone started ringing again. He answered it on the first ring. "Yo, Kev, what's up?" he said. I watched his body language the entire conversation. Matt sat on the other sofa and watched him too.

"What channel is it on?" he questioned Kev, and then he picked up the remote control from the coffee table and began sifting through the channels. When he landed on Channel Ten, he paused and laid the remote control back down on the table. "Okay, I got it," he said, and then he disconnected the call.

The Channel Ten news team was front and center alongside the trap house Kanan ran. The streets were flooded with onlookers and neighbors trying to get firsthand information why the cops bum-rushed the trap house.

The news broadcast was being aired live. A white woman stood alongside the street and spoke into the camera that was before her. I listened intently to the reporter's words and quickly realized this shit was real.

"In breaking news this evening, Norfolk city police are searching tonight for two missing people. The first person is a male by the name of Trevor Glasper, who happens to be a college student at Norfolk State University. The second missing person is a woman by the name of Chantel West. We have no other information for her but that she checked into the Hilton Hotel on the corner of North Hampton Boulevard a couple of days ago and that she hasn't been seen since yesterday. I'm told that the police are combing through all the evidence at this residence, as well as the hotel room at the Hilton Hotel where the woman was staying. I've had a chance to speak with one

of the detectives assigned to this missing person's case and I'm told that they've only spoken to a limited number of witnesses, but they feel confident that their efforts will lead to the whereabouts of the two victims and the arrests of all those involved. So, if you've seen or know where these two people are, please contact the missing person's division of the Norfolk City Police Department. The number you can call is 877-MISSING1," the reporter said, and then two photos of Trevor and me were posted on the television screen. I can't lie, seeing my face on TV spooked the hell out of me. I couldn't believe they used the photo from a copy of my fake driver's license. People like my relatives and old friends would no doubt call into the missing person's unit and let the cops know that Chantel isn't my real name. So now I was fucked!

As soon as the news broadcast was over with Matt and Preech turned their attention toward me. "So, you're using that Chantel ID, huh?" Matt commented sarcastically.

I nodded my head and then I looked down at my baby boy.

"And you were staying at the Hilton, too," he added with a smirk on his face.

I continued to ignore him. "Well, it looks like you won't be able to go back there. The cops are crawling all over that place looking for you," Matt continued.

After Matt made the comment about the cops crawling all over my hotel room, I thought about all my shit that I'd left behind. "Shit!" I cursed under my breath. How freaking careless could I have been? What little bit of money and clothes I had left was at the hotel and I wouldn't be able to go back and get it. How stupid could I have been? I was truly fucked right then.

"Are y'all sure y'all got everything from out of that spot?" Matt asked Kanan.

"Yep. Juice cleaned it out real good," Kanan assured Matt.

"When you got rid of that nigga's body, did you leave it exposed?" Matt needed reassurance that those dumb-ass niggas did what they were supposed to do.

"Nah. We good on that. Ain't nobody gon' find that nigga's body for weeks if not months," Kanan said, and then he cracked a smile. But he was lying through his freaking teeth. He had Preech put a slug in his head after they dragged him out the back of the truck. Then they left his body out in the open so it could be found. I swear, I wanted to burst Kanan's bubble but I left well enough alone. I learned very early that you've got to pick and choose your battles. Well, this battle would be the one I'd leave alone. I wanted to leave so I could get my son and me out of that place and back to New York where he and I belonged.

Preech grabbed the remote again but he used it to turn down the TV's volume. "You know you're gonna have to be extra careful out there while you're doing this last score. You don't want the people in the bank to recognize you and be able to give the cops a good sketch of you," Matt said.

"Yeah, this shit just got real. With your face all on TV ain't no way she's going to be able to do this score," Kanan pointed out.

"Oh nah, she's gotta do this job. I won't have it any other way," Matt protested.

"Do you realize what risk she could pose?" Kanan said.

Matt stood. "Whose operation is this?" his voice boomed.

"It's yours," Kanan replied in a cowardly manner.

"Well, let me run this motherfucker the way I wanna run it!" Matt huffed as he walked toward Kanan. I swear for a moment there Matt was going to square off with Kanan. But when he started explaining how things were going to proceed and lowering his tone, I figured Kanan was no longer in any danger. "Look, all she's going to need is some makeup and a pair of sunshades. That's it. And if you handle things appropriately by getting in there and getting out, this score could go off without a hitch. Speaking of which, call Lisa and see where the fuck they at. I sent them to the store to get an extra pair of gloves, so why the fuck they ain't back yet?" Matt continued.

Kanan pulled out his cell phone and called Lisa. She answered the call on the first ring. Kanan put the call on speakerphone so Matt could hear the conversation.

"Hello," Lisa said.

"A yo, Lisa, this is Kanan, Matt wanna know where y'all at?"

"We just pulled up. We're outside the house," Lisa replied.

"Hurry up," Kanan told her.

"Yeah, hurry the fuck up!" Matt chimed in.

A few minutes later Lisa and Juice walked into the house. Lisa carried a small bag of items while Juice walked inside empty-handed. Matt went straight into question mode. "What the hell took y'all so long?" he asked.

"I got hungry so I told Juice to stop me by Burger King," Lisa explained.

"But didn't I tell y'all to go and get what I asked for and then hurry up and come straight back?"

Lisa and Juice both nodded.

"So then why did you do the total opposite?" Matt hissed as he walked toward Lisa.

Lisa stood there motionless. It was apparent that she was at a loss for words. This pissed Matt off. "So you don't have shit to say, huh?" he questioned, standing face to face with her.

"We only stopped because I was hungry," she tried to explain. But that wasn't good enough for Matt.

"Do you think I give a fuck that you were hungry? I'm running on a time schedule and because you wanted to stop to feed your fucking face, you threw me behind schedule," Matt's gruff voice boomed as he grabbed a handful of Lisa's hair and yanked her head up so that her eyes met his gaze.

"I'm so sorry!" she rasped, flinching at the blow her surprised her with. BOOM! I even flinched after his fist connected to her face. He hit her across the face again. This time blood filled her mouth. Tears immediately sprang from her eyes. I swear, I thought he was getting ready to kill her.

I wanted to beg him to stop hitting her so badly, but I knew I'd be compromising my and my son's safety. So I looked at Kanan, hoping I'd get his attention. It seemed like he should've been the one to chastise Lisa, not Matt. I swear, this shit was so unbearable I had to bury my face in my hands to avoid looking at them.

"Matt, I'm sorry. Please stop! I promise I won't do it again," she pleaded with him through tears and swollen lips.

Tears were running down Lisa's face like a faucet. My heart ached for her. Under different circumstances, I knew I would've jumped to her defense. I couldn't believe the man I once loved was getting a kick out of inflicting pain on defenseless women. His face was filled with hate. He acted like he had something to prove. Something to prove even with me. It was if he was sending a message to me that if I fucked him over again, I might as well kiss my life good-bye.

Matt finally let Lisa's hair go with a shove. The force was so great that she flew backward and fell down on the floor. "Fuck with my time again, bitch, and you're gonna really be sorry!" Matt yelled at her.

Lisa didn't say another word. She sat there on the floor like she was a rag doll.

Normally I couldn't care less about other women, but this case was different. I felt so bad for her and only wished that she and I both got away from this guy before he killed us both.

While Matt continued on with his tirade, I watched everyone's reaction in the room. I found myself looking back up at Kanan. I still could not believe how he'd just let Matt treat Lisa the way she was being treated. I also watched Kanan's body language because I could tell that he wasn't feeling Matt after Matt undermined his authority when it came to hatching the plans out for the bank robbery. So when Matt started talking about how we were going to enter the bank, I saw Kanan give Matt the look of death a few times. He hurried up and changed his facial expression every time Matt turned Kanan's way.

Then I looked at Juice, who was in another world. He acted like he was high or spaced out. Whatever the case was, Matt didn't seem to care because he didn't say a word about it. Next up was Preech. Preech seemed like he was engrossed in every detail of Matt's elaborate plan to rob the fucking bank. And Matt noticed it, which I assumed was why he gave Preech the most attention. If I hadn't known any better, I'd have thought that Preech was trying to take Kanan's place.

Last on the list was Lisa. She was still on the floor but she managed to ease her way back against the wall. She gritted on Matt when he wasn't looking. But she quickly changed her expression when he looked back in her direction. I noticed through my peripheral vision that she looked at me a few times. And when I'd casually turned around to glance at her, she'd turn her head. I wanted so badly to tell her that I wasn't her enemy. She and I were both in a fucked-up position. I just prayed that I would be one of the lucky ones to get away.

"Juice, I want you to go and switch up the license plates on the Charger because that's the car y'all taking," Matt announced.

"I'm on it, boss," Juice replied, and rushed out the front door of the house.

"Lisa, I want you to get up and do Lauren's makeup. Her face was plastered all over the fucking TV so you gotta make her look like somebody else," Matt instructed her.

I watched as Lisa dragged herself up from the floor. She seemed reluctant to do anything for Matt. And still Kanan's bitch ass hadn't said or done anything in her defense. I lost all respect for that weak-ass nigga.

"Kanan, I'm gonna need you to navigate this whole mission. You're in charge. So that means you gotta make sure this shit runs smoothly. You gotta make sure y'all get in that fucking bank, get the money, and get out of there without any hiccups."

"I got it. We gon' be good," Kanan reassured Matt.

By this time Lisa had gotten up off the floor and left the room. She came back a few minutes later with her makeup kit in hand. She walked over to where I was sitting. She stood there for a moment and looked at me. She had a smug look on her face that made me feel uncomfortable, so I asked her what was the problem. She didn't respond to me. She looked back at Matt and said, "I'm gonna need more light than this."

Matt turned around toward her and then he looked up at the light in the ceiling. "That ain't enough light for you?" he asked her.

"It would be if I was just slapping on some lipstick and eye shadow. But you want me to make her look like someone else and I ain't going to be able to do that in this light."

Matt thought for a moment and then he said, "A'ight, you can do that shit in the bathroom but don't take too long. And leave the door open so I can keep an eye out on y'all."

"All right," Lisa replied, and then she looked back at me. "Come with me to the bathroom," she said.

I cradled my baby boy tightly in my arm and stood up

with him while I held his bottle in my other hand. I absolutely avoided looking into Matt's direction by looking
down to the floor as I followed Lisa out of the room. To
get away from Matt was a heavy load lifted from my
shoulders even if I was only in the next room. "Lauren,
don't try any sneaky shit!" Matt warned me while I walked
away.

I totally ignored him and followed down behind Lisa.
Immediately after we entered the bathroom, Lisa instructed me to sit down on the closed toilet seat. So I did.
She turned on the light and prepped her makeup brushes
and colors so she could start on my face. I sat there quietly
for the first few minutes to feel her out. But after I heard
the warmness in her voice when she instructed me to hold
my head back and close my eyes, I knew then that I could
talk to her.

I started off with a few general questions to feel her out.
And I also made sure that I talked as quietly as my voice
would allow me to while Matt ran over the plans with the
guys in the other room. He was pretty preoccupied so he
wouldn't hear our conversation if we turned our volume
up a couple of notches. "Do you do makeup profession-
ally?" I started off asking.

"I used to," she answered.

I thought to myself, *Yes, she answered me. And she did
it without an attitude*.

"Did you go to school for it?" I threw another question
at her.

"Yeah, I went to school so I'm certified," she replied.

I thought to myself, *Yes, she answered me again. Keep
going, Lauren, keep her talking*.

"So, what do you do now?" I questioned her once more.

"Look, you better stop asking me all these damn questions before Matt comes in here and starts swinging on the
both of us," Lisa warned me. I saw fear in her eyes.

"Why does Kanan let Matt puts his hands on you? Why

didn't he stop him from hitting you like that?" I asked her, almost in a whisper. I expressed extreme concern.

"Why would Kanan bitch ass help me?"

"Isn't he your man?"

"Fuck no! He ain't even my type!"

"But I saw y'all together in the car the other night."

"That was because I was making a pickup," Lisa huffed.

"But I thought—"

"Listen, let me tell you something really quick," she interjected. "I'm fucking Matt. And that's why none of those punk-ass niggas in there stopped him from putting his fucking hands on me. Everybody in there is scared of him. Now lean your head back so I can put this makeup on you before he comes in here and sees that I ain't doing what I'm supposed to be doing."

My mouth fell wide open. I swear I couldn't believe my freaking ears. "Okay, wait a minute," I said. "You and Matt are together? Y'all are fucking?"

"Yeah, that's what I thought until you showed up to get your baby."

"He didn't tell you about me?" I continued to whisper.

"Of course he did. He told me everything about how y'all hit it big with that last score and when it was time to divvy up the money, you ran off with it and left him with nothing."

"Yeah, but did he tell you why I did it? And that he fucked another bitch behind my back and got her pregnant?" I spat, but I did it quietly because she and I could still hear Matt in the other room making his list of demands.

"Yes, he told me about Yancy and the baby but he said he didn't love her and that she trapped him."

"He's a fucking liar! He'll tell you anything so he can seem like he's the victim," I hissed through clenched teeth.

"Look, I don't know what happened. All I can tell you is what he told me."

"Did he tell you that he killed my fucking husband?" I asked her. By now tears had filled up my eyes.

"Listen, all he told me was that he was going up to New York to find you and get his money back and pick up a couple of kilos of dope, that's it."

"Did he tell you this was my fucking baby and that he kidnapped him?" I bit down on my teeth. I was freaking livid by this point. This chick was being so fucking nonchalant about Matt's behavior. What the hell was wrong with her? Was I the only one who thought Matt was out of his damn mind for doing what he did?

"We can't talk about this anymore. Lean your head back, please," she said nervously as she pushed my head backward.

I lifted my head back up. "Do you know that he made me have sex with him last night?" I asked her. I wanted her to know the truth.

"I don't wanna talk about it," she replied, dabbing one of the makeup brushes into a slot of golden brown foundation.

"Answer this question, then," I said.

"What?" she asked while she continued to dab the brush in the makeup.

"Do you love him?"

She hesitated for a moment and then she said, "I'm not sure anymore. I mean, he's surely showing me that his heart is still with you."

"I don't give a fuck about him. He and I are over. I just wanna get out of here and take my baby with me. You can have him," I expressed, hoping she'd hear the pain in my voice and know how sincere I was.

"Y'all two are awfully quiet in there. What's going on?" Matt yelled from the other room.

The sound of his voice scared the shit out of me. It struck fear in Lisa too. "Ain't nothing going on. I'm in here working," Lisa yelled back, and then she pushed my head back by giving my chin a nudge.

I held my head back just in case Matt decided that he wanted to come in and check on us. I closed my mouth and I closed my eyes too. I wanted to say something else but I was too afraid to open my mouth. Afraid that Matt would hear me and try to take my life on the spot. No way. Nohow. This didn't stop me from thinking long and hard about what Lisa had just told me. I was shocked to find out that Matt was fucking her. He was either one bold-ass nigga for treating her the way he did, or she was one stupid-ass bitch. Who sits back and lets their man fuck their ex-girlfriend in another room? I wouldn't tolerate that shit under no circumstances. But now it all makes sense, about why she was gritting on me every time I caught her looking at me. Matt was making her jealous by being with me and she just let him do it. What the fuck was he thinking? Damn, I wished I could've asked her more questions. I was interested in knowing how the fuck they met and how long she'd been putting up with his bullshit. Hopefully, I'd get another shot at it.

18

CHANGING FACES

I don't know how Lisa did it, but after we stopped talking she did a total makeover on me. It only took her fifteen minutes to apply the makeup on my face and green-colored contacts to my eyes. I couldn't believe it, but when I looked at myself in the bathroom mirror, I honestly saw a different person. It was scary. I couldn't figure out why this talented chick wanted to be with a loser like Matt. She literally made me look like another freaking person.

"Nice job," Matt said, startling Lisa and me as he peered around the bathroom door.

"You scared me," Lisa said as she held my hand against her chest.

With my son in my arms I jumped a little bit, but I didn't say a word. I did glance at him through the bathroom mirror.

"Turn around," he instructed me.

As badly as I wanted to tell him to kiss my ass, I didn't. I turned around as I was told. He looked at me for a good ten seconds and then he said, "She's gonna need a wig to complete this look."

"You know I only got the long one with the blond high-lights in it."

"Well, put it on her so I can see how it'll look," he told her.

Lisa scurried out of the bathroom and returned a few minutes later with the wig in hand. I sat back down so Lisa could place the wig on my head. While she was working her magic, Matt asked, "Lauren, are you ready to repay your debt to me?"

Why the fuck did he just ask me that damn question? Does he really think I'm looking forward to robbing a fucking bank so he can get back the money I took from him when I left town? I wanna take my baby and leave this place and never come back. That's what I'm ready to do, I thought to myself.

"Lauren, did you just hear me talking to you?" Matt asked me as he stood in the doorway. His tone changed so I looked up.

I immediately plastered a fake smile on my face, hoping this would stop Matt's train from crashing into me. I knew that at any moment he could start throwing punches at me, even while I had my son in my arms. So, I went into Operation Kiss Matt's Ass before he spazzed the hell out. "Yeah, I heard you. I was just thinking about how I'm gonna go up inside that bank and try to take all the cash they got. I mean, that shit is insured anyway. So why not take it?"

Matt smiled. "Now see, that's the Lauren I know. I be telling niggas all the time how you get down. You're about that money. But they don't understand how we used to operate. But we gon' show them, right, baby?"

Nigga, I am not your fucking baby! I thought to myself. I swear it felt like I was about to throw up in my mouth. I wasn't his fucking baby. Those days were over for good.

I only wished Lisa would get up the nerve to leave this bastard. He didn't give a damn about anyone but himself. He continued to disrespect the both of us. He was so fucking evil! I just wished he'd fall to the floor and die right here. No one liked him. So no one would miss him. It would be a win-win for all parties involved.

"Stand up and turn around," he instructed me after Lisa finished arranging the wig on my head.

Reluctantly, I stood up and gave it a whirl, and then I faced the mirror because I didn't want to look at his sorry ass. "She doesn't even look like herself," Lisa commented.

"Nope. She sure doesn't. You did a bomb-ass job, Lisa. I knew you could do it," Matt praised her.

Lisa smiled. But that smile quickly faded away when Matt grabbed me by the arm and said, "Come on, baby mama, let's finish getting you ready so you can go out there and make the doughnuts."

I saw Lisa cringe at Matt through my peripheral vision. She was not at all happy at the way he grabbed me or the fact that he called me his baby mama as he escorted me out of the bathroom. I wasn't happy either, but what could I do? Tell that nigga to go burn in hell and then watch him beat the shit out of me before I get a chance to leave the house? I had just seen how he beat the hell out of Lisa. I wasn't trying to take her place.

While Lisa stayed back in the bathroom to clean up, Matt took me to the bedroom and told me to lay my baby down on the bed. I didn't want to lay my baby down. I wanted to hold him as long as I could. But I knew I couldn't defy Matt, so I did what I was told. Thankfully, he was asleep.

After I laid little Derek down on the bed, Matt handed me a black button-down shirt and a pair of black joggers. I looked at the clothes after I took them in my hands. "Whose clothes are these?" I asked.

"It doesn't matter, so just put them on," he told me in an irritated manner.

That was my cue not to say another word about it. I got undressed in front of Matt and changed into the clothes he provided me with. I looked down at myself and wasn't at all pleased with what I saw. The clothes were a little bigger than I had liked. But I kept my mouth closed and assumed the clothes belonged to Lisa because she was a little thicker than I was. I had the frame of Meagan Good while she had the frame of Kim Kardashian. So there was definitely a difference in the way these clothes fit me versus the way they'd fit her. Matt could care less, though.

"You ready to go over the drill again?" he asked me.

"Yeah," I replied as I stood before him.

"Now, I told you that you and Preech are going inside the bank while Juice waits in the car. I want you to walk in first and walk straight over to the bank manager while Preech stays at least ten feet behind you. He's going to act like he's filling out a bank slip near the end of the counter area while he watches for other bank customers to leave the bank. Then, when the coast is clear, he's going to shut down all the tellers and have them move back from their stations. I want you to stand there with the bank manager just in case she tries to do something. There is a distress alarm underneath her desk, so you're on her before she gets to touch it."

"Okay, I will."

"Good. So then right after Preech gets everything under control up front, I want you to get the bank manager to lock the door. Then I want you to march her ass in the back where the vault is and I want you to clean that motherfucker out. Try to get that half a mil like I told you was there. It's gonna be real simple if you follow everything I say to a T," Matt conveyed.

"I will. I'm running everything through my head right as we speak." I said. But in reality I was running another plan in my head. And it had nothing to do with robbing the bank and bringing all the money back to him.

"Once you get the money, you're gonna duct tape and tie that bank manager up in the vault. She'd fuck up the entire mission if you let her walk out of there freely," Matt warned me.

"Trust me, I've got everything under control," I tried to reassure him, but for some reason, he didn't look fully convinced. I left it alone though.

"Here, take these gloves. You're gonna need them," he told me.

I took the gloves from him and put them in my pocket. "Preech got both backpacks with him in the den," Matt continued.

"A'ight," I said like I was ready to go. But in actuality, I just wanted to get my baby and leave this godforsaken place.

Matt said a few more things to me and then he told me to follow him back into the den area. I looked back at my baby one last time before I left the room and gave him the biggest kiss ever. "I'll be back to get you, little man," I whispered to him before I stood up and walked out of the room.

Matt led me back into the den area. Lisa was in the kitchen cooking something that was smelling extremely good. "Lisa, when you're done with that I want you to go in the room and look after the baby," Matt yelled.

"All right," she replied nonchalantly without even looking up from the pan she was using to cook in.

"So are you niggas ready to get this paper?" Matt asked with excitement as he clapped his hands together.

"You know I'm ready," Juice replied with eagerness.

"You fucking right, I'm ready. I ain't made a lick like this in a long time. So I'm ready to get paid," Preech chimed in.

"Good. Well, let's get this show on the road." Matt jumped for joy. I could see the anticipation in his face. I was sure all he could think about was how much money this score was going to bring him. This was a classic scene out of the *Ocean's Eleven* movie.

All the laughter and excitement came to a halt when another news broadcast interrupted the televised show that was on. "Look, they talking about her and that nigga we wasted again," Juice blurted out as he pointed at the TV. Every one of us including Lisa had walked out of the kitchen to listen to what was being said. The news reporter mentioned that they finally got a chance to speak with someone connected to the case and, several seconds later, turned the camera to Quincy. My heart completely stopped when I saw his face in front of the camera about to be interviewed. He was standing outside of the police precinct with a man who appeared to be his attorney. Quincy looked very worried and confused. He even looked like he cried a lot of tears before he decided to stand in front of the camera. I will say that it was brave of him to do this. I waited there patiently to hear what he had to say. *"So, Quincy, will you please reiterate to all the viewers what events led up to your friend's being kidnapped while you were in the Huntersville section of Norfolk,"* the reporter said.

Quincy took a death breath, looked straight into the camera, and then he said, *"Well, I met this lady named Chantel on the bus coming back from New York City. She told me that she was coming here to visit her grandmother. But after we got here she changed her story and said that she was really here because her ex-boyfriend took her newborn baby and that she wanted to get him back."*

"Did she tell you what her ex-boyfriend's name was?" the reporter asked him.

"No, she never told us."

"Who are you talking about when you say 'us'?"

"My roommate Trevor. He was the one that drove us to the house in Huntersville. It was Chantel's idea to sit in Trevor's Jeep and watch the house to see if she could find some kind of sign that her baby was inside there. But after about thirty minutes, Trevor got tired of sitting there and decided that he was going to knock on the door."

"What happened after he knocked on the door?" the reporter wanted to know.

"Someone opened the door, but Chantel and I couldn't see who it was because of where the Jeep was parked. So after Trevor said a few words to the person standing there in front of him, he turned around to leave but the person grabbed him and dragged him into the house and slammed the door shut. I immediately freaked out and took out my cell phone so I could call the cops but Chantel told me not to. She said that if I called the cops, it could mess her chances up for getting her son back. So I put my phone away and told her that she needed to do something about getting my friend out of that house and do it now. So she got out of the Jeep and went to the back of the house. I got out and followed her and as soon as we stepped on the back porch the back door swung open and someone grabbed her and then another guy started shooting his gun at me, so I took off running."

"Did you get a look at the person who was shooting at you?" the reporter asked.

"No, I didn't. It was completely dark outside and once he started firing his gun I ran and didn't look back."

"Did you get hurt trying to get away?"

"No, ma'am. And I thank God for it because the guy was very close to hitting me with one of those bullets," Quincy said, and then he let out a sigh of relief.

"Is there anything you wanna say to the kidnappers of your friend and the woman Chantel?"

"Yes, ma'am, I wanna say to the guys who took my roommate and Chantel to find it in your heart to let them go, especially my roommate. He's a college student and he has a full life ahead of him. He wants to finish school and become a doctor. I don't know too much about the lady, Chantel, but she seems like a really nice person, so let her go too. And give her her baby back so we can all go home. That's all I'm asking," Quincy said, and then his eyes started shedding tears. The white man dressed like an attorney placed his arm over Quincy's shoulders and gave him a gentle pat.

The cameraman turned the camera back toward the news reporter. After she was given the cue to talk, she said, *"Well, you heard it here first. The young gentleman named Quincy Lloyd is sending a plea to the kidnappers in hopes that they will release his friend and the young lady named Chantel. So folks, if you've seen or know where these two people are, please contact the missing person's division of the Norfolk City Police Department. The number you can call is 877-MISSING1. They have operators on standby to take down any information or leads that you may have. Let's get these two people back home to their loved ones. I'm Sherry Paige with Channel Ten News and this has been an exclusive."*

Immediately after the news segment ended, everyone in the fucking room started looking at one another. Matt opened his mouth first. "Why the fuck is everyone looking at each other like they're fucking stupid or something?" he asked sarcastically.

No one said a word. "So, that's the motherfucker that got away, huh?" Matt's voice boomed.

"Juice told me that he thought he hit 'em," Kanan said.

Juice looked at Kanan like he lost his fucking mind but he didn't utter one word.

"Well, he didn't. And now that nigga is running his fucking mouth on TV, making my fucking spot hot and got the police looking for his homeboy and Ms. Chantel right here," Matt said, and then he pointed at me. "You sure know how to fuck my shit up. You got the whole police department looking for you and that other young boy and they don't even know your real name. And because of all that bullshit you threw in the mix, now my niggas can't go back to my spot and reopen shop. Do you know how much money I'm gonna lose behind this shit?" Matt continued while he stared directly at me.

"It ain't like you ain't gonna get it back once I do this next score for you," I mentioned.

"Yeah speaking of that, I take back the ten percent. Because you and your little young boys made me lose my spot, let's just say that after you make this move for me, we're gonna call it even," he said.

I fucking knew it, I screamed in my head. I knew this asshole was going to renege on the ten percent. It was okay because I planned to take matters into my own hands. If I was gonna risk my life and freedom behind this nigga, I would be compensated for it. "Look, Matt, all I care about is getting my son back. That's it. You can have everything else," I finally said, even though I wasn't telling him the whole truth. I figured it would be best to reveal that to him at a later date.

A few minutes later, I saw Preech look down at his watch. "Yo, I think it's about that time," he said, thankfully, because it seemed like Matt was about to go into one of his rants again.

On our way out the door Matt gave us one final pep talk. "Once you get to the bank let Lauren take the lead. She's a pro at this," Matt told them.

"We got it," Preech and Juice said in unison.

"Juice, you drive that motherfucker straight back here as soon as my money get in that car, understood?" Matt said.

Juice smiled. "You know I'm on it, boss!" Juice assured him.

Matt walked us to the car and right before I got inside he pulled me backward a couple of steps. It alarmed the hell out of me. "Oww, you scared me!" I told him.

He leaned over to my ear and said, "Don't try anything stupid. Remember, I got your fucking son in that house and I will kill him this time if you don't bring me all my money back."

"I'm not risking my baby's life for anything. You can bet'cha life on that," I told him, and then I broke away from his grip.

Immediately after I got in the passenger seat of the Dodge Charger, I looked back at the house and saw Lisa peering out the bedroom window at me. I whispered the words *thank you*, even though I knew she couldn't hear me. But I knew she knew how to read lips. She nodded her head, and then she walked away from the window. By the time Matt had realized what I had done, he looked back at the house but Lisa had already gone. He looked back at me with a weird expression, but he didn't move his lips. He just watched us until the car drove out of sight.

19

THE FINAL SCORE

The drive away from the house became intense by the second. I couldn't fucking believe that I was on my way to rob a bank. I sat in the front seat while Preech sat in the back and made sure our guns were locked and loaded. I looked back at him. He smiled back at me as he held the gun up in the air. "This one right here is going to be yours. But Matt told me not to give it to you until after we walk into the bank," Preech told me.

Juice looked back at the gun through the rearview window. "You think she can handle that big motherfucker?" he commented.

"It ain't nothing but a Glock. She can handle it," Preech replied as he looked the gun over.

"Don't worry about me. I can handle my own," I chimed in after I looked Juice head-on.

"Do you hear her popping that shit?" Juice asked Preech.

"Yeah, I hear her. Matt said she was a rider," Preech commented.

"Yeah, I sure am," I mumbled to myself. These guys had no idea that I was planning to take them out. It didn't matter if I was handed the gun during the bank robbery, I was going to figure a way out of this madness once and for all.

Preech and Juice listened to Lil Wayne's mixtape the entire drive to the bank. They even talked about how they were going to spend their portion of the bank money. "I'm gonna buy me a diamond watch and a big-ass diamond chain," Juice said.

"Yeah, I'ma get me a nice-ass diamond chain too, but I gotta cop me one of them nice-ass Audemars Piguet watches that Jay Z be talking about in his raps," Preech said.

"Oh yeah, I heard those watches was hot as fuck!" Juice commented.

"Yeah, all the niggas around the way be talking about they're gonna get them one and ain't nobody got shit!" Preech added. "So I guess I'm gonna be the first one around the way with one," Preech continued.

"Don't floss too hard. You know niggas will start talking and have the heat on us real quick," Juice warned Preech.

"Man, fuck them niggas out Huntersville. They wished they could be like me," Preech replied.

Juice and Preech went back and forth about what they were going to do with their cut from the robbery. But I knew goodness well that Matt wasn't going to give them shit. Matt was a grimy nigga. These guys would be lucky to get ten dollars and a pack of bubblegum after we made this score. They obviously had no idea what type of man Matt was. But I'll tell you what, after today they would.

Juice finally pulled up alongside the bank. My heart started beating uncontrollably. It felt like my head had begun to spin around. It seemed like my brain just wouldn't catch up to my actions. I couldn't afford to let myself slip into shock, I had to keep myself focused. My son's life depended on it. My life depended on it. I had to go into survival mode because that was who I really was inside. Fighting for my life had been an ongoing thing almost all my life. So I couldn't stop today. *You can do it, Lauren. Little Derek is depending on you.* I gave myself a pep talk over and over under my breath. Finally, it sunk it.

"Let's get this show on the road," Preech insisted as he checked our guns one last time.

"Remember, Matt said y'all should only be in there no more than three minutes," Juice told us.

"Yeah, yeah, yeah, I know. We got everything under control. You just make sure your ass don't leave us," Preech replied.

"Trust me, I ain't going nowhere. Y'all gon' have the golden tickets," Juice joked.

Preech cracked a smile. "Make sure you keep that in mind if you see bullets flying at my head while I'm running out of the bank."

"I gotcha, son. Don't even worry about it," Juice assured him.

I got out of the car first and waited on the sidewalk for Preech to join me. Once we were standing side by side, he instructed me to walk alongside him until we got into the bank. So I did. Immediately after we entered into the lobby, he handed me my gun. I looked at it for a few seconds and thought of putting the barrel of it up to Preech's head and blowing the shit to smithereens. But I knew that wouldn't be a good idea. I'd be in jail on murder charges before I could even see my son again. Couldn't let that happen.

"You ready?" he asked me as he handed me one of the backpacks.

"As ready as I'll ever be," I told him while I threw it over my shoulders.

"Let's do it then," he told me, and then he moved to the side and allowed me to walk ahead of him like Matt had instructed us to do.

I held on to the gun while it was inside my pants pocket. I walked toward the bank manager, who was a white woman dressed in a dark blue pantsuit. She looked every bit of forty years old. She also looked confident. Not your typical run-of-the-mill around-the-way girl. Her looks didn't intimidate me, though. I was on a mission and unfortunately she would be in the middle of it. "Is there anything I can help you with?" she asked me as I approached her.

I smiled. "Yes, I would like to open an account," I lied.

"Sure, I can take care of that for you," she told me, and then she extended her hand for me to shake it. "Your name?"

"Sarah Moss," I lied once more as I shook her hand.

"Nice to meet you, Sarah. I'm Peggy the bank manager, so have a seat right here," she said as she pointed to a chair placed in front of her desk, which was only a few feet away from a row of five bank tellers sitting behind a countertop. There were four women and one male. The male teller was a gentleman who was probably in his early twenties, but looked like he was fresh out of high school. I knew at first sight that he wouldn't be a problem once the shit hit the fan.

After I took a seat, I looked back to see what Preech was doing. I had to admit that he was on cue. He was standing at the help desk area acting like he was filling out a deposit slip. He glanced at me for a second and then he resumed what it was he was doing.

Before I turned my attention back toward the bank manager, I scanned the entire lobby and noticed that there were only two customers being serviced. So as soon as they took flight, it would be game time.

"Do you have your ID so I can key your information into the computer?" she asked me after she sat down in her chair.

"Yes, I do," I lied again, and started patting my pockets like I was really looking for the ID. "Wait," I said, and then I fell silent, trying to stall for time as I continued to pat and search my pockets.

"What's the matter?" she asked me.

"I think I left my ID in my car," I told her, and then I stood. I made sure I did not touch the arms of the chair from the time I sat down to the time I stood back up.

"Do you wanna run outside to get it?" Peggy wanted to know.

"Wait, let me check my back pockets because I could've sworn that I just had it."

While I continued to act like I was looking for my ID, I noticed both customers turn to leave the bank. I looked back at Preech one more time and then I turned back to face Peggy. "You know what, I think I did leave it in the car," I said.

She stood up and said, "Well, run out there and fetch it and I'll wait right here for you."

"I sure will," I replied, and then I turned around like I was about to leave. By now Preech had followed the last two customers to the door and locked it behind them. It was funny how no one saw it but me. The freaking security cop was talking to the one teller at the end of the counter so he wasn't paying attention to anything but that bitch he was running his mouth with. Preech snuck up behind him and stuck his gun in his side. And from there everything went in slow motion.

I turned back around and faced the bank manager. "Excuse me, do you guys have a restroom?" I asked.

"Yes, sure, it's on the other side of the lobby near the exit door," she said as she pointed in that direction.

"Where again?" I asked as I approached her.

But she became mum. And I knew it was because she saw Preech with his body pressed next to the security guard. She took a couple steps backward like she was trying to get behind her desk but I stopped her in her tracks.

I took my gun from my pocket and rushed her. "Don't even fucking try it!" I hissed as I pointed the gun toward her stomach. "Just do as you're told and you will not get hurt," I warned her.

She stood still like she was frozen. "Please don't hurt me!" she whimpered.

"I'm not, so don't cause no scene because if you do, it's gonna get really ugly in here," I told her.

Two seconds later, I watched as Preech took the security guard's handgun and instructed him to lie face down on the floor. Then he jumped on the counter and ordered all the tellers to move back from their quarters. "I want all y'all motherfuckers to put your hands up. And if any of y'all move, I'm gonna put a bullet in your skull and your family ain't going to be able to identify your body when I'm done with you," he threatened them.

"Let's get this paper, Bonnie," Preech yelled over to me.

"I'm on it," I told him. "Show me where the safe is," I demanded.

The woman didn't budge. She looked like she was frozen solid. So I walked up closer to her and nudged the gun in her abdomen. "Take me to the fucking safe now," I was forced to repeat.

She jumped and started walking toward the vault. I walked closely behind her while Preech made his announcement. "If anyone of y'all move or try to be a fucking hero, then shit is gonna end very badly for you. So, do you and me both a favor and stay where you are. We came in here to rob the bank, not you. So as soon as we get what we came in here for, we will be out of here. Got it?"

All the bank tellers nodded their heads simultaneously while the bank manager and I slipped to the back. The vault was only a few feet away. The nerves in my stomach started rumbling. "Let's make this quick," I told the bank manager as we stood before the vault. She was very nervous. She pushed a bank key inside of a keyhole, punched in a numeric code on the keypad, and then she laid her right hand down on a hand scan. It took several seconds for the hand panel to beep. Once it did, the door unlocked and she was able to push it open.

I pushed the door open wide to reveal the contents of the safe. My eyes lit up like a kid at Christmas when I saw all the cash inside stacked up on metal pallets. I felt flushed being exposed to that amount of money. Money was the root of all evil, and trust me, all kinds of thoughts were running through my head at that moment. One thought in particular was me taking as much money out of there and starting my life all over again. From where I was standing, it looked like there was at least $5 million in that pile. I could buy myself a brand new Range Rover, every colored Chanel bag with different pairs of Giuseppe Zanotti to match them. I swore, my life would be so freaking plush. I wouldn't have my hubby, Derek, to share the riches with, but I would have our precious son alongside me.

"Fill up this bag," I instructed the bank manager after I handed her the backpack. One by one she grabbed stacks of $10,000 bundles while I kept my gun pointed at her. I watched her every fucking move.

"Hand me one of those stacks," I told her.

She nervously handed me a stack of money. I grabbed it from her hands and then I held it up to my nose and inhaled deeply. The smell of the money was intoxicating, to say the least. It was the smell of freedom. I was in a stupor. I felt nostalgic holding that money. It was like old times again when I had my own money.

Instead of giving the money back to her to put in the backpack, I stuffed it down inside my panties. "Give me another one," I demanded. So she handed me a stack of $100 bills. I stuffed it down inside my panties beside the other stack. There wasn't any more room down there so I figured I'd be able to stuff a few stacks in my pockets with no problems at all. I ended up being able to stuff $60,000 on my body without it being noticeable.

"Come on, we gotta go," I heard Preech scream from the lobby.

"I'm coming," I yelled back. And then I handed the other backpack to the bank manager. "Hurry up and fill this one up too," I instructed the woman.

Once again she filled up the bag one stack at a time. There was something overwhelmingly powerful about being in possession of a backpack filled with stacks of cash. So much so that I felt dizzy at first. God knows I wanted to take the fucking money, go get my baby, and get the fuck out of Dodge. But I knew it wouldn't be that easy. Or would it? In the back of my mind, I knew I could do anything I put my mind to, and leaving this state for good this time, with some of this money and my son in tow, would be the ultimate blessing. I needed to do this for my son and me.

It took Peggy a minute and a half to fill up the second bag. Immediately after she handed me the backpack, I instructed her to turn around. "Please don't kill me!" she begged as she turned around slowly.

"I'm not gonna kill you," I told her, and then I hit her in the head with the butt of my gun. She fell onto the floor unconscious. At that moment I made a run for the lobby. Preech saw me coming around the corner. "Let's get out of here," I yelled as I proceeded toward the front door.

I heard Preech yell obscenities at the security guard. "Get down on the fucking floor!" he demanded. I looked over my shoulder and saw the guy crawl down onto the floor. "You're taking too fucking long!" Preech spat, and kicked the security guard's ass. The man fell face-first to the floor. Preech laughed at him and made a run for it. The sight of Preech made me sick to my stomach so I waited by the front door of the bank. As soon as he got within three feet of me, I lifted my gun, placed my pointer finger in the trigger guard, and pulled back the trigger. The gun erupted like a cannon in my hand. BOOM! BOOM! I shot him twice. Preech tried to fire his gun back at me but his body wouldn't give him the strength to do it. He jumped. I watched as his body fell back and slumped to the floor. Blood was running out of a hole from his stomach.

"That was for my husband, you bitch-ass nigga! So die, you motherfucker!" I hissed. I wanted to spit on him but I couldn't afford to leave any DNA behind, so I unlocked the door and rushed out of the bank.

The outside breeze hit me in the face. I inhaled and exhaled. I don't know why but I felt free for some odd reason. That all went out the window as soon as I approached the car.

20

ONE DOWN—TWO TO GO

Juice looked a nervous wreck when I opened the passenger-side door and Preech was nowhere in sight. "Where is Preech?" he didn't hesitate to ask.

I hopped inside with both backpacks filled with the bank's money. "The security guard got 'em. So let's get out of here," I expressed my lie with urgency.

"What do you mean the security guard got 'em?" Juice wanted clarity. He didn't budge.

"Listen, a fucking cop came from out of nowhere and shot Preech in the back twice. When he fell down on the floor, his gun fell out of his hand," I continued to lie. I had to make this story sound believable. It was do or die.

"Where the fuck was you at?" Juice grilled me as we sat there in the car like sitting ducks. I had to look around a couple of times just to make sure I hadn't been followed or the police were close by.

"I was running ahead of him. I told him to come on and right when he was trying to get out of the front door a cop came from out of nowhere and started busting shots at us. Preech was behind me so he was the one that took the hits," I explained.

"Fuck! Fuck! Fuck!" Juice roared as he punched the steering wheel of our getaway car.

"Look, Juice, we gotta go. I know the cops is on the way," I yelled, while I started looking around the surrounding area. I figured if this asshole didn't leave in the next couple of seconds, we were both gonna be somebody's bitch in jail. "Do you wanna go to fucking jail?" I yelled once more. I was getting aggravated with this idiot.

"Fuck no!" he spat.

"Well, let's get the fuck out of here then," I roared, and then I turned around in my seat to get a look through the back window just to make sure no one was coming.

Juice finally snapped out of it and sped off in the car. I looked through the back window to see if someone had come out of the bank looking for me, but after driving down two blocks I realized that we were in the clear. But Juice wasn't too happy about the turn of events. "We gotta call Matt and tell him we lost Preech," he suggested through clenched teeth. He was livid that Preech hadn't made it out of the bank. At one point, I thought he was going to suspect that I had something to do with it when he said, "I can't believe Preech got hit and you didn't."

I could tell that he was testing me.

"What the fuck is that supposed to mean?" I hissed.

"I'm just saying that ain't like him because he's always on guard."

"Listen, nigga, I took all the fucking risks. I was the one in the fucking vault getting all the money so of course I'm gonna be the first one to leave the bank. I told you he was right behind me when that fucking cop started busting his burner at us," I replied sarcastically. I gave Juice the evil eye to make my story believable.

He looked at me and then he looked back at the road ahead of us. "Man, fuck this, I'm calling Kanan," he said as he pulled his cell phone from his pocket.

I knew I couldn't let Juice get Kanan on the phone. If he did, then this whole heist wasn't going to end well. It might even cost me my life, so I knew I needed to think of something quick. But what could I say? Then it came to me. "You may wanna wait until we get back to the house to talk to the guys," I said.

"Why the fuck would I wanna do that?"

"Because we just committed a fucking robbery and the cops are all over Preech right about now. So you know they got his phone and since everybody's fucking number is in it, it ain't gonna be hard to track us down with the cell phone towers all around us," I told him. I searched his face to see if I was getting into his head. I could tell he was thinking about what I was saying. "All they have to do is take your number and get the cell phone company to run data on your GPS to see if you were in the area where the robbery took place. And when they find out that you were, you're gonna be fucked. And while I'm thinking, you might wanna turn it off and get rid of it."

"Nah, fuck that, I'm keeping my phone," he protested.

"Well, so be it. But don't say anything to me when Matt jumps down your throat for not taking precautions. Believe me, he knows all about the cell phone towers being able to track down cell phones through their GPS systems. And if the cops get a track on you and you bring the cops back to that house, I know Matt will kill you for sure," I scolded him.

Juice thought for a few more seconds and then he said, "Ugh! Fuck!" And then he took his phone back into his pants pockets. "I can't believe this shit! Fuck!" he growled, and then he tossed his phone from the window.

"Smart move," I commented, hoping he'd think that I was concerned with his well-being. He didn't go for it, though.

"You think what I just did was a smart move?" I knew
he was being sarcastic but I let it roll off my back.

"You fucking right I do."

"Well, it wasn't. The smart move would've been leaving
out of that motherfucking bank with my homeboy Preech.
And now that nigga is hurt all up and getting ready to go
before a motherfucking judge. Dem crackers ain't gonna
ever let my boy out. He's fucked!" Juice roared, and then
he started punching the steering wheel again with his fists.
"I can't believe they got him. This shit ain't right, man. I
knew Kanan should've come with us, then Preech would
probably be with us right now."

"You got this money, right?" I said, and pointed to the
backpacks on my lap.

"Yeah."

"Well, use your part to get him a decent-ass lawyer. Trust
me, he'll be all right if you did that," I suggested.

"Yeah, that's what I'm gon' do. I'm gon' get him one of
those high-powered lawyers that be buying the judges and
shit. He'd be good then," Juice said. He was beginning to
feel optimistic. I guess my pep talk was doing the job after
all. Fucking sucker!

Juice took the highway and put the pedal to the metal.
By the speed at which he was driving I knew that we'd be
back at Matt's hideaway in the middle of the cornfield in
the next fifteen minutes or maybe sooner. So I had to think
quickly. How was I going to get rid of Juice before we got
back to the house? I knew getting him to make a detour
would be out of the question, so I thought of the next best
thing.

"Hey, Juice, get off on this next exit."

"Bitch, are you fucking crazy? I ain't stopping this car,"
Juice huffed.

"Listen, you fucking asshole! I'm gonna need you to

pull over to the next gas station you see so I can check to make sure ain't no sensors on this fucking money in these backpacks," I explained to him.

"Why the fuck can't you do it while I'm driving?"

"Because there might be ink bombs in here. And you don't want that shit exploding in this fucking car, do you?"

Juice thought for a second, and then he said, "Look, as soon as I pull over you better hurry up and check that shit so we can get back on the road. I know them niggas is waiting on us to bring this dough back to them."

"All right," I said, knowing goodness well that I had another plan for this dumb motherfucker!

Juice took the next exit off I-64. The exit was Deep Creek Boulevard. The next major intersection was Military Highway, so I told Juice to pull over on the street before we got to Military Highway. The name of the street was Yadkin Road and on that street was a Baptist church. The facility was closed, thank God, so I told him to pull in the back of the building. As he drove around back, I looked around the parking lot to make sure that there weren't any surveillance cameras visible. When I noticed that there weren't any, I told Juice to stop the car. Immediately after he stopped the car, I grabbed both backpacks and got out. I dropped both bags on the ground while the door was ajar. "What the fuck are you doing?" he questioned me suspiciously.

"Nothing. Just give me a minute. I wanna check the bags out just to make sure that there aren't any tracking devices between the stacks of money," I told him. That was the only logical reason I could come up with that would make sense. So while I reached down on the ground and unzipped the first backpack slowly, Juice sat back and continued to eye me shadily. I immediately felt like a child being chastised. Anger welled up inside of me like a pot about to boil over. I wanted to ask him why the hell was he watching me like that, but I left well enough alone.

Once the bag was opened, I sifted through it with my hands, pretending to be careful but at the same time knowing that there wasn't anything in the bag that could've harmed either one of us. "Is that one good?" Juice didn't waste any time asking me.

I let out a long sigh. "Yeah, that one is clean," I told him as I zipped the backpack back up. Then I reached over to the other bag and unzipped that one carefully too. Once again, Juice watched my every move. I sifted through the bag with my hand slowly and when I completed the search, I looked up at him and told him that we were good.

"Well, come on and let's get out of here," he said anxiously.

While I was zipping up the second backpack, I looked over his shoulder, indicating that I saw something. My actions triggered him to turn around and look back. Immediately after he turned his head, I pulled the gun Preech gave me from my pocket and pointed directly at Juice. And as soon as he turned back around he looked at me. "Yo, what the fuck y . . ." Juice started, his mouth curled like he was about to say the word *you.* BOOM! I didn't give him a chance to say another word. His words were cut short after the shot rang out. One singular shot had landed in his head. It was finally over. I flinched when the gun had erupted in my hand. It was more of a physical reaction, rather than an emotional or mental one. When I saw all of the blood and brain matter gushing from his head, I didn't cringe or barely move, much less scream. I was extremely numb. Numb from all of the mental anguish I'd endured from the hands of his boss.

After his lifeless body slumped over the steering wheel, I felt the powerful reverberation from the gunshot. I sat just there, staring. The sight of him brought joy to my heart.

Now he wasn't able to cause me any harm. Next up was Kanan and then Matt. I hadn't thought about what I was going to do with Lisa yet. But I was quite sure I would think of something. I couldn't have her around messing my chances of leaving, or going to the cops for that matter. I guessed I'd cross that bridge when I got there.

21

TIME TO GO TO PLAN B

I threw the gun onto the passenger seat and scurried around the car to the driver's side. As soon as I opened the driver's side door Juice's body fell out onto the ground, headfirst. I heard a loud thud.

Blood was everywhere. I had no idea how I was going to drive this freaking car with all the blood and brain matter all over the place. "Ugh! Why didn't I lure him out of the fucking car?" I asked myself.

Frustrated, I went to the trunk of the car and searched it for something to clean off the front windshield and the fucking steering wheel. Luckily, I found some old wash towels and an old wool blanket. I tried with all my might to clean off as much of Juice's blood and body tissue with the towels. After much wiping, most of it came up. There was a lot of blood smears, but it was better than how it was before I started wiping the car down. Once I was done, I threw the wool blanket across the driver's seat, grabbed Juice's gun from his pocket while he was still lying dead on the ground, and hopped inside the car. Thank God I had on gloves or else I wouldn't have been able to drive that car anywhere with the residue of Juice's blood smeared all over.

I sped out of the church parking lot and headed straight back to the house Matt, Kanan, and Lisa were hiding out in. I took my time driving back to the destination so I could figure out how I was going to make the trade-off with Matt and make it out alive. I knew he was going to have a lot of questions, especially since I was returning without Juice and Preech. And once he saw all the blood left in the car, I knew he wasn't going to be too happy about the mess I made. I worried this might even send him and Kanan over the edge.

"Come on, Lauren, you gotta think this thing out straight," I said out loud to give myself a pep talk. "You gotta do this thing right. You can't make any wrong moves. No mistakes," I continued while I tried to figure out a master plan.

I looked at the money on the passenger seat and thought about what I could do with it if I was able to get away with it. I would be set for life. And I wouldn't make any slip-ups this time around. No one from this area would ever be able to find me again, especially with all this money. I was talking about living completely under the radar. People with money who don't want to be found do it all the time. So I guessed I'd be added to that list.

Five minutes into the drive, it finally hit me. Since I didn't have a phone to call Matt or Kanan, I decided that I'd pull up to the house and beep the horn. When Kanan and Matt came outside, I'd gun both of their asses down in cold blood and then I'd run into the house and get my baby. If Lisa wanted to play hero, then she'd get a bullet too.

"You can do it, Lauren. You can do it." I pumped myself up as I drove the car down the highway.

Fuck! Fuck! Fuck! I screamed in my mind after I saw an unmarked cop car parked on the side of the road about one mile from the house where Matt was. There was only one person in the car, from what I could see. I was driving up behind him so I only saw the back of his head. My first instinct was to step on the brakes, turn this fucking car around, and go in the opposite direction. I couldn't let him stop me from getting back to my son. This was my last chance to get my baby. But then I realized that I had on a disguise and I was wearing sunshades so the cop wouldn't be able to see who I was even if he wanted to.

I slowed down a bit so the cop couldn't get me for speeding. I kept my head straight, looking at the road in front of me. My heart was beating like crazy. My stomach was twisted in knots too. But I knew I had to remain calm. My freedom depended on it.

As I drove by the cop car, through my peripheral vision I saw him move. It was a sudden move and it caused me to look in his direction; something I was trying not to do. When I peered into his car, I noticed that he looked flushed in the face. He even looked like he saw a fucking ghost. He looked like he was just as surprised to see me as I was to see him. Three seconds after I began searching his face for a reason as to why he was parked on the side of the road, I saw more movement from behind him. I turned my head slightly to the right of him and out popped a chick who looked like a bona fide prostitute. She wiped her mouth with the back of her hand and then she smiled at me. I knew what that meant. She was giving that cop some head. I looked back at him and smiled, letting him know that I was cool with whatever he was doing, especially since he had another agenda. I let out a sigh of relief and continued on toward the house so I could deal with Matt.

22

THE FINAL EXCHANGE

Even though I wanted to get my son and leave, I dreaded driving back up to this freaking house. Going back to the house meant that I was putting my life on the line, as well as my son's. In the back of my mind, something told me that Matt wasn't going to let me go free after I gave him this money. To him, the issue was deeper than money. He was upset that I'd left him and started my life over with someone else. So I knew he wasn't going to let bygones be bygones. He wasn't that type of guy. He was a fucking rebel with no heart. So how was I going to beat him? I knew that whatever plan my mind came up with had to be solid.

With Preech and Juice out of the way, all I needed to take care of was Kanan. But how was I going to do that? He was at the house with Matt and Lisa. There was no way I'd be able to fight all of them by myself. No way. Then it came to me. I needed to lure Kanan out of the house. Then and only then would I be able to eliminate his ass from the equation.

I started down the long dirt road that led to the house. It seemed like the closer I got, the more my stomach turned.

Even the hair on my arm stood up. Something told me that this wasn't going to be as easy as I wanted it to be. Someone was going to fuck up the rhythm. I just knew it.

I finally reached the house. I parked the car about one hundred feet away. I also left the engine running while I blew the horn. I wanted to get everyone's attention in the house. I was hoping that I could make the trade and leave.

Kanan peered out the window on the side of the house in the den area. Seconds later, Matt appeared at the back door. Lisa didn't show her face at all. "Whatcha blowing for? Come on in the house," Matt said.

"Nah, send Lisa out here with my son and then we can make the exchange," I instructed him.

He wasn't too happy with my response. He totally disregarded my request. "Where is Preech and Juice?" Matt wanted to know.

"The cops got them. I was the only one that got away," I lied as I yelled from the driver's-side window.

"That's bullshit! How the fuck did you get away?" Matt yelled from the back door.

"All of us went inside the bank. . . ." I began to say, but Matt cut me off.

"That wasn't how it was supposed to go down. Bring your ass in this motherfucking house now!" Matt's voice boomed.

"Look, Matt, I just came back to give you this money. I don't want no problems. Just send Lisa out here so I can make the trade with her," I asked respectfully.

Being respectful didn't matter to Matt. When he wanted things to go his way that was how it was going to be. "Bitch, bring your motherfucking ass in this fucking house before I snap your fucking son's neck!" he hissed through clenched teeth. I could tell that his blood was boiling.

A few moments later, Kanan came outside by himself. "Get me my money. And bring that bitch in this fucking house," I heard Matt say to Kanan.

"I don't want no problems." I yelled out toward Kanan and Matt both. I was nervous as fuck because I knew that as soon as Kanan got close to the car, he was going to notice all the blood and blow my cover.

"It ain't gonna be no problems," Kanan said while he was walking toward the car. I noticed that he was empty-handed, which was baffling because Matt always required his boys to stay strapped at all times. I figured he was trying to fake me out or something.

The closer he came toward me the more he concentrated on my movement. He knew I was strapped with a gun so he wanted to be very careful. "Come on, Lauren, let's do the right thing. Give me the money and let's go inside," Kanan said the moment he got within three feet of me. But before I could respond, his facial expression changed. He stopped in his tracks and that's when I knew he noticed blood on the front windshield and dashboard. "What the fuck!" he said. Then he turned and looked back at the house. "Yo, Matt, there's blood in the car," he yelled.

It seemed like everything went in slow motion. As soon as Kanan reached his hand behind his back, I knew he was reaching for his gun so I held up my pistol and started busting one shot after another at him. BOOM! BOOM! BOOM! He returned gunshots.

BANG! BANG! BANG! BANG! BANG! BANG! BANG! BANG!

"Aggh! Shit!" I screamed as the sound of shattering glass cut through the car. Glass splintered all over the front seat and rained down on my head and hands. I could feel it cutting the skin on the top of my hands as I shielded my head. I was very lucky that the bullets hadn't ripped through my fucking skull.

Suddenly Kanan's gunshots stopped and when I looked up, he was trying to make a run for the house, but I got a clear shot and let off three rounds. BOOM! BOOM! BOOM! The last shot put Kanan down flat on his face. I watched his body for any movement, but when he didn't move for the first thirty seconds, I knew he was dead.

As soon as I tried to recover from the gunshots Kanan had fired at me, more gunshots started coming from the corner window of the house. POP! POP! POP! POP! POP! I immediately dove back down on the floor of the car for cover. I could barely control my breathing. My legs shook uncontrollably and burned like hell as I crouched with my knees bent. Sweat dripped from my forehead into my eyes, but I didn't dare move to wipe it away. I said a silent prayer for my soul and for my mother. All kinds of thoughts ran through my mind. I knew had to come up with a plan to deal with this situation or else.

Finally, once again the gunshots stopped. Then I heard Matt's voice coming from the window at the corner of the house. I couldn't see him, but I heard his voice clearly. "Bitch, if you don't get out of that motherfucking car right now and bring me my fucking money, I'm gonna kill your fucking baby!" Matt said with evil finality.

I was feeling a mixture of anger and fear. How dare that motherfucker threaten to kill my fucking baby when Kanan started busting his gun at me first? I cringed at the idea of him hurting my son. My jaw rocked so feverishly I was giving myself a migraine.

I swore if he hurt my baby, I wasn't going to have any mercy on his ass once everything was said and done.

My heart thumped painfully against my chest as I tried to figure out my next move. I wasn't about to just get out of that car and leave myself wide open to be shot down like a dog, but at the same time, I wanted to let Matt know I could be trusted. At this point, he had the upper hand whether I liked it or not. My baby was in the house with him, so what was I to do?

"Are you gonna bring me my money or not?" he roared. I could hear the anger in his voice. I could tell that he was on the verge of unleashing his wrath if I didn't hurry up and get out of this car.

"Okay, I'm coming out. But please don't shoot. All I want is my baby. You can have all of this money," I bargained.

"Throw your gun on the ground," Matt instructed me.

"There's no more bullets inside of it," I yelled from the car.

"It doesn't matter. Throw it on the fucking ground so I can see it."

"Okay. I'm doing it now," I assured him, and then I tossed my gun out on the ground. The gun was the one Preech gave me at the bank, not the one I took from Juice. So I was still armed.

"Now get the fuck out the car so I can see you," Matt barked.

I gave myself a pep talk. *Okay, Lauren, you can do this. Remember, this is for your son.*

I let out a long sigh while I started to sweat so badly I felt the beads rolling down the center of my back. I tried calming my nerves while my teeth were chattering. It didn't work. So I said fuck it and got up the gumption to get out of the car. I took all the money I had inside of my pants and stuck it inside of the glove compartment. Then I stuffed one of the backpacks in the backseat. I made sure my gun was tightly secured in the back of my pants and then I grabbed the other backpack in my hand and exited the car slowly. "I'm getting out, so don't shoot," I announced while I exited the car.

I walked around the car door and was fully exposed. I just knew that Matt was going to shoot me dead on the spot, but he didn't. I walked very slowly toward the house while he watched me from the window. As soon as I got within a few feet of the side door to the house, he opened it. "Throw the bag in here first," he instructed me.

I stood there on the bottom step and threw the bag into

the entryway. The backpack hit the floor hard. "Where is the other fucking bag?" he hissed.

"Preech had it with him when the cop shot him leaving the bank," I lied.

"You're a motherfucking liar! I know you, Lauren. You got that money stashed somewhere," Matt barked.

"I'm not lying, Matt. I swear, Preech had it when he got caught."

Matt rushed down the steps, grabbed me by the collar of my shirt, and tossed me inside the house. He slammed the door immediately after he manhandled me and threw me against the wall. I let out another half scream. I heard my handgun skitter to the floor. All hope of protecting myself was gone now. My screams were all for nothing because no one on the outside would be able to hear. "You slick-ass bitch!" Matt growled at me after he saw my gun slide across the floor. He smacked me so hard across my face I saw stars. Wham!

Between the force and the fear, I could not collect my thoughts. I was hyperventilating. I just knew I was going into shock from being so scared. I was being held like a rag doll. I tried to scream *help*, but he muffled my words with his right hand. "Shut up, bitch!" he huffed through clenched teeth.

Suddenly, I felt his muscular arm closing around my neck. He grabbed me so tight, my eyes popped wide open as I gagged. Matt squeezed with intensity. He was like a possessed demon. I had never seen him like that at all.

I gagged from being put in a chokehold. I tried to claw at his arm that was causing me to suffocate, but I could hardly muster enough strength to make any leeway. I immediately felt my air supply being cut off. "I'ma kill you for sure this time, you fucking bitch!" he growled once more.

I knew I was going to die at any moment but before that happened I vowed that I wasn't going to go out without a struggle. I began to flail and kick. But that didn't work for me. It actually tired me out because I wasn't making any headway with this fucking maniac. It seemed like the more I scratched and clawed at Matt's arm around my neck, the tighter it got.

"Matt, please stop!" I murmured, but my words were barely audible. He made it crystal clear that I was staring in the devilish eyes of my ex. My stomach muscle clenched and I balled my toes up in my shoes. He spat as he tightened his grip around my neck. But when he saw that I was losing consciousness, he loosened his grip and grabbed a chunk of my hair with the same hand. Tears were running down my face like a faucet. My body ached everywhere but nothing compared to the thoughts I was having about not ever leaving this house alive.

I couldn't believe it. Matt was finally getting his wish to kill me. And what was so frightening about this was that I once loved this man. His face was filled with hate. I could tell that he really wanted me dead. There was no more love for me.

"You think I'm gonna let you off that easy? I'm gonna torture your ass and let you die slow," he hissed like venom was spewing from his mouth.

Suddenly I felt a sharp pain penetrate the side of my face. "Ugh," I grunted from the pain after he hit me a second time. I didn't have enough energy to scream.

"Shut the fuck up, bitch!" Matt's gruff voice boomed.

"Please," I rasped, flinching. My throat felt like someone had shoved a flaming pole down it. I was hit across the face again. This time the metallic taste of blood filled my mouth. Tears immediately sprang to my eyes. "Please," I pleaded again through tears.

"Oh, now you want to say please," Matt said to me as he grabbed a handful of my hair with his other hand and yanked my downturned head up so that my battered eyes met his gaze.

"Can we please work this out?" I begged him.

"What the fuck can we work out? Bitch, I don't trust you. You're a fucking sheisty-ass ho!" Matt spat, tightening his grip on my hair.

"I'm . . . I'm . . . sorry, I'm sorry for everything. I really am," I gasped through tears.

Matt finally let my hair go with a shove. The force was so great I collapsed onto the floor. He walked away from me and scooped up the gun I dropped from the floor and shoved it down into his back pocket. "You thought you were coming in here to pump me up with a couple rounds of lead, huh?" he gritted at me.

"No, I wasn't going to use it on you," I lied.

"Well, you sure had different plans for Kanan, huh? 'Cause you sho' took his ass out with no problems," Matt pointed out.

"He shot at me first," I explained.

"Shut the fuck up! I ain't trying to hear that shit you're talking. You killed my right-hand man and you probably killed Juice and Preech too."

"No . . . I swear . . ." I began to say, but he cut me off.

"I ain't gonna believe a motherfucking thing that comes out of your mouth. So save it for someone else," he said as he paced in front of me.

A few minutes later Matt was back in my face. I started trembling uncontrollably with fear. He grabbed my face, his strong hand gripping both sides of my cheeks. He squeezed my face so hard I could feel my teeth making an impression on the inside of my cheeks. He forced me to look him in the eyes. "Answer this question," he started off. "What do you think I should do with you?" It sounded like a trick question so I was leery as to how to answer it.

"Huh? What do you mean?" I asked him while he still had my lips pushed out together, so my words sounded foreign.

"Do you think I should let you go?" he asked in an almost cynical fashion.

I was afraid to say yes, but I got up the gumption to say it anyway. "Yes, please. I promise you'll never see my face again," I swore.

Matt let out a sinister, maniacal laugh. "Bitch, whatcha think, I'm fucking stupid? I ought to smack the shit out of you again, for giving me that ridiculous answer," he said as he shoved me backward, then he lunged at me. I jumped, thinking he was going to swing at me again. But he did something far worse. I couldn't believe that he hawked a wad of spit on me, then turned and walked away from me. I felt so cheap and dirty after his spit landed on my face and chest. I used my shirt to wipe it off. But for some reason, I could still smell his spit on my face. It was disgusting. I thought I had hit rock bottom after Matt beat me up, damn near killing me. But nothing could compare to him spitting on me. That was the last straw for me.

23

A MILLION THOUGHTS

I couldn't believe I was still alive. The mere fact that Matt hadn't just killed me with his bare hands gave me hope. I sat alone on the floor of the entryway to the side door. I looked at it for a second getting the urge to make a run for it. But I knew it would be impossible. There was no way Matt was going to let me out of this house. Being within a few feet of this door seemed odd to me. It seemed too easy a way of escape. I knew Matt. He left me here for a reason. He was testing me. So I knew it would be a bad idea to run. And besides, my son was still here. I couldn't bear the thought of leaving him here with this fucking monster. No way.

I sat in this same spot for what seemed like the next five minutes. My hair had been pulled, my lips, my eyes were swollen, and my neck was aching really badly from the pressure Matt applied to it while he was choking the life out of me. I felt like I couldn't move. Then suddenly Matt reappeared with the backpack of money. The bag was slightly unzipped, exposing some of the stacks of one-hundred-dollar bills. "Yo, this shit ain't nothing but $270,000. Where the fuck is the rest of the money?" Matt roared as he threw the bag onto the floor in front of me.

"I told you Preech got caught with the other bag," I lied once more. I knew I had to stick to my story or Matt would crucify me for real this time around.

"You better not be fucking lying, bitch! Or I'm gonna make you pay," he warned me. He snatched the bag back up from the floor and marched out of the room.

About ten minutes later, I heard my baby cry from the other side of the house. My heart started aching. "What's wrong with my baby?" I cried out.

Seconds later, Matt walked back into the room with Lil Derek cradled in his arms. "He's fine. All he wanted was a bottle. And he's with his daddy now." Matt said it to taunt me as he held up Lil Derek's bottle to his mouth to feed him.

Tears leaked out of the sides of my eyes. "Will . . . you . . . please . . . ," I started, but I let the sobs flow freely.

"What? Let you go?" he barked. "Bitch, you are out of your damn mind. You ain't never going nowhere. You gon' be with me until I get tired of your motherfucking ass! Me, you, and this lil nigga right here in my arms is gon' be a family whether you like it or not," he continued as he paced back in forth in front of me. He was rocking Lil Derek back and forth in his arms to console him.

"But you have Lisa. She's a nice girl. So why don't you settle down and have a family of your own with her? She loves you. She probably loves you more than I ever had," I mentioned. I made sure I said it loud enough that Lisa could hear me. I wanted her to know that I was on her side and that I didn't want anything to do with Matt's ass. I wanted him to be her problem and not mine.

"Shut the fuck up! I don't need you to tell me what the fuck I have. I know what Lisa is to me. I had her here to do the shit you were supposed to be here doing. But nah, you took my motherfucking money and ran off to be with the next nigga," Matt pointed out. He was getting agitated with each word he uttered.

"Matt, please, just listen to me," I begged him.

"Fuck you! I don't wanna listen to shit you gotta say! Everything that comes out of your mouth are lies and pure nonsense. And do you think I wanna hear about you leaving me again? You took away my chances of ever having a life with you when you left with my money. And then to go off and start another life with a fucking FBI cop and then have his fucking baby? Do you know how fucked up that made me feel when I found out about that shit? That shit fucked my head up. Men can't take hearing about their woman going off to be with another nigga. And then to have a baby by him was damaging in itself. Yo, you fucked my heart up, Lauren, when you had this little nigga right here with that fucking cop. You can't fuck with a nigga's heart like that. You just don't know how you fucked me up forever. And that's the reason why I can't let you go. Do you think I can let you go off and be with another nigga? The thought of you being happy with someone else makes me sick to my stomach. So that's why I gotta keep you here with me. I'll die first before I let you get away again." I could see the sincerity in his eyes while he poured his heart out to me. And from there, I knew my chances of ever leaving this guy were very bleak.

"Let's be honest here," I began to sob uncontrollably, "our relationship will never be the same. You don't trust me. And you know you never will."

"Oh, so now you're a fucking relationship specialist?" he spat.

"I just know that this right here will never work because all you're gonna do is try to keep me locked up in this house. You and I are both wanted, so how will we ever live happily ever after?" I asked him. I wanted him to finally listen to me. Our situation was really fucked up. So he needed to be rational about the decisions he was going to make from this point forward.

"Look, I know what the fuck I'm doing. So you let me run this shit here," he replied, avoiding the questions. He was good at that. But he and I both knew that this little fairy tale he had concocted in his mind was going to fall apart quicker than he could put it together. There was no happily ever after for us. So the sooner he figured that out the better we'd both be. "Get the fuck up and take your ass into this next room," he instructed me as he jerked his head in the direction he wanted me to go.

He ended up taking me back in the bedroom that he and I had slept in the night before. He gave me Lil Derek, and then closed the door on me and locked it from the outside. I took a seat on the bed and began to wipe my tears away from my ears. I wanted to get a clear look at my baby boy while I held him in my arms. It was good to have him with me again. Having him gave me a sense of hope even if I would never ever got a chance to leave out of here alive.

While I cradled Lil Derek in my arms and rocked him back and forth, I heard an argument start between Matt and Lisa. I could barely hear Lisa, but I heard Matt clearly. "What the fuck do you mean, do I love you?" his voice boomed. "We ain't married so don't be asking me no questions like that," he continued with finality. I knew this cut Lisa deep. To hear a man avoid the question if he loved you or not was damaging to the heart. But then for him to pour salt in the wound and make it known that you two

weren't married was a clear indication that y'all's relationship didn't mean shit to him. Lisa had to see that this relationship between her and Matt wasn't going anywhere.

"So this is how you treat me after all I've done for
you?" I heard her say.

"What the fuck did you do for me?" he huffed. He
sounded like a raging bull. I knew that in any moment he
was going to be attacking Lisa.

"I risked having my freedom taken away by helping you
break out of jail. I even helped get you this fucking spot
we're in right now. And I've done shit for you that no
other bitch has. I put my life on the line for you, Matt, and
this is how you repay me?" she expressed. I could tell she
was crying because her voice cracked a few times while she
vented.

"Bitch, please! Get the fuck out of my face with that
bullshit! You ain't did a motherfucking thing for me! My
nigga put that shit together. All you did was drive me away
from the fucking jail. Speaking of which, you almost fucked
that up," Matt spat, minimizing her role in his escape.

Surprised by what I was hearing, I couldn't believe that
this chick would risk her freedom for Matt. She couldn't
have known him that long. Damn, I had only been gone
for a little over a year. And you can't fall in love that much
with a man that you do stupid shit like that in such a short
period of time. But if that was in fact the case, then she
was gullible as hell! Now, I'd done some crazy shit for
Matt, but never to that extreme.

"Matt, I was the one that got my friend that works in
the jail to get you that CO uniform. She was my connect,
remember?" Lisa tried to jog his memory.

"Who gives a fuck whose connect it was. That bitch got
paid, didn't she?" Matt roared. I could tell he was getting
tired of his conversation with Lisa. And at any minute he
was going to snap out at her.

"Look, are you going to keep her here against her will?" Lisa abruptly changed the topic.

"What?!" Matt replied. He sounded like he heard her the first time, but for some reason needed clarity.

"She has told you over and over again that she doesn't want to be with you anymore, so why won't you let her go? I mean, she did rob the bank and brought you the money back," Lisa pointed out.

"Lisa, you better stay in your lane and shut the fuck up!" Matt growled.

"Just answer my question, Matt. Why are you keeping her around when she doesn't want to be with you anymore?" Lisa pressed the issue.

I waited for Matt to respond to Lisa's question. But nothing came. And then I heard a loud thump. BOOM! POP! BOOM! I laid Lil Derek down on the bed and jumped to my feet. It sounded like Matt had attacked Lisa. Then I heard another boom sound. This time I knew it was Lisa falling down to the floor. I placed both of my hands on my head as I listened to all the noises in the next room. At one point it sounded like a herd of lions stampeding through that room. I could feel my entire body vibrating with tremors. My chest was heaving up and down as I flattened the left side of my face against the wall to get a better handle on what was going on since I couldn't see a thing.

At one point, I could barely gather my thoughts when Lisa started begging Matt to stop hitting her. "Matt, please stop. You're hurting me," she started screaming. I was beginning to regret the fact that she brought up my name in the first place. I truly appreciated Lisa for questioning Matt about why he wanted to keep me against my will, but the consequences that she was enduring made it not even worth it.

"Bitch, you gon' learn today that you can't talk to me any kind of way," Matt roared in the midst of all the chaos.

"I'm sorry, Matt! I'm sorry," I heard Lisa scream, and then I heard more chairs being turned over, bumping sounds against the wall, and objects falling down on the floor. Her voice droned on like she had totally given up on her own life. It was like she was repeating words she had rehearsed a thousand times. "I'm sorry, Matt! I'm sorry!" She was like the man's robot now, doing whatever he told her to do. She seemed brainwashed, like she was going through the motions but wasn't really herself. I was really afraid that Lil Derek would wake up from all the commotion.

I wanted to break out of that room and help her so badly, but unfortunately, I couldn't. I could still hear Lisa's cries ringing through my head as I stood on the other side of the door. I closed my eyes tight to try to keep the screams from haunting me too bad, but it didn't work. The sound was stuck in my head. I walked away from the door and sat on the edge of the bed. I looked down at him and thought to myself that it was now or never. Matt was losing his damn mind. I could tell that he was cracking under pressure because he was all alone. Preech, Juice, and Kanan were all dead, so who was left to have his back? He was too stupid to see that Lisa had his back. No. He wanted to have things his way. That was just Matt getting in his own way and he was going to cause his own demise. I just hoped that I wasn't around when it happened.

I lay back on the bed and thought about the likelihood of me getting out of there. I looked at the bars on the other side of the window and thought about how impossible it would be for me to get out that way. Then I looked back at the bedroom door and thought about how impossible it would be for me to leave that way too. The only way I'd be able to get out would be if Lisa helped me. But how, though? She'd made it perfectly clear that I shouldn't be here. She even tried to reason with Matt, so it was obvious that she felt my pain. Or she just didn't want me here because she knew that Matt favored me over her. Regardless of the reason, she was my only shot. Trying to convince her would be very hard to do. I just hoped God would continue to work on her heart.

24

IT FINALLY MADE SENSE

Finally, everything calmed down. I guess Matt got tired of whipping Lisa's ass because he just stopped. Either that, or Lisa convinced him not to kill her. Either way, the house became quiet so I was able to hear myself think and go back into planning mode.

After I put Lil Derek back to sleep, I checked to see how secure the bedroom windows were in the room. And when I saw that they were completely nailed shut, I knew there was no way in hell I was going to be able to make my escape this way.

I hadn't realized that I had fallen asleep until Matt burst into the room. "You slick-ass bitch! I just got a fucking call from my peoples! You fucking shot and killed Preech! Then you took the money and shot Juice and Kanan! And now you trying to rob me again?" His voice boomed while he held the other backpack of money in the air for me to get a good look at it. "I knew you were lying to me, you fucking sneaky-ass whore! I ought to kill you right now." He tossed the backpack on the floor.

"What are you talking about?" I tried to act surprised but I knew where he was going with this.

"Lisa, come in here and get the baby!" Matt yelled at the top of his voice.

In a flash Lisa came running in the bedroom. I looked in her face and saw all the bruises Matt had just inflicted on her. Matt was a fucking monster. And I knew my turn for a lashing was coming. I jumped up when she reached the bed and tried to grab ahold of my baby. I blocked her hands and scooped Lil Derek up from the bed. I tried to cradle him in my arms but my strength was no match for Matt's. He intervened by grabbing me by my neck with one hand. "Let 'em go, you dumb bitch! Or I'm going to snap him in half," he hissed.

I had no fight in me so I opened my arms and allowed Lisa to take my son from me. She looked at me and whispered that she was sorry, and then she sprinted out of the room. I was left to fight Matt on my own, and I knew that no one was going to come and save me. So I braced myself for the inevitable, because this time I knew it was going to be bad, especially since he knew I intended to steal the other backpack of money from the bank robbery.

Without warning he threw the first blow to my face. His fist connected with the right side of my head after I blocked it with my arms. That made him furious. He attacked me with a vengeance.

"Ahh!" I screamed out as multiple punches pounded my head and face, knocking me backward onto the floor.

"Matt, please stop. I didn't . . ." I screeched and tried to finish my sentence but I couldn't. I was no match for Matt. It was clear that he wanted me to kill me this time around. But that didn't deter me from giving everything I had. I was still going to fight to the death.

I quickly scanned the room for something to help me fight Matt off with. And that's when my eyes landed on his all-black leather Gucci belt. I don't know how I did it but I was able to get away from Matt for three seconds, so I dove for the leather Gucci belt I saw lying on the dresser whip and at the same time Matt tried to grab me by my hair again. I swung my free arm and caught him across his face. I felt my elbow connect with the bone in the bridge of his nose.

"Aghh!" he yelled, throwing his hands up to his face. I had caught him in the right spot, obviously. He stumbled backward a few steps. The look in his eyes and the look on his face told me he was about to unleash the beast on my ass.

Once I got the belt, I grabbed its buckle tightly so it wouldn't slip out of my hands. I eyed him evilly and let a snarl curl on my lips. He came storming toward me so I swung the belt at Matt's face with all the force in my body. The long leather strap caught him across his face. POP! The belt crashing into his face gave off a loud sound. It stung too because he went crazy.

"You fucking bitch!" he roared as he charged at me head-on. He looked like a raging bull, so how was I going to defend myself from that? I knew this guy was about to draw blood from every inch of my body. I wanted to ball up into a knot and run for cover, but I knew that wouldn't help me. I was going to have to fight for my life.

I braced myself for the head-on collision that was about to take place. I squeezed the belt tighter in my hand and swung it at Matt as soon as he leaned forward to hit me with his fist. Both blows connected. I was stung with a blow to the head and he got hit in the neck with the belt buckle. But I didn't stop there. I staggered a second or two and then I when I caught my balance I dove on top of his head and managed to wrap his belt around his neck.

"Arrgh!" he gagged, and he struggled, trying frantically to free himself. I yanked the strap of the belt as hard as I could, but he was too powerful for me so I couldn't get him to fall.

He growled and yanked on it, causing me to fall. I was on the floor now, panicking as Matt struggled to free himself from the belt strap.

"Bitch, I'm . . . gon' kill . . . you when I get my . . . hand on you," he gurgled, finally freeing himself. His hands were curled into fists and his lips were drawn tightly. He looked at me with his nostrils flaring and his chest bumping up and down from breathing so hard. He squinted and zeroed in on me like a bull seeing a matador's red cape and charging for it. Before I knew it, Matt was charging forward toward me at full speed.

"Shit!" I huffed, jumping aside. I whipped my head around real quick. I needed something that I could use as another weapon right away! Then, without thinking twice, I picked up the lamp from the nightstand and as soon as Matt was in front of me, I slammed that lamp into his head. The thick porcelain lamp base shattered against Matt's head and face. I felt little sharp pains as the sprinkles of porcelain sprinkled onto my feet.

"Ahhhh," Matt let out a sickening gasp. Then he crumpled to the floor in a heap and blood spilled from a newly opened gash in his forehead. He was moaning, but he clearly couldn't move. I guess I was more powerful than I had given myself credit for.

When I realized that he was down for the count, my heart revved up as I raced for the door. I tried to open it but it was locked. I started banging on it, hoping Lisa would unlock it and open it from her side. BOOM! BOOM! BOOM! "Lisa, open up the door!" I yelled as I jiggled the doorknob. BOOM! BOOM! BOOM! "Lisa, come on, I knocked him out so hurry up, before he gets up," I yelled once again. I was beginning to get frantic. Here was my only chance to get out and this stupid bitch wouldn't open the fucking door. What the fuck was going on in her freaking brain? Was she deaf or something? BOOM! BOOM! BOOM! "Lisa, what the fuck are you doing? Let me out before he wakes up!" I screamed. "Please let me out of here," I begged her as I panted like crazy. I couldn't believe that I had knocked Matt unconscious. I knew I had to take this small window of opportunity to get out of here before he woke up.

In addition to trying to convince Lisa to open the door, my mind was having all kinds of thoughts about what Matt would do to me if I didn't hurry up and get out of here. None of my thoughts had a happy ending so I forced myself to knock even harder. BOOM! BOOM! BOOM! "Lisa, please, I need your help! Open the door before Matt wakes up and kills me!" I begged her. But my words fell upon deaf ears.

After several more knocks I realized that she wasn't going to let me out of this room. I had looked back at Matt at least a dozen times, but now I noticed he was regaining consciousness. I knew this wasn't good. I cursed as I saw my time running out.

My heart started hammering against my chest bone so hard it felt like it was going to explode inside of me. I said a quick, silent prayer while I watched Matt slowly regain consciousness. And then I thought to myself, *How could I be so stupid as to put myself in this type of grave danger?* There was no way for me to turn back now, but worse, there was no way for me to know what was to come. Matt had clearly lost his damn mind and was now more deadly and dangerous than I could have ever imagined him to be. And now I was in a situation with nothing and no one to protect me. I was in this hellhole alone. And no help was in sight.

I gave myself a pep talk. "You gotta find a way to get out of here," I said over and over under my breath. Finally, it sank in. I looked around one last time and tried to assess what I might need to make my escape. "Shit, there's nothing in this fucking place!" I cursed, still trying to think what I could use. There was nothing I could fashion into a weapon big enough to break down this fucking door, but I was suddenly hit with an idea. Maybe Matt had the key in his pocket to unlock this door. So I tiptoed over to where he was lying on the floor and started sifting through his pants pockets. I dug into every pocket he had but there was nothing in it but a small, folded bunch of cash. I took the cash, along with his wallet and his cell phone. Better to have something that might help me get out of there than nothing at all. I didn't know it then, but I would surely find out later that my quick thinking with taking that stuff and those few little things I had stolen were going to be my keys to freedom.

Immediately after I realized that he didn't have anything else of use, I stood up, and when I was about to step away from him, he grabbed my ankle. "Come here, you fucking bitch!" he hissed, and snatched me back down to the floor. BOOM! I hit the floor like a ton of bricks. I tried to get underneath the bed but my body wouldn't fit. I knew my life was over now.

Matt snatched me back toward him and I started scratching and punching him in the face. He tried to grab my hands a couple of times but they were moving too fast. So he punched me dead in the nose, forcing me to see stars. I swear I felt the hot blood trickle out of my nostril and down my lips. And before I could react he started flailing his fists at me one after the other. He was up on me within seconds. I stood defenseless as he advanced on me so fast. I threw my hands up, trying to shield myself from what I expected to come when he reached out for me. But I was too late. I felt like a punching bag. "Aggh! Matt, please stop! Please Matt . . ." I screeched, trying to fend off as many of the blows as I could. I had never envisioned an impending death to be like this but now I knew.

While Matt continued his reign of terror, Lisa finally burst into the door. It was a little too late to try to save me now. Matt had me down on the floor, beating me to a pulp. Lisa saw this and started begging him to stop. She started acting in a frantic manner. "Matt, please stop. Two police cars just pulled up to the house," she whispered.

Matt stopped beating me at that very moment. He jumped up to his feet. I couldn't see him that clearly because of my tears and the swelling around one of my eyes caused by the impact of his fists, but I could see the fear in his face.

"Why the fuck are they here? Did you call them?" Matt asked through clenched teeth.

I looked at Lisa, waiting for her to answer. "No, of course not," she replied. She looked very worried. Then I thought about the cop I saw on the side of the road getting his dick sucked by the prostitute. I wondered if someone near the bank reported the license plates on the getaway car and that cop realized I was driving that vehicle and had his boys come here. What were the odds of that? *Please let that be the case, because I really need some help getting away from this maniac now,* I thought to myself.

"Where are they? Have they gotten out of their cars yet?" he whispered. He looked like he had seen a fucking ghost.

Before Lisa could reply, we all heard knocking on the front door. "Oh shit! That's them knocking on the door," he commented, and then he looked down at me. "Try to scream and I will put a fucking bullet in your head and your fucking son's head. Do you hear me?" His face looked merciless, so I believed every word he'd just uttered.

I nodded and then I turned to Lisa. She looked like we shared the same sentiments. She gave me this pitiful look like she was sorry for what I was going through. But I wasn't feeling her right then. So I turned my head toward the wall because I felt like she should've opened the fucking door and let me out of here while we had a chance. She had the freaking power to help me get out of here and she didn't. Now we were both back at square one.

BOOM! BOOM! The sounds were coming from the cops knocking at the front door. "How many cops are out there?" Matt continued to whisper to Lisa as he tiptoed quietly toward the window in the bedroom.

"Four," she whispered back.

"Where is the baby?" he wanted to know.

When Matt mentioned my son, I turned my attention back toward Lisa. I wanted to hear her response. "I just laid him down in the back room. He's drinking a bottle," she replied, continuing to whisper as low as she could while looking at Matt. A few seconds later, she looked down at me.

I saw Matt trying to be very careful not to be caught looking out the window. He peered around the dark curtain and then he jumped back really quickly. "Oh shit! I just saw one of them walk by the window," he whispered to Lisa.

"Did he see you?" Lisa asked.

"No, I don't think so."

"Do you think they're gonna stick around since my car is out there?" she wanted to know.

"Hopefully, they won't. But I will say that if we hadn't gotten rid of that car Juice's blood was in, they'd be coming in here on our asses right now, instead of knocking on the fucking door," Matt explained.

Hearing that he and Lisa got rid of the bloodstained getaway car crushed my hopes of the cops kicking the door down to this house. For the first time in my life, I was sick to my stomach that the cops weren't coming for my rescue. I knew I was a wanted woman. But guess what? I didn't care at that moment. I just wanted to get me and my baby out of there while we were still alive. Because everything I'd done thus far hadn't worked. So I need a fucking plan B.

The knocking continued. "I wonder why they came here," Matt whispered to Lisa like she knew the answer. All the while, I was hoping they're here because of me. *Please God, don't let these cops leave without me,* I prayed silently.

She hunched her shoulders and stood alongside him while he stood still by the window. They both looked shell-shocked. I was hoping Lisa would do something stupid to make noise so the cops would hear it and refuse to leave. Unfortunately, she didn't. I swear, I was about to lose my freaking mind.

In all, I think the police officers stuck around the house for about five long minutes. I had lost all hope after I heard Matt announce that they were leaving. It seemed like right after he said that, his superior demeanor resurfaced.

His voice changed. "Yo, I'm gonna need you to pack some shit up because they coming back and I ain't trying to be here when they come."

"What do you want me to pack up?" Lisa questioned him in a mild manner.

"Just get all the guns and shit together and throw them in that dark blue backpack with a few pairs of pants and shirts for me. You can pack up whatever you want for yourself. Just don't try to bring a lot of shit 'cause we ain't gon' have no room for it."

"When are we leaving?"

"Now?"

"But what if the cops are parked on the other side of that cornfield, waiting for us to come out of the house? We'll be fucked up then."

Matt thought for a moment. "Yeah, you right. It'll probably be better if we wait until it gets dark."

"I think so too. But even then, we could still be driving into an ambush. We can't see on the other side of that cornfield out there. So, what if I drive us out of here and the cops are waiting for us? We'll be in a shitload of trouble."

"I don't wanna think about it," Matt expressed. He had the look of a man whose life was about to fall apart. And guess what? I didn't feel sorry for that fucking loser.

"Okay, well why don't you call one of your boys and

get a couple of them to drive down the main road and let us know if the cops are posting up out there."

Matt looked at Lisa suspiciously. "You know what? You might be smarter than this dumb bitch on the floor after all," he commented, and then he leaned forward, grabbed Lisa's face with both of his hands, and kissed her on the forehead. Right after he left her go, he grabbed the backpack of money off the floor and said, "Let's go. I'm hungry as fuck. Plus, we got a few phone calls to make."

I looked at Lisa, she looked back at me, and then she turned her head and followed Matt out the bedroom door. Immediately after they closed the door, one of them locked it.

I was starting to believe that Lisa was this wishy-washy chick who didn't know if she was coming or going. One minute the bitch was taking up for me and the next minute she sided with Matt. If she wanted him to let me go, then why hadn't she opened the fucking door when I was begging her to do so? What kind of drugs was this lady on? Ugh! I just wished she'd take one of our sides and stick with it.

To make light of the situation, I felt a little optimistic that I might get another chance to escape. To know that we were about to leave this place put me in a mindset that I needed to figure out how to get away from Matt's psychotic ass! I prayed the cops were somewhere nearby. At that point, I didn't care if I ended up going to jail—I just wanted to get as far as I could from Matt before he killed me.

While I went over a couple of scenarios in my head, I thought about the possibility that I could get locked up if the cops were actually waiting on Matt to leave the house. But then I also thought of the possibility that if the cops were waiting for us to leave the house, Matt wasn't going to let them take him alive. He would pull out his pistols and have an all-out war with them. It wouldn't shock me if Lisa joined in with him. I could definitely picture them doing a Bonnie and Clyde shoot-out while my baby and I got caught up in the crossfire. That whole scene would be a fucking disaster. So I needed to figure out a way to prevent that from happening. It would be tough, but I had to do something before we all ended up in body bags.

25

TWO WAYS TO SKIN A CAT

Several hours rolled by and I noticed we had about an hour left of sunlight, which meant that we were going to be leaving this place very soon. Anxiety began to engulf my entire body all over again. I didn't know whether to be happy or be sad. My feelings were all over the place. But I knew that whatever move I made to make this heist successful, it had to be on point and precise. I couldn't make any mistakes.

I figured that if the cops weren't staking this place out, then I was going to have to cause Matt and Lisa to have a car accident without damaging myself or my baby. And if that didn't work, I was going to have to convince them to stop the car at a public place and try to escape then. But that would be too farfetched because Matt wouldn't ever permit that. Stop at a public place? No, never. So, I thought, maybe I could get the attention of passengers in passing vehicles. If I drew their attention and gave them some type of sign that I was in distress, then maybe they'd help me escape.

I swear, coming up with different ways to escape started draining every ounce of sanity I had left, so I lay back on the bed and tried to relax. Ten minutes into my relaxed mode, I heard Lisa and Matt talking in the other room.

"Keep watching the house and I'll be right back," I heard Matt say to Lisa. He sounded like he was standing by the bedroom door.

"Why are you going back in there?" Lisa asked him.

"Bitch, don't question me. Just do like I said," Matt boomed, and then I heard him tugging away at the doorknob. At that moment, I knew that he was on his way back into the bedroom. I figured he was coming in here to help me get ready so all of us could leave the house, so I sat up on the bed.

As soon as the door opened, I looked directly at him. He gave me this creepy look that made my skin crawl. "I'm back," he said, smiling. This nigga was acting like we were old buddies or something and like he was glad to see me. It was weird.

He closed the door and locked it behind him. "Ready for another round before we get out of here?" he asked me.

I swear I instantly felt sick to my stomach. How the fuck did he want me to answer that question? Was he freaking serious? Did he really think I wanted to go another round and give him some pussy? Hell no! I didn't want him touching me at all. I wanted to leave out of there with my baby and never look back at him or this godforsaken place. "Stand up," he instructed me.

"Are we getting ready to leave?" I asked while I scooted to the edge of the bed.

"We will be soon enough," he replied as he stood before me.

"Do you want me to pack my stuff up?" I continued questioning him as I moved closer toward him.

"I'll let you know when I'm ready for you to do that," he told me.

I stopped midway on the bed. "What's going on?" I wanted to know.

"Shut the fuck up with the questions and bring that ass here," he demanded. His facial expression changed. His nostrils flared up so I could tell that he was getting aggravated. He reached over and snatched me up from the bed aggressively. My heart skipped a beat as he pulled me close to him. He then grabbed me and hugged me tightly. He began kissing my neck with his big mouth and then moved to my breasts. I could feel his dick getting an erection while he was pressing it up against me. A feeling of disgust came over me and I wanted him dead.

He pushed me back gently on the bed. My mind started swirling with all kinds of mixed feelings. He started pulling off my clothes and I immediately started crying because I knew if I didn't fuck him, he'd want to kill me for sure this time around. I continued to let him undress me. Then I watched him undress himself. A few seconds later, he climbed on top of me and slid his dick straight up inside of me. "Ahh," I let out a loud sigh. "Yeah, you like that, don't you?" he asked. Oh, he was so lucky I didn't have a knife or a gun. It was like I had left my body. Matt had become an uncontrollable animal. He grunted and groaned and sweat dripped off him. He pounded on me like a maniac. I lay there and didn't say one word. I had to take my mind away from this bedroom and focus on how I was going to get out of there with my baby. This was the only way I was coping with what was going on inside this bedroom. "This pussy is so fucking good! I swear you got the best pussy in the world!" he moaned loud. "Baby, tell the truth, don't you miss this dick?" he asked me between moans. "I know that other nigga wasn't fucking you like I be doing it. I'm the only one that can handle this shit," Matt bragged. I swear I wanted to throw up in my fucking mouth. Instead of answering his question, I nodded my head.

I couldn't believe that I was in this predicament. I could feel his dick deep inside me now. It was the most horrible feeling in the world. It was like he was trying to pull my pussy inside out. No fucking condom at all, and I just lay there and let him fuck me over and over again. Matt had stripped me of the bank robbery money and now he was holding me against my will. I guess I was what you would call a fucking puppet. I was living in a nightmare with no sign of it ending.

By the time this nasty motherfucker finished fucking and ejaculating inside of me, he was ready to move on to the plan set before him. "Get up and get ready because we're gonna be leaving this spot in about thirty minutes," he instructed me while he stood alongside the bed putting back on his clothes.

I sat up in the bed naked, holding part of the bedsheet up to my breasts, waiting to hear him tell me where we were going, but the explanation never came out of his mouth. For the life of me I couldn't figure out how I was going to get my mind right after being raped by this bastard once again, but I was willing to try.

While Matt was rambling on about how and at what precise time we were going to leave this place, Lisa knocked on the door. Matt ignored the first couple of knocks. That didn't stop Lisa from continuing to knock on the door. This aggravated the hell out of Matt. He stopped in mid-sentence and leaped toward the door. He snatched it open, posturing himself to unleash the beast on Lisa, but he was taken aback when he saw that she had a gun pointed directly at his face. "What the fuck . . ." he gasped, his eyes almost bulging from his head. He was shocked that he ended up on the other side of his own fucking gun. He threw his hands up. "Yo, what the fuck are you doing? Why are you pointing that gun at me" Matt screamed at Lisa.

"Get the fuck back, you demented motherfucker!" she spat as she held the gun steadily at him, tears beginning to fall from her eyes.

"Lisa, you're playing, right?" he asked her, trying to play it cool. He seemed confused. Shit, I was even confused. I mean, she was just talking to him a few hours ago and now she was acting like she was about to shoot him. What a sudden change.

"Matt, didn't I just tell you to get the fuck back?" She squinted at him evilly. She was looking like a woman scorned.

He took a couple steps backward. She followed him, keeping a firm stance with the gun. "Lauren, get up and get dressed right now," she instructed me, refusing to take her eyes off Matt.

I hesitated because I didn't know where she was going at with this. "Do you wanna get out of here or not?" she roared at me, taking her eyes off Matt for one second.

"Yeah," I said, barely audible. I think I responded like that because I was caught off guard. But I was happy nonetheless.

"Well, get the fuck up and get dressed," she continued. This time she didn't look at away.

Without hesitation, I jumped up from the bed. I was completely undressed but that didn't matter. Lisa took another quick look at me from head to toe. I guess she wanted to see why Matt couldn't get enough of me. Well, she definitely got it. After she felt like she had gotten an eyeful, she set her sights back on Matt, who looked like he was about to take a leap toward her. She caught him just in time. "Nigga, I wish you would move." She stared him down. She didn't flinch.

"You know you're making a big fucking mistake, right?" he warned her while grinding his teeth together. I felt like holding my breath because it seemed like at any given moment this guy was going to charge toward Lisa, take the gun from her, and start beating the crap out of her. Lisa looked like Jada Pinkett Smith standing up against LeBron James. She was definitely no match for him.

"Fuck you, Matt! You've been making fucked-up choices since I let you come into my life. Now move back some more before I blow your fucking head off your shoulders. I am not fucking playing," she continued.

Matt took Lisa's advice and took a couple more steps backward while I was trying to slip my clothes back on. I had never gotten dressed so fast.

"If you let this bitch leave out of here, I am going to kill you with my bare hands," he threatened her.

"Shut up! You ain't gon' do shit to me! I'm tired of you putting your fucking hands on me! I've never done anything to make you treat me the way you do. All I've ever done for you was love you and have your back. That's it. But instead you continue to treat me like a dog by talking shit to me and putting your hands on me. But that shit stops today," she roared. She was an emotional wreck.

"Oh, so now you wanna grow some balls?" Matt gave her a sly smirk. Anger was welling up inside of him ready to boil over like a pot of hot water. I saw the veins around his temple rise up. I knew I needed to hurry up and get out of there while I had the chance.

"You can smile all you want to, nigga, because I'm gonna have the last laugh today. Now, you if try and play games like I won't waste your ass right now, then go ahead. Try me. I've put up with your shit for the last time, Matt. I've sat back and let you fuck your ex-girlfriend while I was in the next room. Do you know how painful it was for me to sit back and listen to you fuck her like you were enjoying yourself? I heard you moaning and shit. I heard what you were saying to her while you were calling it making love to her. You don't think that shit didn't fuck my head up? Did you think I was really all right with you walking around here playing house with her and her fucking baby?" she screeched, her voice trembling. I could hear the pain through her words. I started feeling so sorry for her.

"Bitch, please, I ain't trying to hear that shit," Matt

huffed, as he stood there like he was trying to plot his next move. I could see it in his body language; he was waiting for the perfect opportunity to jump on her and take that gun from her.

"Nah, I ain't your bitch no more. That ship has sailed," she told him. Then she looked at me because I was just standing there fully dressed and waiting for further instructions. "You ready?" she asked me.

"Y-yeah," I stuttered.

"Well, go in the living room and get your baby. I've already dressed him and packed all of his stuff up so he's ready to go," Lisa told me.

When I took the first step to leave the room, Matt's thunderous voice boomed and startled me. "Leave this room, bitch, and I'm gonna jump on your motherfucking ass!"

I nearly stumbled, listening to Matt's warning. I stood there frozen, not knowing what to do. "Don't listen to him, Lauren. Get out of here right now and get your baby! Run!" she ordered me. So I took off like a lightning bolt. I didn't wait for Matt to say another word. On my way out of the bedroom I looked at her and whispered the words, "Thank you."

"Lauren, you think you're gonna get away with this? Bitch, I'm gonna kill you as soon as I catch you!" Matt yelled at me as I exited the bedroom. I rushed into the living room and picked my baby up from the sofa.

"Shut the fuck up! You ain't gon' do shit to her! You ain't gon' do shit to nobody else, you evil motherfucker! Today will be the last day you put your hands on anyone," I heard Lisa huff, and then I heard a loud slam. BOOM! With Lil Derek in my arms, I looked around the corner to see what was going on and saw Lisa standing outside the bedroom door. She locked it and turned around toward me. Before she could utter a word, Matt started punching the door with his bare hands. It was a roaring sound. The strength behind his blows shook the door and its frame.

"I'm gonna kill both of you bitches when I get out of here! I'm gonna make you wish you were never born, you fucking cocksuckers!" I believed him.

See, Matt was a man of his word. If Matt said he was going to do something, then nine times out of ten, he would make it happen by any means necessary.

"That door isn't gonna hold him very long," I whispered loud enough for her to hear me, but at the same time being quiet enough so he couldn't.

"Don't worry about him. Take your baby and go," Lisa said as she walked toward me carrying the two backpacks of money I'd robbed from the bank, and then she handed them both to me. "Take these with you."

I was puzzled why she was giving me both bags of money. "Why don't you take one for yourself?" I asked her. Matt was still trying to knock the door down with his bare hands. I could hear the door getting weaker by the minute while Lisa and I were talking.

"For what? I'm not going to be able to spend it. So you take it and take care of yourself and that little baby of yours. You're gonna need it." She smiled. Her gesture toward me was so genuine and sincere but with finality.

"What are you going to do?" I wanted to know. For some reason, I wanted more answers. She wasn't giving much to draw a conclusion from.

"Don't worry about me. I'm gonna be fine," she assured me as she walked over to the kitchen. But that was it. She didn't give me anything else.

"How am I going to get out of here?" I wondered aloud.

"Take those keys near the lamp. It's to my car. Take it as far as you can and then drop it off wherever your heart desires."

I ran over to the end table where the lamp was and snatched up her keys. "Are you sure you want me to take your car and abandon it?" I was trying to figure out where she was going with this. But my question was answered quickly enough after I witnessed Lisa turn on all four knobs on the gas stove. I looked at this bitch like she was out of her damn mind. "Wait a minute, you're not about to do what I think you're gonna do, are you?"

"I told you to hurry up and get out of here now. Get as far away from this place as quickly as you can. And don't look back," she warned me for the last time.

"Why don't you come with me? You don't have to go through with this. And especially behind that piece of shit in the next room. You're a beautiful person, Lisa," I told her. I really didn't wanna see her kill herself, especially not over that nigga Matt. She was better than that. He was a fucking loser, not her.

"It's over for me, Lauren. I've done a lot of shit for that nigga in that room. And when the cops catch me, they're gonna try to lock me up for a very long time. So I might as well end it now. I mean, it ain't like I got something to live for like you do," she replied as she pulled a cigarette lighter from her pants pocket. The sight of the lighter spooked the hell out of me. I knew then that it was my cue to leave.

"Thank you for saving me and my baby's life." I turned to leave. I heard Matt's voice while he was trying to tear that bedroom door down.

"I'm gonna fucking kill both of you bitches! I swear, I'm gonna make you pay if that's the last thing I do!" he roared. But all of that ended after I opened the front door, walked outside, and closed the front door behind me. I couldn't hear his voice anymore. It was like I had experienced freedom all over again. A nice breeze came through and whisked by my face. It felt so good.

I rushed over to Lisa's car. It was a midsize sedan. It was just perfect for me. I tossed the two backpacks of money in the backseat and then I hopped in the front seat with Lil Derek in my arms. I didn't have a car seat for him so I laid him down on the passenger seat and hurried to start up the engine. I put the gear in drive but before I sped off I looked back at the window and saw Lisa peering out at me. I whispered "thank you" once again, hoping she could read my lips. Immediately after I uttered the words, she backed away from the window and I didn't see her face anymore. I didn't waste another second and sped away from the house. As soon as I got to the edge of the open field, I heard a loud explosion and when I looked back through the rearview mirror, I saw a mushroom cloud of smoke in the distance. I knew what that cloud of smoke meant. My heart sank into the pit of my stomach knowing that Lisa took Matt's life as well as her own. The thought of her actually going through with the murder-suicide fucked my head up. Anyone who could take someone else's life and then their own is a mental case. I just hoped she got what she was searching for. If not, then all was definitely lost.

26

SAFE PASSAGE

I still couldn't believe Lisa helped me get away with my baby. She was heaven-sent. Without her I knew I wouldn't have gotten away from Matt. He was for sure going to kill me. So as I continued to drive away from the house I watched as the flames literally engulfed it. This scene was like something you'd see in a movie. Never thought I would experience anything like that. I thank God I got out of there when I did.

Now, even though I was out of the house, I still wasn't out of the woods. It was still dusk outside, but slightly darker than it was fifteen minutes before, so while I was driving away through the dirt road, I left my headlights off so I wouldn't attract any attention if cops were in fact waiting alongside the street. But then I thought about it: If the cops were parked alongside the street, they would've seen the explosion and would've driven up this path by now. So without further hesitation I bolted down the dirt road in less than twenty seconds flat. When I reached the end of the road, I looked in both directions to see if any cars were coming and when I realized that the coast was clear, I sped out onto the main road and traveled in the opposite direction I figured help would come from.

I looked down at my baby at least ten times before I could even get a mile away from the house. I mean, I'd traveled a long way to get him back with me, so I just want to make sure that I wasn't dreaming. He was all I had left. And he was all I had left to remind me of Derek. I just wished that Derek was still alive to move into this next phase of my life. Matt's psychotic ass took away the only man who sincerely loved me. Now look at him. Burning to death in that locked bedroom. The fate he suffered was destined for him. He was a lying, cheating, conniving dog. The love of money consumed him. He didn't give a damn about anyone but himself. I hoped he burned in hell!

Three miles into my drive Lisa's face kept crossing my mind. I remembered her telling me she did a lot of stuff for Matt that would put her behind bars for a long time, but that wasn't enough cause for her to kill herself. She seemed like such a reasonable person. So why did she get hooked up with Matt? Matt must've fucked her good because any woman who would take her life because a nigga didn't want her is fucking insane. I only pray that she made things right with God!

After driving five more miles, I finally hopped on the first highway I saw. It was I-64. And the first thing I thought about was seeing that young guy Quincy before I left town for good. I wanted so badly to let him know that I was fine and that I got my son back. But I knew that wouldn't be the smartest thing to do because the cops were crawling all around him. I was sure the news media was down behind him too. So I couldn't jeopardize myself to play hero. But then again, I felt like I owed it to him to let him know that his friend Trevor was dead and where Preech and Juice dropped off his body, so his family could give him a proper burial. Knowing that his body was lying underneath an underpass where bums lived didn't sit well with me. I mean, they threw him out of the truck like he was a piece of trash. How coldhearted and callous can a person be? Matt and his boys really did a number this time around. Just think how this whole thing started. They all went to New York and found me. Then they kidnapped my husband and son. Killed my husband, after they took what money I had left from the last score. Then they took my son and brought him back to my hometown, which lured me back to Virginia. And then when I got back here, I had no other choice but to do another score just to keep my baby boy alive. Now everyone who had a hand in my family's kidnapping was dead. Karma is definitely a motherfucker!

I had to drive another twenty miles, and then I headed south. I was thinking I'd be okay if I started over in one of the small towns of Tennessee. No one there would know me so that would be a win-win situation for my son and me.

En route, I stopped off at a gas station to fill up Lisa's gas tank before I crossed over the North Carolina and Virginia state line. Immediately after I got out of the car, I locked the doors just to make sure no one tried to steal my son while he was asleep in the front seat. Once I felt he was safe and secure, I went inside the convenience store to pay for the gas. While I was walking up to the counter, I noticed the black store clerk watching TV. She was glued to the news station. She was facing me but her attention was focused on that news broadcast. "Can I get fifty dollars on pump three?" I asked her.

She looked at me and then she took my money from my hands. "I'm sorry, which pump did you say again?"

"Pump three," I told her, and then I waited for her to give me change from the $100 bill I gave her.

Once she gave me the change she owed me, she put her sights back on the TV screen. "What's going on?" I asked her while I stood there for a few seconds. I looked outside at the car just to make sure no one was standing near it.

"You didn't hear about this?" she asked me.

"No, what's going on?" I asked her. But I could clearly see that the news broadcast was about the house that blew up with Lisa and Matt inside of it. Chills instantly bubbled on my arms while anxiety filled up my stomach. From the way the news camera was facing, it looked like at least a dozen cop cars were at that house, along with paramedics and two fire trucks. That area that was surrounded by a cornfield and dimly lit by only two light poles was now lit up like a Christmas tree. It looked like pure mayhem.

"A couple of Chesapeake police officers went to this house earlier this afternoon because they received a tip that the two kidnapped victims they were looking for were there. But they said that when they got there and knocked on the door, no one answered. Fast-forward to now, someone calls nine-one-one saying that the same house was on fire. So the police, paramedics, and fire and rescue rushed out there and discovered that a male and female were trapped inside the house. The firefighters were able to pull the guy from the house and rush him to the hospital. But they said he was burned pretty badly so they aren't sure if he's one of the kidnap victims or if he's even going to make it," the store clerk explained.

"What about the lady?" I asked the clerk, hoping to hear that Lisa was still alive.

"I don't think she survived the blast," the woman said.

No! No! No! This can't be true! I screamed inside of my head. The shock of the possibility that Matt could still be alive was tearing me apart inside. No words would come out of my mouth. I felt like someone had set all of my organs on fire. I watched in horror while my jaw dropped wide open. I even winced trying to imagine how in the hell Matt was that fucking lucky to get pulled from that house fire. He was in the back bedroom. So how were the firefighters able to get him out of there? Now he was on his way to the hospital, *so does that mean he's going to survive?* Whatever the case, I didn't need to stand around and wait to see what happened. I needed to get me and my baby out of Virginia and never look back.

I swear I hoped he didn't live through this. He couldn't. If he did, he'd find a way to find me. And I couldn't have it. Not then, not ever.

I didn't thank the store clerk for her time or the information she gave me. I just rushed off and left the store. I returned to the car and pumped my gas. Immediately after, I got back in the driver's seat and started up the ignition. I looked down at my son. He was still sound asleep. "Son, Matt may still be alive. So we've gotta get out of here and never look back," I said aloud, even though I knew he didn't hear me nor could he understand a word I said. "I promise I'll never let anyone else take you from me. I'm gonna protect you from this day forward. I'll die before I let someone else take you away from me." I continued. I got teary-eyed just looking at my son lying in the passenger seat with his eyes closed.

I quickly got myself together after the car behind me beeped their horn. I looked through my rearview mirror and noticed that I was in their way of getting to the gas pump. Without hesitation, I put the gear back in drive and drove off. I got back on the highway and took it until I saw I-95. I took the ramp and merged onto I-95. Yes, I was on my way down south. No one would find me down south. So that's where I was going.

EPILOGUE

IN NEED OF A LIFELINE

"We're not sure if this is the kidnap victim or one of the kidnappers but we have a male burn victim around the age of thirty with first- and second-degree burns covering the right side of his face and neck, his right arm, and half of his torso area. Fire and rescue pulled him out of a bedroom of a burning house. They found him lying underneath a mattress that was barricaded by the bedroom door. We did a defibrillator one time," the lead paramedic said as he and his partner rolled the stretcher into the ER unit.

"Do we have a pulse?" the woman from the respirator unit asked.

"Yes, but it's faint," said the lead paramedic.

"Let's transfer him over and start compressions," a male doctor said. "Continue compressions and let's verify airways. Do you know if he's allergic to anything?"

"No, we don't have any of that information. There were two people inside the house and he was the only one who came out alive," the same paramedic replied.

"I see he has gray under his nostrils and some nasal singe," the doctor said.

"His pupils are dilated," the lead nurse noticed.

"He's gonna need oxygen therapy," the doctor pointed out.

"What was the last EPI?" one of the female nurses asked.

"Stop for one minute and check pulse please," the doctor instructed.

"I have pulses. His pulse is ninety-two," the lead nurse announced.

"What's his temperature?" the doctor wanted to know.

"His temperature is ninety-eight point six," another nurse replied.

"And his respiration?" the doctor questioned.

"His respiration is twenty-six," the same nurse replied.

"We need to intubate him now," the lead nurse stated.

"Start the IV," the doctor said.

"What are the vital signs?" the male surgeon asked as soon as he stepped in the burn unit.

"His vital signs are one-twelve over sixty-five and his CO-two level is twenty-six," one of the female nurses said.

"We're gonna need to put him on a ventilator now before we take him down to surgery," the other doctor announced.

"Let's move this along, you guys," the surgeon demanded.

"I'm administering five mgs of morphine now," the lead nurse stated.

"All right, let's keep this man alive," the surgeon's voice boomed as he watched the nurses and the other doctor prep for surgery.

"Alexandra, will you call down to surgery and make sure that they're ready for us?" the surgeon said to the lead nurse.

"Sure, doctor," the woman replied, and then she left the room.

"How are his pulses now?" the other doctor asked.

"His pulse just dropped " the Nurse Alexandra answered.

"We've gotta get him out of here now," the lead doctor spoke with urgency.

"Let's go before we lose him," the surgeon agreed.

"Are we clear?" the lead doctor asked.

"Yes, we're clear," the same nurse replied, and then every medical staff person standing around unlocked the wheels of the hospital bed and began to roll it out of the examination room.

"Let's go! Let's go! We gotta get him to the OR. We're losing him. His blood pressure is dropping," the lead doctor announced while they were wheeling the hospital bed down the hallway.

"Stay with us, sir. Stay with us," I heard a male's voice say, and then I didn't hear another sound.

Kiki Swinson, the bestselling author known for "fast, tension-packed" (Library Journal) novels featuring the glamour and grit of Virginia's most notorious streets, shows what happens when a criminal partnership takes a detour that puts its members on the road to jealousy, revenge, and murder....

THE SCORE

On Sale Now

LAUREN

Present Day

My feet moved at the speed of lightning. I could feel the wind beating on my skin so hard it made snot wet the inside of my nostrils. My entire body was covered with a thick sheen of sweat and I could feel it burning my armpits. My breath escaped my mouth in jagged, raggedy puffs and my chest burned. My heart felt like it would burst through the front of it. Even feeling as terrible as I did, I would not and could not stop moving.

"Move!"

"Get out of my fucking way!"

"Watch out!"

"Move!"

I screamed command after command at the nosy-ass people who were staring and gawking and being in my damn way. My legs were moving like those of a swift and agile cheetah as I swerved and swayed through the throngs of people on Virginia Beach Boulevard. I was met by more than one mouthful of gasps and groans and I could faintly see more than one wide-eyed, mouth-agape stare as people gawked at me like I was a crazy woman. I guess I did look crazy running through the high-end shopping area with no shoes on. I had run straight out of my Louboutins, my expensive embellished Balmain skirt was hitched up around my hips, my vixen weave was blowing in the wind, and my Chanel caviar bag was strapped around my arm like a slave chain. I could feel that my makeup was a cakey, smudged mess all over my face and eyes. But I didn't give a damn. I wasn't going to stop running. No matter what. Looking crazy was the least of my worries.

I had run track in high school and it was still paying off now, but clearly I wasn't in the same athletic shape. Still, I wasn't about to go out like this. I wasn't going to get captured on the street and probably murdered for something that wasn't totally my fault. I had been pushed and provoked to do everything that I did. All of the mistakes. All of the grimy shit I had done over the years. All of it was because I was born at a disadvantage from day fucking one.

I didn't want to die. I had always seen myself growing old with a few kids and grandkids surrounding me when I was ready to be settled. I would've given anything to be old and settled at this moment. But, of course, life threw me a curveball.

I could hear the thunderous footfalls of the three men chasing me. If they weren't so damn gorilla big and slower than me they would have caught me by now.

"Hey! Are you okay?" I heard a man on the street yell at me as I flew past him, nearly knocking him over. Why the hell was he asking me such a dumb question when you could clearly see that I was being chased by three hulking goons dressed in all black with their guns probably showing on their waists or maybe even in their hands. Thank goodness I am always so alert or they would've walked right up on me while I unsuspectingly ate my lunch at the posh restaurant and grabbed me. It was the fact that I had only been back in town for a few hours, the disappearance of my lunch companion, and the suspicious looks that had alerted me in the first place. How could I have been so trusting? So naïve and stupid, too.

I could feel the look of terror contorting my face, so I know damn well passersby could see the fear etched on every inch of it.

Finally, I dipped through a side alley and the first door I tried allowed me inside. Thank God! With my chest heaving up and down I rested my back against another cold metal door inside and slid down to the floor. My legs were still trembling and my muscles were on fire in places on my body I didn't even know existed. I tried to slow down my rapid breathing so I could hear whether the men had noticed me dipping into the alley but the more I tried to calm myself the more reality set in about the grave danger I was in. I was probably about to be murdered or worse, tortured and then murdered right in a dank alleyway in the place I thought I would never return to. If I hadn't gotten that call, it would have been years before I crept back here. I thought about Matt and wondered if he was the one who had sent these men after me. But how would he have known I was back? I knew Matt had a lot of selfish ways about him and although shit had gone south with us, I never thought he would try to do something like this to me. I expected that if he wanted to confront me, he would come himself. Even if it was Yancy who had sent the goons, I would think Matt would have tried to spare me.

CLANG!

A loud noise outside interrupted my thoughts and caused me to jump. I clasped both of my hands over my mouth and forced the scream that had crept up my throat back down. Sweat trickled down my face and burned my eyes. My heart jackhammered against my chest bone so hard it actually hurt. My stomach knotted up so tightly the cramps were almost unbearable. I dropped my head. Suddenly I felt like vomiting.

"I don't see her! She's not down here!" I heard one of

the goons outside of the door scream to the others. I swallowed hard and started praying under my breath.

Dear God, I am sorry for all of the things I've done. I don't know how things got so far gone. I never meant anything by any of it. I just wanted to live a better life than I had as a child. I guess with the mother You gave me and the hand You dealt me, I should've just handled it. I should've worked harder and not try to take the easy way out all of the time. I knew stealing is wrong. Since the first time I stole a credit card from my foster mother's purse, I'd known it was wrong. But I got addicted to the feeling that I'd gotten over on someone. I felt powerful. I remember the times I'd hear her talking to my foster father about some of the fraud scams she witnessed by working as a bank manager. It was interesting to hear how bank and credit card frauds were being committed on a daily basis. It all seemed too easy, too intoxicating. I had to test the waters. . . .

So here I am today. I'm literally running for my life. Maybe this is Your way of teaching me a lesson. Trust me, I hear You loud and clear. If You let me get out of this, I swear I will change my life. I don't even know how things got this far . . .

MATT

"Ooof," I gagged as another fist slammed into my stomach causing all of the wind in my body to involuntarily escape through my mouth. Acidy vomit leapt up into my throat and spewed out of my mouth right after.

"Hit 'em again!" a deep baritone voice commanded. With that, another sledgehammer-sized fist slammed into my left jaw. I felt the blood and spit shoot from between my lips. The salt from the blood stung the open cuts on my split bottom lip.

"Until he tells me where the fuck every dime of my money is I want his ass to suffer," the deep voice growled. "Break every bone in his body if you have to."

"Agh!" I belted out as a heavy-booted foot crashed down on my ribcage. I think hearing the crack and crunch of my own bones disturbed me more than the excruciating pain I felt.

I coughed and wheezed trying to will my lungs to fill back up with air. Each raggedy breath hurt like hell. I knew then that some of my ribs had been shattered. More fury came right after.

"Ugh!" I coughed as a front kick with a pointed, steel-toe boot slammed into my back. I swore I heard my spine crack. My insides felt like they were being shuffled around by the punches and kicks I'd been subjected to since these dudes had snatched me from my hideout in the thick of the night. I had tried to bounce before they could get me, but I was too slow. Thank God Lauren had up and left or else she would've been there when they broke the door down to get me. Although I wanted to kill her myself right now, I could only pray that she was someplace safe ... maybe with the police or back on the run. But if these dudes were after me, I would think they would be after her and Yancy as well.

"Where is my fucking money!" the voice boomed again. This time, I forced my battered eyes open and looked at the sharply dressed man that was standing over me. In dim light I couldn't make out his face. But I could see from the flash of his sparkly diamond pinky ring, solid-gold cufflinks, and a clearly expensive tailor-made suit, this dude hadn't even broken a sweat. He obviously took great satisfaction in commanding his goons to torture me over and over. And like good little soldiers, they did just enough to hurt me, but not kill me.

"I'll ask you one more time, Matthew Connors ... what the fuck did you and your bitch do with my fucking money?" the boss man growled. His money? Me and my bitch? What the ... It finally hit me like a hammer to my head. My entire body went cold like my veins had been injected with ice water. The score that was supposed to put me back in the game and set me and my woman up for life had turned into my worst nightmare.

The man who'd been our mark let out a raucous, maniacal laugh. "You petty fuckin' thief," he spat as he moved closer to me. "Stealing instead of going out there and working for your own shit. I can respect a man that hustles for himself, but a man who steals from another hardworking man is a waste of fucking sperm. Your mother should've just swallowed."

The heat of anger that lit up my chest from his words was probably enough to make me kill him with my bare hands. I bucked my body out of anger but that just made shit worse. . . .